Wood Duck

Wood Duck

A Western Double

Levi Johnson Mountain Man Scout

Book Nine

Ash Lingam

Wood Duck
Paperback Edition

Wolfpack Publishing
1707 E. Diana Street
Tampa, Florida 33610

www.wolfpackpublishing.com

Paperback ISBN 979-8-89567-573-1
Ebook ISBN 979-8-89567-572-4

Contents

Wood Duck

The Last Rendezvous

Wood Duck

Wood Duck

Levi Johnson Mountain
Man Scout 17

This book is dedicated to my grandchildren, Kai, Ziggie and Kalani.

"Knowledge isn't free. You have to pay attention."

RP Feynman

Boot Hill

The smell of fresh dirt floated on puffs of air as the sharp blade of the spade sliced through the earth. Piles of waist-high soil stood beside the hole where the gravedigger worked. Crosses covered the ground to the top of the hill. The white contrasted with the thick green grass. Birds fluttered in the chestnuts as hummingbirds buzzed from flower to flower, more like giant bees than birds.

An aging Indian with a face wrinkled like an old dog sat before a White man on the opposite side of the cemetery. His pale skin looked sick compared to the man with Comanche blood. Indian camp dogs snapped and barked at each other, waiting for their master to whistle and throw them a bone. He spooned hot beans into his mouth as he watched and waited. Every time Rory cried out, the outlaw smiled. When he didn't, he kicked him in the kidneys to make Rory suffer more.

Wood Duck had captured the White man, tied him to four stakes, spread-eagled, facing the sun. He didn't want him to miss a second of his show. Rory Breaker struggled to free himself from the bindings, but the wet leather tightened. The Indian had stripped off his shirt, leaving his pale white skin bare to the elements. The White man craned his head, trying to see what the Comanche planned.

The captive's eyes spread wide in terror. The warrior's brown face had red and blue stripes down his cheeks. His gray hair was pushed back with a matching chin beard, twisted into a long braid. This is where his mother's genes showed—that and his blue eyes, which seemed out of place. Colorful feathers hung from his long hair.

Waiting a respectable distance away sat his eight warriors. They came from the Ute, Pawnee, Sioux, Apache, and Blackfoot tribes—all outcasts from their people. There was also a White man in the gang. More than a decade before, the gang members turned their backs on their people and families to ride with the most dangerous outlaw of them all. He was Wood Duck, born to a White woman, Doris Dailey, and a Comanche Indian father.

He captured her from a wagon train and made her his wife. She was one of the lucky ones because she was claimed as Quana's spouse and not his slave, although there seemed to be little difference at times.

The Comanche outcast squatted before the young man. He knew who he was and had searched far and wide to find him. He worked for Marshal Joseph Walker. Capturing the cowboy would make it easy for Wood Duck to draw the lawman into his trap. He held a knife between his thumb and finger, dangling over Rory's stomach. Light glittered off the honed blade. Breaker knew if Wood Duck let it go, it would pierce the skin.

The renegade Indian eyed the cowboy as he slowly moved the knife over his face, making Rory wince.

Finally, he delicately sliced a two-inch incision in Rory's abdomen and inserted his index finger. He carefully hooked a piece of intestine with his finger and slowly pulled it out, stretching it to the nearest cross as it dangled in the air. Four yards of guts strung from his body to the painted marker as it swung back and forth in the breeze. Rory's eyes opened so wide they nearly popped out of his skull. He shook his head repeatedly no, but Wood Duck silently smiled and nodded his approval. He was a master at his trade of torture. He knew the key was patience.

"I'll ask you one more time before I call the dogs," Wood Duck whispered. "Where is Marshal Walker? I know you were going to meet him to organize a wagon train. Everybody knows because of the marshal's big mouth. Maybe he should learn to be more discreet in the future. If you tell me where he is, I'll let you go—I promise." Wood Duck's smile alone proved it was a lie, and Rory knew it. He could see it in his wicked glare. The cowboy could only pray for a quick death.

Breaker was bordering panic. He didn't want to tell the Comanche where the marshal was, but he didn't know how much longer he could hold out and not talk. His eyes kept roaming from the Indian's painted face to his guts hanging on the cross. He closed his eyes and shook his head again. He couldn't believe this was happening. When he opened them, he saw it was true, and it wasn't a nightmare after all. Shortly, he was going to die, no matter what he said.

"Sarii!" Wood Duck called out, and the Comanche camp dogs came running.

The gang's canines must have been used to such practices because they didn't hesitate to dig in as they tore the intestines from the bloody cross. Three dogs' jaws snapped at the slimy guts as they gobbled up their warm meal, eating their way toward Rory's stomach. He was tied to the ground; he couldn't move—all he could do was stare. He wiggled and pulled as hard as he could, but to no effect. He was forced to lie there while wild animals ate him alive.

"Tell me, and I'll let you die quickly!" Wood Duck chuckled over the growling canines. It was apparent he was enjoying himself. "If not, I'll let them eat. It's up to you to decide."

Rory finally screamed, "He went to the Yellowstone Valley with some mountain men! He's spending the winter in the mountains above the valley floor!"

"Who was he going to visit?" Wood Duck asked, brimming with curiosity. "Tell me now, and I'll cut your throat, so you won't suffer more." He moved the blade in his hand as sunlight flashed off the honed steel again.

"No, no! Shoot me, shoot me, please!" Rory pleaded. "He's with Rusty Steel! I told you what you wanted. Now kill me, scum!"

"I wouldn't waste a bullet on a rat like you," Wood Duck spat. "You betrayed your friends."

The outlaw clicked his tongue, and the dogs went wild and tore Rory Breaker to pieces. The Comanche sat patiently while his pets devoured the cowboy while still alive. With their bloody snouts dug deep into his stomach cavity, Rory finally gave a last scream. He was near death, so his torturer became bored, got up, and walked away.

The renegade Indian had found Rory Breaker

waiting for the marshal along the trail to The South Pass. He was waiting for his boss as agreed. It was as easy as stealing chickens. He had caught him off guard. Wood Duck had been looking for the sheriff for months. When he disappeared, the renegade Indian believed maybe he was dead, but after he found his right-hand man, and he didn't mention Walker's demise, he knew Walker was still alive.

This made the Indian smile. Now, Wood Duck was one step closer to capturing Marshal Walker. He wondered how he would torture him. He was going to have to get inventive. His death couldn't be ordinary at all. He hoped to make it a memorable moment. The Kansas lawman thought he was chasing the outlaw when the truth was Wood Duck would be tracking him.

The gang leader silently walked away from the damaged and torn body, which was already growing stiff and cold. At least what was left; now that he had the information he wanted, he was ready to throw his dogs that bone he promised them—Rory Breaker's bones. He smiled, listening to them snap and growl at each other as he departed. A final scream was stifled as a set of massive jaws clamped down on the dying man's windpipe. When it snapped, it sounded like breaking wood.

"Did he talk?" James Wilson, the White gang member, asked. He scratched his coal-black beard. He wore his hair in braids like an Indian, and his skin was burned from the sun.

"Of course, he talked," Wood Duck replied, smiling. "No man can resist my will."

The renegade cocked his head to listen to his dogs, and his smile turned into a grin. Shortly, there was hardly a sound. He looked up and saw the vultures circling lower and lower. Some swooped down and perched on crosses a short distance away, waiting for the dogs to finish.

"He's with Rusty Steel," Wood Duck said, raising his eyebrows. "We're gonna get to torture two of my oldest enemies while they watch each other die. It's going to be more fun than expected. I had Steel in my clutches once years ago, and he got away, but I swear that won't happen again. I thought the old fool was dead since I hadn't heard anything about him for years. Now, he apparently lives above Yellowstone Valley. I didn't know he was friends with the Kansas sheriff. This will make it more interesting—even fun."

"If he's in the Rocky Mountains, you ain't heard nothing about him because he's lost in the wilderness. I wonder what he's been doin' up there all this time," Wilson said. "With the weather warmin' up, I reckon we can climb those hills with little to no problem. We can have a look for ourselves. That marshal needs to die soon, or he's gonna change his mind and start chasing us again if he ain't at it already."

"He doesn't even know we're near Fort Boise." Wood Duck chuckled. "He's gonna get the surprise of his life when we show up unannounced. I'm sure that old man, Rusty Steel, will be shocked, too. I promise you his time is comin' soon. We're gonna get to finish something that we started long ago. Make sure you collect the head before we leave. I'll need proof of what we've done. Make sure you put it on salt so it don't stink. I've got a plan."

The following morning, they broke camp, loaded their mules with supplies, and mounted up. They trotted toward Yellowstone Valley as three dogs ran around the riders, barking endlessly. Dried blood still covered their muzzles. A leather pouch hung from Wood Duck's saddle horn. It was the size of a human skull.

When they drew near the fort, they stopped short and made camp in a dense stand of bushes and trees. Luke Dawson rode on to Boise alone. He was the only one who they wouldn't recognize. Before leaving, he unbraided his hair, rubbed off his war paint, and pulled out a heavy wool coat. Suddenly, he looked like a White traveler and wouldn't be suspected when he showed himself before the army soldiers.

"Do you have that list I made?" Wood Duck asked. "Get our supplies, and don't linger. I want to get where we're going before Walker decides to run off. With the weather warming up, he won't stay much longer. If we can catch the two together, it will be twice as much fun." He smiled gruesomely.

Flames danced in the gang members' eyes as they sat around the fire. Waves of heat radiated off the orange embers. The Ute and Sioux Indians were in the dark, taking turns as guards. Being so close to a fort was always dangerous. Their reputation followed them around like the stink of a skunk. Wood Duck was known and feared far and wide. His face was on dozens of wanted posters in a dozen states and territories.

The bounty on his head had steadily climbed over the years. Now, it stood at two thousand dollars. There were another five hundred on each gang member, but few lawmen or bounty hunters were stupid enough to try to collect. Many believed that catching Wood Duck was a nearly impossible task. All those who had tried before were dead and buried—everyone except Joseph

Walker and Rusty Steel. If the Comanche renegade had his way, they would follow the others soon.

Late that night, the other men snored as Wood Duck sat near the fire and prodded the cinders with a stick. It popped and crackled as flames lashed out. He searched for some message from the other side. It was nearly dawn when the gang leader finally slept, and even then, his dreams were restless and full of dead faces.

While sleeping, his past haunted him at night, but he didn't care. He believed he was the chosen one by the evil Comanche spirits. Many of his old tribe members thought he was some sort of wicked male witch. Nobody could understand how he had survived so long.

Levi Johnson

Levi's superhuman will and determination to recuperate at record speed surprised everybody. Of course, in the first couple of weeks, he was too weak to focus on rehabilitation. When the claim jumpers had shot him, he nearly died, so the road ahead was arduous and full of pain. But Johnson pushed the agony aside and got down to business. Three weeks later, he had his first try at chopping wood like he had done only a month before.

At first, it was nearly impossible. Johnson couldn't lift the heavy axe above his head. With no other option, he sat on a stump and feebly chopped up kindling with a hatchet until he couldn't move his arm—but he wasn't done there. He took a thirty-minute break and would be after it again, chasing it like a wolf after a baby lamb.

At first, every day, his energy returned very slowly, a little bit at a time, but now it was coming back in leaps and bounds. While he ate like a bird during the first two weeks, he now devoured every thick elk steak and bowl of potatoes Dahteste fed him. Johnson was obsessed with his recovery and hated feeling like he was a handicap for his family and friends in the compound.

He had always pulled his weight and more and was tired of being cared for. It was time he took care of himself. Still, it was too early, and he knew it, but his mindset was focused on the target, and he was determined not to fail.

He briefly remembered back when he felt he was dying and, after that, when the lights went out and silence befell him. Those moments where he appeared dead after his cardiac arrest were too hazy to remember. But he did recall the expressions on his friends' and family's faces. That was when the realization came to him. They had all believed he had passed, just like he did.

Virgil told him all about autoresuscitation and where such things happened in the Bible, but Levi was still confused. He obviously didn't die, at least not as far as he could tell. He liked to believe he was in a deep sleep of some sort, and just by luck, he squeezed by and dodged death. He felt it was as simple as that. He believed if he had died, he would have had some memory of Heaven or angels, but there was nothing but darkness with wavy images behind the curtain.

Levi thought his limitations were what he set in his mind, not what somebody else thought or claimed. He had always felt this way. He knew his focused determination when attempting to reach a goal was unrelenting, and he didn't plan to do any different with the new challenge before him. He would attack his recovery like he had everything in life.

Johnson always invested himself one hundred percent, and he saw this would be the same. In fact, it was the most critical challenge he had ever faced to date. If he wanted to stay in the Rocky Mountains and continue to live in the wilderness, it was imperative that he recuperated well and as quickly as possible.

They never knew what the wilderness would have in store for them just around the bend. He had to be ready just in case. The last months had been exceptionally complicated, and he had a gut feeling that it wasn't over yet. Surprises seemed to be waiting for them at every turn.

Levi's wounds were still fresh, so he knew he could only go so far, but every day, he pushed the limits to the very edge before backing off and giving himself time to rest. Still, the bleeding had long stopped inside and out, and the scabs were hard and dry. Soon, they would fall off.

Levi resisted the urge to scratch and pull at the dead skin and crusty covering. They itched night and day to add discomfort to the agony. What caused the most pain were his broken ribs, front and back. Both sides of his body were still completely black and blue, bordering on purple.

The sound of Levi chopping wood made all the compound members happy, especially his Crow wife. Johnson, the mountain man's favorite, looked like he would tackle the task as he had everything else during his life. Even now, in his convalescence, he pushed the envelope further daily without busting open any recent injuries. Not everyone could survive a gunshot wound to the chest, but then again, Levi wasn't like most men.

Rusty sat on the porch, watching his apprentice work through the smoke billowing around his head. His ceramic pipe protruded from one side of his mouth, and a quid was in his other cheek. His fingers unconsciously kneaded a beaver pelt, making it soft and supple. Occasionally, he removed the stem of his pipe, spat a stream of brown juice into the dirt, and had another sip of whiskey-laced coffee as he pulled on his long gray beard.

As the temperatures rose, the men and women in the compound spent their days outdoors. Angus, Dennis, and Rusty were easily found at their daily roost; Virgil and Marshal Walker wouldn't be far. Betty spent hours alone with her husband in the cabin. Despite the warm weather, she wanted their privacy to last. She wondered if she would ever see him again every time he disappeared. Either one of them could die any day, and this fact was hard on her nerves.

Dahteste, Levi Beaver Johnson's wife, worked beside her husband, cutting wood. The sound of blades hacking into timber rang out all through the day. Even though it didn't appear so, his wife kept a close eye on his every move. Since she nearly lost him, she hadn't let him out of her sight. Even when he went to the outhouse, she waited nearby on the trail. It was as though his wife believed if he moved out of her sight, he would escape her again and this time he would surely die. Unlike before his near-death experience, she was as possessive as a mama with her baby ducklings.

Angus pulled up a chair and sat beside his friends, grinning. "It looks like Levi's gonna be well enough to go to the Rendezvous."

"Ya think?" Dennis replied doubtfully. "I believe he's pushing too hard. I don't see why all the hurry. Whatcha think, Virgil?"

"What do I think about what?" Lovejoy asked as he crossed the last bit of grass-covered yard.

Boot heels hammered on the wood plank floor. Virgil sat at the long table. It was visible where it had been added onto over the years as the numbers of the compound varied. The porch was dotted in chairs except the rocker Dennis made. Now that Levi was better, he didn't like the rocking chair anymore, so Breed claimed it for his own, and nobody objected. Rusty didn't like it because it made him sit too far from the table, and it was too low.

Horsehair floated in the air above the stables in the back corner of the compound near the outhouses. A five-foot-tall buck-and-rail fence surrounded the entire compound with gates north and south. Another narrow gate stood on the west side, just wide enough for a single rider. It was the old trail to the nearby creeks, but they were all trapped out. The beaver had long gone deeper into the mountains. Three cabins stood in a row in the compound. The largest log building belonged to Angus McFarlin and Rusty Steel. They gathered every evening on their porch.

"Is Levi pushin' himself too hard with such fresh wounds?" Mountain Dennis asked, eyeing Lovejoy.

"I only go as far as the mendin' and stitchin' up," Virgil replied. "After that, it's up to y'all to care for yourselves. There's nothin' I can do now. Dahteste sees that he gets his fill of grub and he's already makin' headway with his recovery. Every man's gotta take responsibility for what he does, and we should respect him rather than cluckin' around like a bunch of old hens. Some men take time to heal, and others less; we're all different. If anyone can break records when it comes to getting well, Levi Beaver Johnson is your man."

"I reckon you're right," Dennis replied. "I'd say we've gotten carried away with all this fussing around. I know Levi is snappin' at us lately, so we must be gettin' under his skin."

"I only had the best intentions," Rusty grumbled. "I treat him like a son."

"Y'all gotta give 'em some rope." Kansas Marshal Walker smiled. "If you keep him all tied up, he's gonna turn on ya, and he might bite. He's plenty smart enough to know what he's doin'. I know if I was him, I'd be plumb fed up with yas."

Will Forrester stepped out of the far cabin nearest the stables and stretched into a yawn, arching his back. He patted his chest with open palms and walked toward Rusty's cabin. He casually saluted his friends and sat.

"If anybody knows what's goin' on his Levi's mind, it'll be the captain." Rusty grinned.

"What about Levi?" Forester asked.

"Do ya think he's pushin' himself too hard?" Rusty replied. "We're worried he's gonna bust open his wounds again, then we'll all be back in the same mess."

"I thought by now you all would know Levi's ways," Captain Forrester said. "You could talk to him until you were blue in the face, and he wouldn't change his mind once he has it set on something. Right now, he's focused on recuperating, and for Levi, *focus* is not defined the same as the rest of the world. What he does is something else far more intense, so relax, sit back, and watch. He'll break a record getting well if there is one available."

"I guess you're right," Angus said, "but it seems too

early for some of us. I know I scratch in the dirt and cluck like a hen, but somebody has to take care of him. Dahteste can't do it on her own."

Will shook his head and said, "No, you don't get it, do you? I don't know why it's so hard for you to understand. You *do* know what the definition of crazy is, right? It's when you keep doin' the same thing over and over again, expectin' a different result. Give it a chance and watch how he'll be able to get down to business without you hens in the way."

"Watch who you call a hen," Rusty growled. "I ain't beyond whoopin' youngsters."

Will chuckled, but he didn't say anything. Soon, Angus was rushing in and out of the back of the cabin to the cookstove. The smell of fresh biscuits floated in the air as stomachs growled. The more Angus cooked, the better he got. Now, when it came close to mealtime, everyone would gravitate toward the cabin closest to the south trail.

When asked, they would make up elaborate excuses that tickled McFarlin pink. He loved all the attention, especially at his age. He believed if older people weren't careful, they could become invisible and nobody would notice them anymore. It was a danger that he no longer feared.

"At least things are back to normal," Rusty said, "or almost, anyway. With all those bullets flying from those foolish prospectors, it's a wonder more of us didn't get shot."

Crow Stronghold

Will Forrester and his wife, Betty, accompanied Angus McFarlin and his wife, Pine Needle, to the large Crow camp just a half-day ride up the mountain. In a couple of months, Angus would head for the coming Rendezvous, and his wife was homesick and didn't want to wait in the compound for her spouse to return. This wasn't something new because she did the same every year, just at a different time.

Usually, she spent the summers with Angus in his cabin, and he would spend the winter with her in the Indian stronghold, snuggled up inside her teepee. Since she hadn't seen her family all summer, she decided to go home and forget the chaos at the Rendezvous and what it brought when they returned.

She had no desire to mingle with so many drunken White men in one small place at the same time. Pine Needle had heard that they came in the hundreds, and most of them weren't anything like Rusty, Angus, or the other people in the compound. She believed they would be as different as night and day, and she wouldn't be far from right.

Of course, there was gossip in all the Indian camps and many stories about the ugly White people. Some Indian tribes even gave their children demon-like descriptions when they looked pretty much like everybody else, except that they were White or Black and not Red. As a child, they taught Pine Needle White people were evil. But when she saw Angus cutting up the rug at a powwow they attended, she and half the women in the stronghold instantly got a crush on the fancy dancer.

A man's dancing skills were fundamental to the Crow women, and they had never seen anybody as good as Angus. He was even skilled at Indian specials like the Grass Dance, which nearly all Indian nations of the Great Plains embraced. From that moment on, he had the pick of the tribe's women. He married two others but divorced one, and the other died. He finally settled down for good with Pine Needle. He had met his other half and looked not further. Still, the women were dazzled every time he took the floor and did his thing, much to their delight despite his age.

They rode in single file up the narrowing trail with Angus in the lead, and Pine Needle closely following. After them came Betty with her husband, Will, riding drag. The wind ruffled his shoulder-length blond hair, and a long saber hung from his belt. His blue eyes flashed as he traced their surroundings for danger. Betty eyed her man like the newlyweds they were. Her face blushed red every time he touched her.

As they got nearer the stronghold, they felt eyes on them, but nobody showed themselves. Suddenly, they noticed Crow spies everywhere they looked. Pine Needle wasn't afraid for their lives, not even her husband's, who would be an enemy in many tribes' camps.

Still, something important was brewing with so many guards spying from every blind and lookout spot. As a tribe member, Pine Needle knew of many but not all. Some tribe members could be standing next to you; you wouldn't see them as they shadow-walked.

"I wonder what is happening in the stronghold?" Pine Needle asked. "I hope my family is safe."

"I ain't ever seen so many warriors guarding the path north since the big war with the Blackfeet ten years back," Angus replied. Concern etched his wrinkled face.

Halfway to the camp, mounted men stopped them. Three painted warriors blocked the narrow path. They waited with expressionless faces. After sitting silently for fifteen minutes, Wanata, the Crow tribe's war chief, rode into view. Until then, nobody dared ask the braves any questions. They knew from experience they probably wouldn't answer them anyway.

"Sho'daache Kaee, Dahteste, Angus," Wanata said, nodding. "Hello, to you too, Captain Will," he added in broken English.

"Sho'daache Kaee to you," Angus said. "What's up, Chief? So, you're wearin' war paint, are ya? You did a fine job, too. You look as fierce as the dickens."

"You must turn back, but Pine Needle will come with me," Wanata said in Crow—he wasn't asking; he was telling. "Chief Hachta ordered all our people to safety inside the camp. An old enemy lurks in these mountains, and no Crow is safe until this devil is dead. We want to ensure there are no captives, either. She will be safe with her mother and father, brothers, and sisters in the stronghold."

"That sounds pretty danged serious to me," Angus said. "But Will and I were just escorting my wife home to her family for a spell. We weren't stayin' anyway. We'll just turn around and mosey back down the trail if that's all right with you."

Without another word or explanation, they wheeled their horses and silently led Pine Needle away. In minutes, they disappeared up the winding trail and into stands of trees. The wind whistled through the pines, spreading the thick odor. Birds sang as they fluttered from one branch to another high above. The sky was void of vultures for a change.

"I wonder what in the world that was all about," Angus said as hooves clopped on the hard path. "They could have at least told us what they're so worried about, but I didn't dare ask. Indians are funny like that, sharing secrets and all. The Crow Indians are particularly tight-lipped. I reckon it don't concern us or they would have said somethin'. At least, I believe they would, but lately, everything has turned upside down, so I ain't all that sure anymore. Just the same, nobody asked what we wanted to do, so it's as clear as day. When you have no options, and the Crow wants it, we follow orders, like it or not. It's still their mountain we're livin' on."

"I have no idea what's going on, but it looks serious to me," Will replied. "The warriors seemed nervous and apparently meant business. There were lots of angry faces. At least, that's the feeling I got. I've found it's unhealthy to hang around anxious Indians. I didn't mind leaving at all."

"You better believe they meant it," Angus replied. "When I saw the look in War Chief Wanata's eyes, I knew it was best to follow orders and keep my mouth shut, but I'm curious just the same. What was it all about? I guess we'll have to wait to find out."

By then, any trace of Crow warrior braves had vanished, but they both felt and knew they were there even though they couldn't see them. The mountain men wheeled their horses and made the uncomfortable ride down the steep mountain.

"Sometimes I believe it's better to walk down this trail, yet a horse is mighty handy on the climb up," Angus said as his head bobbed back and forth with his body.

The captain's stallion, Midnight, gracefully made his way along the rocky, worn path. Sparks flashed as iron shoes hit stones. Both men kept looking around, and Angus had a rifle cradled in his arm. In anticipation, Captain Forrester thumbed the hammer on his pistol as his other sleeve flapped empty in the wind.

An hour later, they saw stains on the rocks in the middle of the trail. They pulled up for a moment, studying their surroundings. When they got near, they saw it was blood. If somebody else got trapped there, they could get bushwhacked, too.

"Where's the body?" Will asked as he looked around at the ground. "There's no signs of a carcass. I suppose it might have been a hunter. The strange thing is I don't see any tracks."

"Why don't I feel like that's what it was?" Angus asked, raising an eyebrow. "Somethin' smells rotten, and I feel like if we wait around to see what it is, it might be curtains for us. Somethings eatin' at my stomach like a couple of rats."

The ex-army captain stood in his stirrups and looked around three-hundred-sixty-degrees but saw nothing other than vultures. They had suddenly reappeared a few hundred feet above the claret. A bad feeling came over both men, and they nudged their horses' flanks despite the downhill grade. Something told them they better distance themselves from the blood, be it from man or beast.

"Let's get back to the cabins," Angus fussed. "I feel too vulnerable out here when something's up. Lately, we never know what's gonna hit us next. Then again, maybe this is an Indian thing, and that's why I didn't go into detail. Now, I don't feel so good with Pine Needle going with 'em back to the stronghold, though. I'd feel safer if she was with me."

"It seems like everything is changing constantly," Will complained. "We haven't had a quiet week for over six months. I never knew being a mountain man was such a complicated profession. We seem to have enemies coming out of the cracks everywhere we go."

"Well, nobody ever promised you were one hundred percent welcome up here in the Rockies, did they?" Angus said. "If you want to live in the wilderness, then it is what it is, and it's always changin'. That don't just go for now, but we've been subject to constant change ever since I came up here."

"I'm lookin' forward to the Rendezvous," Will said. "Betty's coming with me, aren't you, darlin'? I don't believe Levi will be in good enough shape to enter the sharpshooter's contest, if he goes at all. Rusty's going to win yet another year."

"Do you think they'll have dresses for sale at the trading post?" Betty asked. "Once in a while a woman wants to fancy up."

"You just never know with Levi," Angus said. "Then again, you know him better than I do. But if any man can make a quick recovery after a busted lung from a gunshot wound and a heart attack, it'll be Beaver Johnson."

They tightened the formation and put Betty in the middle as they quickly descended the path leading to the north gate of the compound.

Rendezvous

"Who said there won't be a trappers' meet this summer?" Rusty asked, shocked. "Why, last year, there must have been over five hundred frontiersmen, hunters, fur traders, Indians, and every kind of thief you can think of. How is it nobody's gonna go to somethin' that's been growin' every year? I find that kind of hard to believe, old friend."

"It's not about the trappers because they're still here, although there is half the beaver there was two years ago," Chief Hachta grumbled. "I doubt anybody knows about the cancelation yet. I don't even know how everybody will find out unless, when it comes time, they see it as they arrive and nobody's there."

"I can't see such a thing disappearing in a single year, though," Rusty said. "There are no White men's newspapers in the Rockies like there are in Fort Boise. I was wonderin' when they were gonna announce where it was this year."

"That paper is nothing but lies anyway," Angus replied. "Remember what it said about the fake gold strike? Without that headline, all the ruckus with the miners would have never happened."

"I learned about the Rendezvous from the smoke signals," Hachta said. He and a hunting party were passing by and had stopped to see his old friend. "They are much more reliable than White men's method of providing information. I'm surprised you didn't see them. They relayed for hundreds of miles. It is an important change we face. We rely on the fur traders meet for our supplies. Now, we will have to take the dangerous journey to Fort Boise, with enemies all along the way. Blackfeet rule the land in the eastern Yellowstone Valley. We'll have to trespass, so we will have to ride in large numbers, and it will make the soldiers nervous. This creates new dangers on all sides. We have managed to maintain a peace treaty between all tribes during the meet so all Indian nations could buy coffee, sugar, and steel tools—sometimes a few guns."

"You still ain't told me the which of why there's gonna be such a big change for the worse," Rusty said. "Where're we gonna sell our beaver pelts without the Rendezvous? If we take 'em to Fort Boise, they'll give us half of what the Canadian fur traders paid, if that. If we wanna make good money, we'll have to take 'em to Kansas."

"You *do* know that all those beaver pelts went to make smokestack hats for White people to wear back east and over the great waters," Hachata said. "I cannot tell you why, but the smoke signals said they no longer wear tall hats, so nobody wants the beaver pelts. Today, they are worth little to nothing. It doesn't surprise me that they don't like them. I never did. It looks like small tree trunks on their heads, and the brim is too small to ward off the sun. Cold-water beaver is warm, though, but tree branches must knock them off all the time. White men never cease to surprise me. Indians have been wearing the same clothing for centuries, and White men change what they wear every summer or two."

"There ain't no trees in the cities back east to knock your top hat off," Rusty said. "White folks ain't as practical as Indians. I reckon they wear 'em to show how rich they are. How is it that you know all about top hats, anyway? I ain't ever seen an Indian wearin' one."

"I have eyes, don't I?" Hachta replied. "I have been to the trappers meet to sell our furs. Few people see me because I don't linger, leave as soon as I get paid, and never drink. There, you can see samples of fancy hats in the fur trading companies' tents, and some of the traders wear them, too. They stick out like a skunk in a bed of roses."

A sudden look of bewilderment crossed Rusty's face. He stared into space, looking at nothing as his mind tried to wrap itself around the new information. The loss of beaver pelt trading would devastate men like him who lived high in the mountains. He began to wonder how they would make money to survive. A million questions bombarded his mind, leaving him overwhelmed. They would have to make significant changes in how they lived and provided the goods they needed.

"This is gonna be a problem that'll affect us all," Rusty whispered as he looked over his shoulder. "Who else knows about this?"

The chief unconsciously craned his neck to see who was close. He wasn't sure himself.

"Maybe we best speak English, so your people don't

understand what we're sayin'," Rusty said. "If we keep talkin' Crow, they're gonna put it together quick. We might wanna think about what it all means for a spell before lettin' the cat out of the bag."

"I am not the only man in camp who knows how to read smoke signals," Hachta said, giving Rusty a jarring look. "By the end of the day, the entire stronghold will know."

"I reckon I've been dotin' on Levi too much of late and not payin' as much attention as I should," Rusty said. "I saw the signals you sent me first thing this morning and knew you were coming straight away. Things have been chaotic in the compound since the gold hunters passed through and Levi died and returned to the livin'."

"What? I know he got shot and was near death, but I didn't hear he died," Hachta replied, confused. "Which is he then? Alive or dead? You can't be both."

"He's just as alive as you and me, but I swear we saw 'em die on the cabin table," Rusty said like he could hardly believe it himself. "Virgil listened and later even put a mirror to his mouth but there was no sign of life a-tall. We were just about to bury him in Dennis's coffin. It took the captain and me the better part of a day to pick out the frozen earth to dig a grave. It was a miracle."

"I've never heard this word you say, miracle. What does it mean?"

"That's a hard question, Chief," Rusty replied. "I don't rightly know how to answer. I reckon it's when something impossible happens, no matter what ya think. I believe that God brought 'em back. It was like Indian spirits came to this side and breathed life into his mouth."

The chief nodded, but he obviously didn't understand by the expression on his face. White men often perplexed him—even Rusty Steel, his blood brother.

"Do you think the army chief in Fort Boise heard about what happened with the gold seekers?" Hachta asked. "They don't mind killing Indians, but they get angry when we kill one of them."

"I don't see how they couldn't have found out by now," Rusty huffed, vexed. "Since it wasn't about killin' one man but better said a few hundred, I doubt it'll pass lightly. Believe it or not, some of them fellas got away despite havin' several tribes with hundreds of warriors after 'em. Don't get me wrong; I understand why y'all did it. Trespassin' is different up here than it is back east unless you're on rich peoples' land without permission. Then it's probably more or less the same. Wealthy folks like havin' big iron fences all around what's theirs. In the end, I'm afraid I think it was overkill when we should have somehow showed 'em they weren't welcome, sendin' 'em off packin'."

"And what kind of message would that have been?" Hachta asked. "These were not rational men, and most of them were violent. Wasn't it a prospector that shot Levi Johnson?"

"Yes, sir. The problem was, all of 'em arrived more or less at the same time," Rusty grumbled. "We didn't have a spell to ponder on the matter and figure out what we should do before they were at our door. We had no warning until they were already camped on the mountain not an hour from my cabin, and they were fightin' mad from the start. I don't know how many of 'em attacked the compound like only men crazed by gold fever could. Most of 'em were so green they walked into chaos and didn't know how to get out."

"There were too many tribes to steer them away from the bloodshed," Hachta replied. "My voice was one of many, and my lifelong enemy was our host. Even if we could have found another plan, it would have fallen on deaf ears."

"I was wonderin', have ya ever heard of a half-breed Comanche outlaw named Wood Duck?" Rusty asked.

Chief Hachta's face suddenly changed into a mask with no apparent emotions. It was as though chiseled into stone.

"What's the matter, Chief?" Rusty asked. "Oh, you must know who I'm talkin' about then, don't cha?"

"The evil spirit walks the earth," Chief Hachta whispered.

"Why, that's just what I said," Rusty replied. "The Devil walks the earth. There ain't no other description for Wood Duck. He's done things to people that I won't even repeat. They give me nightmares."

The chief's controlled expression broke—he flinched when he heard the name. It obviously meant as much to him as it did to Rusty and Walker. Everybody else who had crossed Wood Duck's path with ill intentions had died.

A steady breeze whistled through the pines, filling the air with the natural odor. The snow had melted entirely except for the higher peaks. Green grass covered the valleys, and wild game was readily visible in the distance. Cirrostratus crossed the sky like wisps of hair as woodpeckers hammered against trees. Millions of blades of grass swirled like ocean waves as gusts of wind crossed the valley floor.

"When do you think the soldiers will come?" Hachta asked. "Maybe they won't begin to look for us until next year. With times like these, who knows where we will be in twelve moons."

"Well, I reckon they'll come in the spring and spend the summer lookin' for signs of what happened and exactly who did it. They know they can't take on all the tribes," Rusty replied, "but I doubt they'll be waitin' until next year, either."

"The only thing we have going for us is the caravan got attacked on Blackfoot land, so they will have to fight through them before they get to my Crow tribe," the chief said.

"Remember what the Blackfeet did when the prospectors arrived?" Rusty asked. "They let the first hundred pass right on through and didn't even try to stop 'em. They may well do the same with the army, although the cavalry ain't run by a bunch of fools like them men with gold fever. That's why so many died. Still, we better be ready to get hit first, just the same. There's a bunch of dead men who put off what they should have done today until tomorrow."

"What will you do now, Rusty Steel?" Chief Hachta asked. His face had new wrinkles every year, and this one had been exceptionally hard on the leader of the Crow stronghold.

"I reckon I'll get everybody together and talk things over with my clan," Rusty said. "We can't travel yet even if we wanted to. Not with Levi still on the mend. Plus, I doubt the cavalry will be too hard on us, as we're White. We're gonna have to think up a good story to tell 'em if we want 'em to leave us alone. You just never know, though. It all depends on the officer they send with the soldiers. If we get somebody new who wants to make a name for themselves, we might have a problem."

"Every White soldier I've met wanted to make a big reputation," Hachta said.

"Yeah, it's true. Some of 'em volunteer to come to the frontier just so they get a chance to shoot at somethin'. And that somethin' usually be an Indian of one tribe or another. I've heard of some real mean fellas that killed elders, women, and children and then burned the camps. If they want your land, there's no such thing as goin' too far. But to keep the law over a bunch of crazy folks with gold fever, I doubt they'll be willin' to give up their lives. Then again, it is about the officer in charge. A crazy leader can make for some crazy followers, too."

Marshal Walker

"I wonder how Rory Breaker's doin'?" Marshal Joseph Walker pondered. "I hope he ain't given up on me. That would put my wagon train in a spot. Actually, I miss my old friend. I suppose I'll have to plan on packin' my mule and headin' down the mountain and up to The South Pass any day now."

"How long has Breaker been ridin' with ya, Marshal?" Levi Johnson asked.

"It must be near on a decade now," Joseph replied. "He's the best right-hand man I've ever had. He's as brave as they come and don't talk back—I've never heard him sass. I'll need him on the journey across the Oregon Trail. If we make this trip, it'll just be the start. Maybe next time we'll drive four or five hundred wagons and the animals and people that go with such a large wagon train."

"If you saddle up and load your mule, you can make it out of here by noon." Rusty chuckled. "There ain't nobody here stoppin' ya. I'll even help ya with the saddle."

"There ain't nothin' shy about you, is there, Rusty?" Joseph spat. "Don't worry, I'll be out of your hair soon enough, you grumpy old fart. You don't have to push. I can pack my mule and saddle my own horse. I can't get away from that mouth of yours until I light out. I feel sorry for ya, Angus, and you too, Dennis. Virgil, I reckon you can leave anytime ya wanna. You're welcome to come along with me."

"I still don't know why a man would want to put himself in such a position of responsibility," Angus fussed. "I'd never be able to put up with all the chaos without shootin' somebody. What gave you such a fool notion, anyway?"

"I'd be more bothered about all those who'll die along the trail," Rusty said. "With two hundred wagons, you're gonna have well over a thousand people to take care of. Do you think you and Rory can manage such a large group on your own? All of 'em will be green, and half won't speak English."

"Why do you speak so badly of a noble cause?" the marshal asked. "When I make it to Oregon City and back, the newspapers will say I'm a hero. Now, whatcha think of that?"

"I think you've been smokin' too much loco week for your own good." Rusty chuckled, which quickly turned into laughter. Both old friends joined in. "You've got to stop goin' to see that witch doctor. He's turnin' your mind into mushy mud."

"He's a medicine man, and he gives me herbs to eat to make me strong while I prepare for the trip," Marshal Walker said. "He's one of Chief Hachta's men. I ain't no fool."

"I figure all of them medicine men and shamans be

witch doctors at night," Mountain Dennis said. "I've had nothin' but bad experiences with 'em in the past. Even if they act all friendly-like, I know for a fact that none of 'em like White folks."

"What makes ya say that?" Rusty asked.

"When have we met a medicine man that didn't look down their noses at us?" Angus asked. "Dennis is right. You best be careful. They might be feedin' ya poison for all you know."

"If he wants to sidekick up with a witch doctor, I reckon it's his right, but this whole deal with taking so many people across what you say is gonna be the Oregon Trail is bad for everybody but you, Joseph," Rusty said, but now he wasn't hacking on his friend—he was serious. "You saw how the Indians took to the prospectors on their land without permission. Whatcha think they're gonna do when you go traipsing across their country with a thousand people or more? The next thing we know, they'll be showin' up here, tryin' to take Crow land, not to mention our own right here in the compound. You saw how those greedy White folks came at us with guns a-blazin'. I believe you're just openin' a can of worms."

"You still don't see the writin' on the wall, do ya, you old fool?" the marshal growled. "It ain't about what I do or what you want. What's wrong with you is that you believe that the world doesn't change. Especially if you hide out up here in the mountains. Like it or not, that change you ignore is gonna come and bite ya in the butt if you ain't prepared."

"Yeah, and with your Oregon Trail, more Easterners will be snoopin' around here in two shakes of a lamb's tail," Rusty moaned. "A couple of weeks' ride from The

South Pass to Yellowstone Valley and another seven days to climb this high. They'll be so many folks wanderin' around the countryside that they're bound to stumble onto us, and what then?"

"You've got your head buried in the sand, old man," Joseph said as he began to rile.

"If you call me an old man again, you won't have to walk off the porch 'cause I'll throw ya off," Rusty retorted. "You won't be so pretty if I break your snoopy nose."

"You sound like a couple of young kids full of testosterone and nowhere to go." Virgil laughed. "Y'all ought to be ashamed of yourselves."

"Test-what?" Joseph asked. "Just because you been readin' up on what doctors do don't mean you need to throw them fancy words at us. We're just common folks."

"Speak for yourself, moron." Rusty chuckled. "Go ahead and admit it, Joseph. You're dumb as a dog's foot."

"Maybe you ought to look in the mirror once in a while, and you'll see how old the both of ya are." Dennis laughed. "You're no spring chicken either, Marshal. The young folks are still in their cabins with their young wives. All that's sittin' here on this porch are aging men. Some a little younger and others a little older, but there's no youngsters here, so don't go hackin' on Rusty when you're on the front steps of the same age."

"I guess Rory will be there waitin' for me in a couple of weeks," Marshal Walker said. "I'd like to get there before he arrives, so I have some time to check out how the winter weather has affected the trail. It was as rough as a gator's back the last time we crossed. Then we'll ride back, pick up the folks and their wagons, and begin headin' west so we'll have good weather on the way."

"And what are ya gonna do if he ain't there waitin' on ya?" Rusty asked, now serious. "It's been a long winter, and a lot of things could happen, and your man will have a passel of miles to ride. Anything can and will happen. You know that as well as any of us."

"There you go again with all that negativity," Joseph retorted. "Why can't you give a friend some encouragement for a change? That's what buddies are supposed to be for."

"There you go with that friendship bull again," Rusty replied. "I still haven't decided if I like ya or not—even after all these years." But then he was laughing. He didn't know why, but he had always enjoyed hacking on Marshal Walker because it was so easy to rile him up.

"Since you've been here all winter, how do you know if you have interested clients to travel across the country or not?" Virgil asked.

"Rory Breaker is gonna take care of all that," Joseph said confidently. "I know I can rely on him. He's good at organizing things, but he ain't all that great with people, so that's where I come in."

"I still say you're gonna start somethin' that nobody is gonna be able to stop," Rusty complained.

"Like I said before, nobody can stop the progress machine," Joseph said. "It's just as unstoppable as a roarin' locomotive."

Rory Breaker

Rusty and Angus were the first two up, but the other unmarried men followed shortly. As always, McFarlin was busy making coffee and breakfast. Unlike in the past, since Levi got shot, Dahteste made him stay in bed until she had his breakfast of five eggs, a quarter pound of bacon, and a half dozen freshly baked biscuits. She wouldn't let him leave the cabin until he ate the last bite.

Each day at sunrise, his wife brought his meal to him on a tray. Even though he hated it when the others pampered him, he loved how his wife doted on him with the day's first and most important meal. A man who had a demanding schedule ahead of him had to have the required nourishment. Especially a person recovering from a gunshot wound from a heavy-caliber rifle.

The Crow woman cooed and cawed as she gave him one last cuddle before beginning another tiring day. She, too, was exhausted from chopping wood, even if they were only working on the light stuff. Now she realized how strong her husband was and would soon be again. She smiled every time she saw the determined look on his face and felt lucky to have found such a good husband. He had changed his life for her, and she sincerely appreciated it. It made her respect him all the more.

The unmarried men all walked onto Rusty's porch and took a seat. The sun dangled just out of sight over the world's edge, ready to bring a new day. Still light warmed a dark sky. As dawn came, direct sunlight arrived with it. One of their favorite things was to watch the sunrise on a warm spring day. They lit their pipes, hiding behind curtains of hazy gray smoke. The mountain men patiently waited for the show of beautiful lights and waves of warm rays.

A long shadow stood from the pike to the end of the split-rail fence around the corral, but they all knew it wasn't supposed to be there. They blinked their eyes as they stared. The lawman gasped a sigh in reverse. Joseph rubbed his eyes with the heel of his hands and looked again in disbelief.

"What the hell is that?" Marshal Walker asked as he pushed back his chair and stood. He growled and spat a stream of juice off the porch.

"How did somebody get into the yard?" Dennis asked. "Who would dare?"

The lawman steadied himself, placing his hands flat on the tabletop as he narrowed his eyes and stared at the initially unidentifiable object at the end of the pike. The sunlight spilled across the yard as the shadows shrunk and the sun began to edge into the sky.

"It looks like it had ears," Rusty whispered. "I believe it's somebody's head. Go in and grab some more guns, boys. Somebody's been inside our compound while we were asleep. How did that one get by ya, Dog?" He frowned at the canine at his feet.

With a pistol in each man's fists, they crossed the yard to the post protruding from the ground. Torn pieces of skin at the ear holes said it was a head: that and two empty eye sockets. There were bite marks everywhere—even scratched into the skull. What was left was primarily white bone.

"Look at the foot of the pike," Will whispered. Danger filled the air as they swung around with their pistols, ensuring nobody was behind them, ready to pounce.

The sun was high enough now for rays to bounce off the shiny badge. It said: US Deputy Marshal.

"Rory Breaker," Marshal Walker croaked like an old frog. "What have they done to ya, boy?"

"Are you sure that's Rory?" Will asked. "I didn't know he was a deputy marshal."

"Unfortunately, he ain't. I reckon I just never got around to it and kept puttin' it off because of all the paperwork, but I paid him just the same," Joseph said. "He told me he got the badge to remind him what was at stake, and it would make him be a better lawman. But I reckon I didn't pay enough attention. I didn't think it meant so much to him, and now I reckon it's too late. I should have made him my deputy a long time ago, or he wouldn't have carried that badge all these years. I admit that sometimes I'm blind to other people's feelings. I just figure they're all as hard as I am when they ain't."

They could all see the marshal felt somehow responsible. He squatted and studied the ground as though he was looking at the tracks when he was trying to blink back a tear.

"Let me have a look," Rusty said. He stared at the crushed grass and over to the edge of the narrow gate and down the worn path. He crumbed dirt in his hand, then grabbed a fistful and smelled it, frowning.

"The gate was unlatched so he must have walked right in as bold as could be," Rusty said. His eyes raced all along the fence around the yard. "I only see the tracks of one man, and he's wearin' moccasins. He must have tied his horse back in the woods, or Dog would have barked. Whoever it is, he's good at sneakin' up on folks 'cause one of us should have heard it."

"I've always thought everybody has a little of the devil and an angel in 'em too," Virgil said. "But not this one. There's not a hint of anything but evil here."

Steel began studying the pike Rory's head hung on. "This here's Comanche markings," Rusty said. "I haven't heard of any boys from that tribe around here, have you?"

Marshal Walker removed his jacket and gently laid it over the decapitated head. Then he pulled it off the pike and laid it on the ground.

"I'm gonna need a spade," Joseph moaned. "I wanna bury what's left of my friend. God knows where the rest of him lay. At least we've got enough for a little ceremony."

"We've got a hole already dug right here in the yard," Angus said. "It's the one we made for Levi when we thought he was gonna die. So, at least you won't have to do the hard labor. We did it when the ground was frozen. All you can do now is mourn."

"That ain't all I'm gonna do, and you can bet your

life on that," Marshal Walker growled. "Whoever did this is gonna pay and pay plenty."

"Joseph, come with me, and the rest of y'all stay right here and defend our homes," Rusty said. "I don't know who did this, but I believe we're lookin' at a whole new threat. I ain't even seen the Blackfeet do anything like this. And why bring him here?"

"Whoever did it obviously knows I'm here," the marshal said. "This is for me in particular. He's sendin' a signal is what he's doin'." The lawman stopped for a moment and exchanged stares with Rusty. "You don't think it could be *him*, do ya?"

"Who else could it be?" Rusty replied. "I don't know anybody other than him or one of his men could sneak into camp like that. This is just the sort of torture and butchery I'd expect from such a villain. Do you think it could be one of his boys?"

"No, it wasn't one of his gang members," Marshal Walker said. "He came to do this himself. You know him; he's a hands-on kind of outlaw."

"Whoever this fellow is that tortured Rory," Will said, "probably forced him to tell him where we are. Do you want to let the rest of us in on all this before our heads end up on pikes, too?"

"I reckon it's Wood Duck who done this," Walker said. "He's a half-Comanche, half-White renegade outlaw. He's terrorized ten or twelve states for the last thirty-five years."

"It has his name written all over it, don't it?" Rusty said. "Come on, let's get to it, or his track is gonna get cold. While we're gone, Angus can fill you in about Wood Duck. He'll have an earful for ya. If we ain't back straight away, don't fret. It might take us a spell to find him. When I get near, I'll whistle and send Dog to ya to make sure it's all clear. If you don't hear me whistle, shoot anybody that gets near the fence. And mind ya now—one bullet ain't gonna do it. I reckon it would take three or four bullets to put the madman down."

In minutes, Rusty and Joseph had their traveling gear, and Angus prepared grub for a day or two. Pistols showed from belts and pockets, and they carried a rifle in each hand. Goatskin water bags hung over their shoulders. Virgil led Socks, the marshal's beige quarter horse, and Rusty's horse, Flossie, an Andalucian Gray, to the edge of the porch.

"Tell Levi and the ladies we've taken off to run to ground a bad outlaw, but we'll be back soon enough," Rusty said, full of confidence.

From the look on Marshal Walker's face, he didn't appear as though he was so sure about what they were heading out to do.

"Maybe it would be better if we took an army," Joseph moaned. "Remember, there're nine of them."

"Just because we're gonna track 'em down don't mean we're gonna pick a gunfight," Rusty replied. "The only way to catch or kill an outlaw like this one is by using our brains, and he ain't a tiny bit dumb, either."

"I don't know how a renegade outlaw without the least bit of education could turn out so danged crafty," Joseph grouched. "It would befall us to take care with this scoundrel."

"He picked us," Rusty said. "We didn't pick him."

They slipped their rifles into their scabbards and mounted their horses, wheeling them toward the gate. They, like the Blackfeet the month before, took the west gate and the old trail from the compound. Dog raced around the horses, glad to get back on the road.

"Hush up now, or you're gonna let every Indian in the Rockies know where we are," Joseph growled at the mountain man's dog. He reached down to smack the canine on the snout.

When the marshal heard the gun's hammer click, he turned his head to find Steel had a pistol in his hand.

"Don't you ever raise your hand to my dog again, or I'll shoot ya, friend or not," Rusty said in a husky voice. He clucked his tongue and rode off, riding point with his canine racing around his horse, having the time of his life.

Joseph chose to ignore Rusty's threat. He knew he was on edge, just like him. Chasing down outlaws was one thing, but hunting for Wood Duck was something entirely different. Either of them could die in the process if not them both—maybe even his dog.

The Outlaw Gang

"The last time Joseph Walker saw Rory Breaker was at The North Pass, so he won't know a thing," Wood Duck said as an evil grin crossed his face, and his eyes lit up with delight. It was clear the outlaw renegade loved his job. He lived for the sport of hunting humans. "Up in those mountains, they're pretty much out of touch with the rest of the world, so I doubt anybody but the marshal will know we're even still alive. We were running west the last time he saw us, and he and his posse gave up the chase. For him, we could be anywhere by now, The marshal won't believe it when we pop up right before his face high in those mountains." He nodded toward the vast range above them.

"I doubt it will be a happy reunion. I wonder what the Crow and Blackfeet will say when they see us?" Nashoba, the Choctaw from Mississippi, said with bloodthirsty eyes. His name meant wolf. "They will probably run away when they hear we are in the valley. They know we have killed scores of braves from all tribes, and none have killed even one of us. That includes all the lawmen, too. Half of them died, as well."

"If we corner the marshal and Rusty Steel in the mountains, where are they gonna run?" Wuyi, the Miwok Indian from California, asked. His name meant Soaring Turkey Vulture.

"Over the range of snow-covered peaks?" Nashoba laughed.

"They better, if they value their lives." Wood Duck snickered. "Right now, we must make sure we don't let too much information leak into the Indian gossip, or we'll scare them off. I doubt the Blackfeet will warn their lifelong enemies above the valley floor. I wanna have a go at some Crow hunters to get Chief Hachta's attention first. We can do that on the way up to wherever Steel has made his home. That's the tribe that governs this part of the Rockies. This is going to be some fine sport."

The famous renegade outlaw gang crossed the Yellowstone Valley unchallenged. As they had expected, the Blackfeet, Bannock, and Shoshone warriors watched them hidden in the distance, but nobody attempted to confront them. They all hoped the troublemakers would continue and not stop, other than camping for the night. Even without a powwow, they declared a temporary truce between the valley Indians. What happened high in the Rockies was of little concern to them.

The renegade warriors wore animal skins, pieces of fine silk, bits of White men's clothing, and the occasional article of a blue uniform. One was a frogged and braided officer's jacket worn by the only White man in the gang, and even he was raised in an Indian stronghold from the age of thirteen.

Others wore rawhide helmets with buffalo horns, with their faces painted black, dark green, and blood-red shades. Their horses' manes and tails were braided with brightly colored fabric, fluttering in the breeze. The coat of hair on the gang leader's horse was dyed orange and had white handprints all over its body.

They left the valley floor and climbed the trail they tortured out of Rory just before he died.

"Lucky for us, after a long session of torture, Rory spilled his guts." Wood Duck chuckled. "Then again, with our skills, don't they all? Now we know from here we have a seven-day ride. Hopefully, we will run into some sport before we get to the three-cabin compound high above."

As soon as they hit the trail, it became steep for the first half day, then summits would dip into lush valleys and then up to another mountaintop. The worn path curved and turned like a switch-back trail.

Wook Duck pulled his painted horse to a stop and sniffed the air. "I already smell burning wood. That is our first sign of humans." He carefully looked across the sky above the treetops and pointed. "Over there, it's just barely visible. As soon it reaches the open air, it vanishes with the breeze."

"I see it, too," Luke Dawson said. "I'd say it's less than an hour away."

"Distances are deceiving in the mountains," Wood Duck said. "It will take us two hours to travel what would usually take one."

The White gang member was born and raised in Texas

until the Comanche kidnapped him and made him a slave when he had just turned a teenager. In his mind, he was more Comanche than a White man and was one hundred percent diabolical like the people who raised him. The day he met Wood Duck, he and his gang of renegades attacked the camp, and as they slaughtered his capturers, he joined in and slayed a dozen braves from the tribe himself.

This pleased Wood Duck, especially as he came from the Comanche and lived by their ways of life. He was also as violent as the tribe that raised him. When the gang leader asked if Luke wanted to join the gang, he immediately agreed. For the first time since he was a small boy, he again had a family of sorts, and all of them were very much like him. They all enjoyed killing for sport. Hunting men was much more amusing than hunting wild game—even mountain lions and grizzly bears.

When they neared the smoking fire with stealth only the Indians and mountain men possessed, they saw a black stain on the side of a canyon wall. Before the dark opening sat a family who was just beginning their meal. As they said grace with closed eyes, the killers closed the distance silently. Only their smell was noticeable to the trained frontiersman but not by innocent Easterners who had taken a chance and set out to strike it rich in unknown lands. They were more green trespassers without the slightest notion of the dangerous land on which they trespassed.

All the tribes had missed them and mountain men alike, while the family worked daily in an adjacent spring. Despite the fact they hadn't found an ounce of the valuable golden dust, they believed this was where they would make their fortune. Then, they would continue across The South Pass and east until they hit Oregon.

As he clasped his hands, the father said, "Bless us, O Lord, and these, Thy gifts, which we are about to receive from Thy bounty. Through Christ, our Lord. Amen."

Wood Duck gigged his horse, and it lunged for the White family. The leader of the assailants grabbed the husband and father by his hair and scalped him, standing as his wife and children watched. He screamed a howl of outrage as he watched his family murdered. They left him for last, so he would have to see it to the end.

The only American outlaw in the renegade gang slipped his boot back and out of the stirrup and kicked the mother square in the face. Bones cracked, her nose bent, and teeth flew—the white objects stared back at her from the ground. Her husband tried to reach out for her, and the rest of his hair broke loose in the gang leader's fist.

An instant later, his wife, son, and daughter suddenly tottered on broken arrows as they tried to make themselves as small as possible without success. Despite the blood streaming down his face and into his eyes, he blinked as he watched his family slaughtered.

As he shook his head and tried to make sense of what was going on, Wood Duck deftly slipped a loose slipknot over his head as Nashoba tossed the other end over a low branch of a tree standing beside the cave and looped it around his saddle horn and pulled him into the air. His arms flailed over his head and his feet kicked in the air. The gang members sat on their horses and watched him struggle with bulging eyes for twelve long minutes.

"Burn him!" Wood Duck ordered. "I soaked the rope in water and mud, so it won't burn." He grinned evilly.

"But he's already dead, boss," Luke Dawson replied. "He won't feel a thing. I thought torture was all about making 'em scream and thrash about. He's already done all the wiggling and yellin' he's ever gonna do."

"Yeah, but anybody that sees him hanging there, all carbon black and charred, will remember what they saw," Wood Duck said. He couldn't stifle a chuckle as it escaped his thin lips.

It was easy to see he enjoyed spreading fear and vicious violence. The renegade gang leader was one of a kind. Yet, his men were a close second when it came to wicked minds. They were all masters of torture and murder in the most unusual ways.

In minutes, the other three family members swung in the air with the soft breeze. Finally, the father remained with a frozen gesture of pain and terror on his red and bloated face. The young boys and women got scalped for their blond hair. In minutes, their bodies were stripped of all their clothing as the renegades poked at the lifeless bodies with long lances.

Bottle flies buzzed and clamored over the wigless skulls and walked into open mouths around bloated tongues and into noses, ears, and eyeholes as the vultures flapped their wings, hissed, and battered nearby. Wolves slunk in the shadows, carefully awaiting their turn. Low grumbling growls were heard from deep inside the wild canines.

Wood Duck leaned slightly toward the dead as he studied his handiwork. Later that night, he would play the scene over and over in his mind's eye, enjoying it time and again. Behind him, his gang members began to hoot and holler, pummeling each other on the backs like gorillas as their eyes danced in delight. They watched as the father burned.

The half-White man and half-Comanche warrior wheeled his horses smartly, trotting through his eight men, who all turned and followed their leader. There was no question who was in charge.

As soon as they vanished into the trees and rode toward the path they had been following, the wolves raced from their cover in the shadows, and the vultures' great wings flapped, making whooshing sounds as they deftly lighted on the dead, and they began by pecking out their eyes, but not the husband's. His popped like water-filled ballons when the fire reached his face. The villains could hear them burst as they rode away.

Three Crow hunters silently followed the elk into the dense forest well off the beaten paths. They had tracked them for hours but knew patience would win the day. The braves squatted silently with two arrows between their fingers and another clamped in their mouths. Their focus on the elk intensified as they slowly grazed their way. They crouched behind bushes as the wild game innocently closed the distance between freedom and certain death.

The Crow hunters took deep breaths to steady their nerves, their bodies coiled for the moment they would spring to their feet and loose well-placed arrows. They were now so near they could hear the animals pull at the long grass and slide their jaws. The hunters were startled when one of the elk bugled an eerie high-pitched sound, signaling the bull's virility and desire to mate.

It wasn't rutting season, but he was following his three six-year-old females in their prime. The smell of urine-soaked mud floated on puffs of air. The seven-hundred-pound, nine-year-old male made it clear he was ready to rut with his harem.

Despite the fact it was too early in the season, it was warming up, and the bull's testosterone levels spiked. Yet, the females were unreceptive, as they would wait until late August or until the end of October when the actual rutting season came.

Both Crow hunters stood suddenly, letting three arrows each fly as they targeted the animals' hearts. Legs doubled, and the elk kneeled as blood poured from their mouths. Death came quickly and cleanly. It was time to butcher the meat and pack it on their mule's back. They had tied their animals far enough away from the wild game they wouldn't hear them when they neighed, nickered, or whinnied into a heehaw.

The Indian hunters were so focused on their task that they only noticed the presence of someone else's shadows who suddenly stood beside them. When they looked up, they locked eyes with devils. Rifle butts slammed into heads as the hunters fell unconscious to the ground. Chuckles turned into laughter that echoed across the valley and bounced off the sides of the mountains. Wood Duck's men patted each other on their backs as they took swigs from a jug of corn liquor.

After fastening their preys' hands and ankles together, they threw the Crow braves across the backs of their horses. Santana, the Kiowa outlaw from Texas, had watched them as they had tied them far from their targets, the elk. His name meant White Bear, and he had trailed the hunters since early that morning. Now, they would awake with a surprise. Horses hooves filled the air as they hammered on the soft earth. All four outlaws grinned as violence flashed in their eyes.

Shilah, the Navajo renegade from Colorado, tied their hands spread-eagle on a bed of gravel on a creek's bank. His name meant brother. Viho, the Cheyenne outlaw, tied their legs. His parents from Oklahoma named him Chief with big expectations. But things hadn't worked out as they had hoped, and he had become an infamous outlaw instead.

Wood Duck walked up to the Crow hunters with greedy eyes. He raised his arm without a word, and the sun flashed off the White man's hatchet's steel blade. It happened so quickly that even his men were surprised. Four hands and four feet remained attached to ropes and stakes as bodies thrashed on the creek bank like beached fish.

The smell of blood, vacated corpses, and death rose from the ground like poisonous weeds. Coyotes howled, and they moved toward the slaughter. The smell of blood was fresh in the air, and the scavengers could smell something to eat from four hundred yards.

Before the innocent hunters bled out, the gang leader pushed them into the water with his foot so he could watch them drown. Face down, they silently drifted downstream as laughter filled the air. Strips of skin hung from blood-matted beaks and faces as wings whooshed six feet wide. The vultures floated with the bodies as they dined.

Fort Boise

US Cavalry Captain Dallas Sutton was the officer in charge of the patrol that was preparing to search for over five hundred dead or captured prospectors. Some estimates were as high as a thousand, but the captain didn't believe exaggerations and lies. The rumors had been full of hostile Indians and violence. He thought it impossible for men with bows and arrows to defeat so many White men, even if they had a few old muskets; it just didn't make any sense.

How could the local natives so easily defeat that many heavily armed men in what was said to be minutes? Some witnesses claimed it took seconds, while others swore it was hours, so the officer made his own guesstimate. Panic and fear could make a man imagine things and play the devil with time. The officer believed every man west of the Missouri River knew how to shoot because their survival depended on it, and even the Indians who had guns never had enough black powder and lead to practice enough to become marksmen, not alone sharpshooters.

If there were four to five hundred prospectors, how many Indians did it take to render them defenseless in such a short time? Finally, the captain decided there must have been thousands of hostile Indians. Otherwise, it made no logical sense.

Of course, an inexperienced man in battle had a different notion of time than the veteran fighter. Some things that passed in seconds were perceived to take hours. Confusion and chaos added an exaggerated space and time, so he had to carefully pick what he chose to believe or not. There were also some who made up out-and-out untruths. These men the captain considered of questionable nature and dismissed them immediately with a threat of punishment if they mistakenly took him for a fool again.

Where there was a supposed gold strike, you would find outlaws and thieves, too. Everybody was interested in easy money. For over five hundred gold seekers, it wasn't as easy as they had expected. There were more Indians living in the valley than initially believed. The captain and his men were ridiculously outnumbered, but then again, they always were, and they were still alive. They depended on their skills and their leader's plans to repeatedly succeed and win the day.

The reports from the most reliable soldiers had been full of terrifying acts and hundreds of White men's scalps. Those who relayed the event said the hostiles were so numerous they looked like termites as they moved as one, from both sides of the mountains, leaving hundreds of enemy warriors standing on their flanks.

Now, he had to find the supposed location of the attack and those responsible for the violence. Dallas wondered which of the five tribes in the vicinity would be most likely. All the signs pointed to the Blackfoot Nation and their warrior braves. It was common for them to behave with total disregard for life. Only the Comanche had a worse reputation. The captain and his patrol had witnessed this firsthand.

Of course, the officer knew there were several more Indian tribes between the fort and Yellowstone Valley, and most of them, if not all, were hostile. The proof was in the recent attack. Over fifty men staggered back into the barracks, asking for the surgeon after striking off to look for gold. Of them, fifteen died after medical attention.

They were all shot to pieces with both arrows and bullets. Some appeared to be hacked with tomahawks or beaten with clubs. The myth of the Native Americans not having firearms was just that—a myth. It didn't matter when they acquired the weapons; the only important fact was their possession. This changed the situation substantially.

Still, even with the fastest men reloading, it made their defense limited when the hostiles appeared to have an unlimited supply of arrows, and some could shoot as many as three projectiles every seven seconds. If only the army soldiers could do the same with their firearms. Their current solution was to carry as many rifles and pistols as possible. The fact the government supplied weapons in such numbers was why they could stand up to the resistance of the Indian tribes to give away their land to the US Government.

Yet, they seemed to be at an impasse regarding strength in combat, so Dallas knew he had to tread carefully while heading for the crime scene. Even with twenty-four veteran soldiers and an experienced Indian fighter to lead them, it could still be risky. His information on the valley and mountains above was minimal. It mostly came from the prospectors who were not precisely intellectuals, so he took much of their reconnaissance information with a grain of salt. The captain believed the best way to find out what was going on was with boots on the ground, and he intended to be the first one.

The following day, a cavalry patrol would head south for the valley and the location the fleeing prospectors described. It didn't sound like it would be too hard to find. The problem was it sounded like a perfect location for another ambush. It was obvious why the hostile Indians had picked it, and Dallas was aware of the fact and planned to prepare accordingly.

Captain Sutton wasn't new to the duty of Indian fighter. He had fought Comanche and Apache from Mexico overland all the way to Kansas. His battle-hardened face and thousand-yard stare told the story and was impossible to miss. Dallas wasn't the kind of man people overlooked when he walked into a room. It was quite the opposite. With only a stare, he demanded respect, and everybody listened when he talked. Timid people dropped their eyes when he locked their stare.

Sutton's face was a roadmap of tiny scars, as were his arms and legs, but his uniform was impeccable even though it was dusty from the long ride. All his soldiers wore complete uniforms, and the officer permitted no variations. He would never allow his men to look like ragtag lowlifes. They were the US Cavalry, and Dallas believed it was no small thing. He considered them the best the army had to offer, no matter what military branch.

The break of dawn saw them in a tight formation as the army patrol trotted out of the fort in single file. Men moaned at the early hour as horses sniffled. The dull thump of hooves, squeaking leather saddles, and the endless soft jingling of harnesses accompanied creaky boots.

A whirlwind made scarves of dust far ahead as it raced across the ridges. The cloud kicked by the twenty-four-man patrol vanished in the immensity of the land. This far west, the earth seemed to blend in with the sky, making it all endless. A man could see for twenty miles.

The captain led the way. In the officer's scabbard was a high-powered, round shot, flintlock percussion, 56-caliber Hawken rifle with an effective range of over five hundred yards. It was an expensive gun with only a thousand produced, weighing fifteen pounds. It had a worn walnut beaver-tail stock.

The captain's rifle had a double trigger, and a long Morgan James telescopic sight sat over the blade sight on the end of the octagon barrel. His sergeant carried a spyglass to lead him to his targets and indicate if the shot was high or low with the nudge of his hand.

Of course, the officer didn't have to fight on the front line as a sniper, but Dallas enjoyed the contact. For him, it was more sport than a battle; war was contagious and had cursed him most of his life. He had survived so many battles he made the dire mistake of believing he was indestructible, or an angel was looking over him, so he sometimes flaunted death despite the danger. So far, it hadn't caught up with him.

Dallas Sutton remembered when he was young and

how he felt the fear before an engagement. But after he risked his life, time and again, his brain rewired and assured him he could continue to do as in the past. After being the victor of so many battles, he began to take both his courage and his superior skills for granted. He was a proud alpha male and West Point graduate and felt larger than life compared to others.

The officer also had a brace of flintlock pistols in scabbards mounted across the pommel and horn of his saddle. This made them readily accessible when mounted, with two more crossed in his broad saber's belt. So much iron and steel would weigh down the average man and horse, but there wasn't anything common about either. Both were big and strong and had challenging characters.

A week down the trail, the first two men fell sick, and within hours, one died, then another became ill, replacing the dead man. The patrol medic couldn't make an accurate diagnosis. It wasn't cholera or small-pox, but there could have been a dozen other diseases. Hopefully, it wouldn't run through ranks like poop through a goose and leave the captain shorthanded for an already difficult task.

The sun in the west flashed pale streaks of red, which deepened in color until it looked like blood. The fiery disk sat squat as it pulsated light in the day's final minutes.

When they made camp, they shaved sticks and used them to skewer slabs of elk. Military issue tin canteens clanked unceasingly. They still had a reasonable distance to go before arriving at Yellowstone Valley, so they didn't have their guard up and weren't on alert. That would all change soon, though. That night, twenty-four soldiers wrapped in blankets stared at the stars with their eyes spread wide. They all knew they were in the middle of enemy territory.

After two weeks, twenty-four tired men rode with their heads down against the now blazing sun, faceless under the shade of their hats' brims. It was like an army asleep on the march. They had ridden hard, and the horses dragged their hooves as they walked, with their tails swishing at bothersome flies. It was spring and everything was blooming, and all the insects were active and hungry, just like every other living thing in the mountains.

Finally, thick stretches of wind-twisted grass seemed endless as they rode into Yellowstone Valley. Mountains surrounded them, and the green color of vegetation climbed up to the tree line with distant snowcapped peaks beyond that in the distance.

The following afternoon the earth turned into the sky at the edge of creation. The red ball of fire became magnified by the humidity in the atmosphere, making it appear three times its size. It quickly disappeared over the edge of the earth. Shadows stood long from small stones like ink lines across the valley floor. The men and horses' shadows elongated like strands of the darkness to where they headed.

That night, the captain decided they would make a cold camp and eat dried meat and stale biscuits. He set out six guards on three-hour shifts. Still, Dallas couldn't sleep as he stared at pulsating stars light years away. Despite spring, the temperatures dropped as soon as the sun set. The wind rose, and the thin air grew colder. Falling stars dotted the sky, but the officer didn't have a superstitious bone in his body and didn't believe in wishes, but the Indians silently spying on them did.

Large, shaggy, gray wolves with yellow eyes followed them at a safe distance just out of pistol range. When the column of soldiers stopped, the wolves squatted, bathing in the spring sun. As soon as the patrol mounted again, the pack ambled behind them with their long muzzles to the ground, hunting for their next meal.

The following day, when the cavalry mounted their tired horses yet again and set out, they could hear the wolves snapping and snarling as they ravaged anything edible remaining in their camp.

The Cavalry

As they rode down-country, they stumbled across what looked like had been a sizable battle. Strangely enough, there wasn't a single arrow seen, but there were dark blood stains even after the last snow and weeks of sun—bleached-out bones contrasted with the green grass. Weeds began to weave in and out of skulls' eye sockets, nose, ears, and mouth holes. In a month, the vegetation would envelope all the remains of the recent battle, erasing all signs of life and death.

The sunburned bones of dead bodies littered the next two hundred yards. Later, they found some as far away as a mile. The horses shifted their hooves and stomped nervously as the riders leading them pulled down their jaws with their reins and froze in place as they all wearily looked around.

The officer stood with his thumbs in his belt as he surveyed the land with a sense of vigilance. He was obviously an alpha male and felt superior, even separate from the rest.

The sergeant squatted on his heels as he studied the

track, then spat a brown stream of juice into the dirt and shook his head. "There was a bunch of 'em all right, Captain. It's impossible to decipher how many, though. I doubt there are so many of one tribe, though. Maybe they got together for a common cause. That'd make things a might riskier in my opinion."

"From here, it looks like there were more men on both sides of things," Captain Sutton said. "There might have been more than five hundred that died. I would say the number of Indians had to be several times that. There were thousands of braves in my opinion."

The army patrol left the killing fields behind. The horses trotted off without encouragement. They could still smell death and blood despite the weeks that had passed and were nervous to leave. The captain knew the location could be a death trap, as well. He looked at the sun, and it said an hour till dark. They had to move quickly to distance themselves from the killing field before they made camp and got some much-needed rest.

Dallas saw his soldiers were getting anxious around so many fallen men and sensed it was time to leave.

"Mount up!" Captain Sutton called out.

Leather boots mounted noisy saddles, squeaking as the men prepared to ride on into the unknown. They quietly pulled themselves into formation as each soldier had their place in the patrol. Only the sergeant rode out front with their captain.

The patrol column rode past sunset and slowed as they pressed into the night, riding by the light of the stars. Later, a sliver of moon cast a dim glow across the landscape, allowing them to make better time. Finally, they stopped sometime late into the night and prepared camp. Now, a fire was preferable because if anybody was there, they would have already known of the soldiers' presence. At least it gave them some light around their campsite to see their enemy if there was an attack. The men slept with their weapons cradled in their arms.

Wolves' eyes winked on the edge of the light provided by the campfire's flickering flames as shadows danced on the trees around them. The predators lifted their snouts in the air and sniffed. The pack leader sat a few yards closer to the humans. She growled deep inside; hackles rose on the canines' backs, and lips snarled. Their tails and ears pointed straight up. They were ready to defend themselves at any moment, and they would attack if they saw the opportunity.

As soldiers rode through the night, they watched electrical storms so far away that they couldn't hear the sound. Sheet lightning lit up the sky to the west. As the evening waned, thunder began to rumble overhead. Within the hour, the air cooled, and raindrops the size of grapes fell on their heads, denting their hats.

Suddenly, the soldiers heard hammering hooves on the valley floor and could feel the ground shake like a small earthquake. At first, alarm raced through the patrol like electricity, but as the animals ran by, coming into view, they soon realized it was a herd of buffalo.

Lucky for them, the captain had them camp in a stand of trees, and the mass of fur and feet veered away, narrowly missing the patrol. For several minutes, tens of thousands of massive beasts raced by, trampling everything in their paths. The rumbling was so loud, they couldn't hear each other's shouts.

One moment, the air was filled with hair, dust, and noise; the next, it was as silent as an empty church.

A few hours before dawn, the army horses fed on the lush grass as they slid their jaws and bottle flies lit on their eyes. They shifted their ears trying to shoo away the bothersome insects. The animals blinked their gray eyelashes.

Like a ghost army, they rode through the night. In the sliver of moon, their wavy figures looked like images erased from a chalkboard—wavy and hard to see.

As the sun blushed rose on the eastern horizon, the sergeant gigged his horse, catching up with the captain. In minutes, the daylight chased away the darkness, leaving shadows to the west of every object before them, creating endless places for their enemies to hide.

Both men's eyes followed a worn path upward until it quickly was swallowed up by trees and vegetation.

"How much blood had to be shed to still leave a stain on the earth like that?" Captain Sutton asked. "The bones scattered from here to the horizon are a dead giveaway. The battle happened from here to way up there. The caravan of prospectors appeared to be long. I would have expected them to ride in separate groups. I wonder why they all bunched up like that. That was what secured their demise. Experienced men would never travel in a tight group when that large. Clearly, none of the victims had a proper burial. Look at those skulls. They still have patches of hair here and there, but you can see signs of the hostiles' knives, too. See those cuts where they were scalped?"

No birds save vultures and crows cawed and stared from nearby branches. More buzzards circled hundreds of feet above in the sky. All the while, they patiently waited and watched for their next dinner.

Captain Sutton dismounted along with Sergeant

Penny Money as they carefully stepped over a scattering of bones of every size and shape. The stiff valley wind had pushed many of the skulls across the ground hundreds of feet from where they died. Coyotes were responsible for scattering the rest as they tried to take more than they could carry back to their dens.

"In a few months, there won't be much sign of a battle at all," Captain Sutton blew. "But I believe the reports were true after all. There are the bones of hundreds of bodies here. This was every bit the massacre the survivors claimed it was, and here I was sure they were exaggerating. If anything, it was the opposite, as it looks worse than I was told."

"Don't you think we need some backup, Captain?" Sergeant Penny Money asked. "We could be walkin' into a bee's nest, sir."

"It would take too long for that," the captain replied. "I believe we will miss our chance if we don't strike first. They don't know we're here right now, so we must take advantage of the situation. I plan to give them a good dose of their own medicine. Did you bring the dynamite, as ordered?"

"Yes, sir," Penny Money replied. "We have fifty sticks and fifty fuses. I have the man riding drag, keeping an eye on it. The pack mule with the explosives is right in front of our drag man, so if it goes off unexpectedly, the damage would be minimal."

"Give me my spyglass, Sergeant," the captain said. "Maybe we better have a look around before we move on any farther. Once we know the area is free of the enemy, then we can drop our guard and have a rest. That was a tough two-week ride."

"As we rode at night for the last few days, I doubt

we've been seen," Sergeant Penny Money said. "Then again, with heathens, you just never know. If nothin' else, they're sneaky."

The captain collapsed his telescopic spyglass and tapped on his gloved hand. He smiled grimly. "We might see some sport before the end of the day, Sergeant Money. Get a few men over there by those bushes east of us. Don't look now, but I believe somebody is spying on us. Move slow and easy, so they don't suspect we know they're there."

In a few minutes, two soldiers dragged an Indian from the bushes. They dropped him at the captain's feet as he lay prone, moaning from a quick beating. They didn't want him lashing out at the captain. The officer stared at the captive with his spyglass hanging from his neck like a crucifix.

After looking at the Blackfoot Indian from the top of his head to his toes, the captain noticed a bulge. He reached into his buckskin shirt and pulled out a small mirror.

"It looks like they're communicating with their superiors, too," Captain Sutton said. "Indians don't use mirrors for their vanity like Easterners do. It has become a communication tool and works as well as smoke signals and is harder to spot. I'd say the tribes are raising the ante."

"Maybe we just got here at the wrong time," Penny Money said.

The captain looked at the Indian again, then nodded to his sergeant, who pulled his pistol, aiming as he drew back the hammers and pulled the trigger. A neat round hole instantly appeared in the center of the Blackfoot's forehead. He stood like he was a dead tree trunk, then he began to waver. He lifted his leg to take a step, but his knee buckled under his weight, and the hostile dropped to the ground.

"We had to make sure he didn't get away and tell anything more about our position," Captain Sutton said as he gave his sergeant a piercing look. "I don't linger when it's time to send a message. Hang him from the tree right there beside the trail—not from the neck, but his feet. We don't want to be distasteful, after all."

Horses' hooves softly padded on the grass as the dead man swung to and fro in the wind. A brown piece of paper was pinned to his chest.

It said... 'Beware as you walk through the valley of death because the US Cavalry walks unseen at your side. Captain Dallas Sutton.'

As they rode toward the mountain trail, Penny Money said, "That trail up the mountain looks like the high road to hell, if you ask me."

"I guess this time you're right," Captain Sutton replied. "I feel like we're walking into the mouth of the beast."

The tight formation of men snaked through the valley toward the trail that climbed the mountain and disappeared into the trees. After they vanished into the dense vegetation, you could still hear the horses' hooves against the stone trail.

The iron shoes and stone made sparks fly. The soldiers saw movement in their peripheral vision. The wolves were back on the march again.

Overwhelmed

As the cavalry patrol began to climb the mountain, the steep trail slowed their pace. Visibility was limited due to the dense growth of vegetation and trees. The column had spread out to make each one a target harder to hit. The captain didn't want what happened to the prospectors to happen to them.

He had seen enough to evaluate the danger, and their risk of some sort of attack by one of the local tribes was high. He knew it could happen any day, hour, or minute. They had to be in a state of readiness twenty-four-seven.

"Don't you find it strange that we haven't seen a single sign of Indians or people for the whole day?" Sergeant Money asked. "In the valley, there were tracks every little bit, but up here, I haven't seen a trace of anything or anyone, save the wild game."

"Don't think for a moment they aren't out there watching," Captain Sutton said as they continued to advance. More sparks flew from iron-shod horses on rock trails. "After what we've seen, it's only a question of time before we run into some sort of enemy or other. Ride the line and make sure nobody bunches up. We don't want a massacre like we saw back there."

"Those folks weren't US Cavalry soldiers, Captain," Sergeant Money replied. "There's a world of difference between their skills and ours."

"Overconfidence is as dangerous as the lack of, Penny—don't you forget that," Captain Sutton said. "Ride to the back of the formation and check on our drag man. Replace him with somebody fresher. He'll be tired from all the stress. I know our men, and I doubt any of them have seen anything so shockingly violent as the massacre back there. I imagine a few of them are shaken up, if not most."

Penny Money wheeled his horse around and gigged its flanks, launching into a quick sprint, heading for the back of the string of twenty-two men. With he and the captain there were twenty-four in all. When Dallas Sutton gave an order and said jump, his men asked how high, such was their confidence in the West Point officer.

Without any warning at all, suddenly, there appeared to rise a fabled hoard of men on the ridge right before them, and the front of the patrol was nearly at the top. The leader carried a shield covered in broken mirrors reflecting the sun into the cavalrymen's eyes. The gray-haired older man looked like the devil in a nightmare. Tombstones reflected in his eyes as the edges of his mouth curled down.

"Why, it looks like a party of circus clowns all dressed up in bright colors." The sergeant snickered. "We'll go through that little bunch like crap through a goose."

Everybody else's confidence fell away like autumn leaves. Only the sergeant appeared totally convinced they were not that big of a threat. He even laughed in the face of possible unexpected death.

"Yeah, but these aren't like any clowns I've ever seen," the captain replied, getting more serious by the second. "This war party looks oddly dangerous, despite their fancy getup. Look at all those guns in sheaths and belts and quivers of arrows on their backs." He suddenly felt he knew a hell worse than the brimstone land of Christian reckoning was coming.

In reality, it was only nine members of an outlaw gang of mounted lancers, archers, and marksmen, but everything began to happen so rapidly that nobody had the time to count. They came on them like they were ten times their numbers, and everyone in the patrol got thrown into doubt.

A rattling mass of arrows as thick as rain passed through the cavalry company, and men tottered on their horses before dropping to the ground with a thud. Their mounts staggered as they turned into arrow pincushions instantly while they squealed and groaned and died.

The patrol sent their first volley of return fire at their attackers, but they had chosen rifles when Wood Duck and his men were already too close. Many couldn't swing their barrels in time. Dark gray gun smoke rolled through the suspended dust as the outlaw gang quickly breached the patrol's ranks under its cover. Now, they were cast into the middle of the melee, fighting hand-to-hand.

Captain Sutton's horse sank beneath him as he heard the long pneumatic sigh of a dying animal. He rolled over, pulling his flintlock pistols and firing both blindly. A couple of lucky shots left two Indian renegades horseless.

One of his soldiers lay close by with arrows in his neck, chest, and legs as the fletching ruffled in the stiff breeze. Dallas could hear the man mumble the Lord's Prayer as he prepared for his demise. For the briefest of seconds, he saw his sightless eyes.

Men scrambled as dead and dying horses dotted the ground, some rocking their bodies, trying to get up and flee. Other soldiers sat in bloody puddles as they fumbled with their shot pouches over empty pistols despite the arrows jutting from their arms and legs. They were fighting for their lives, and their adrenaline boosts and fear overrode every other feeling.

Wood Duck rode into the fray in a wild frenzy with arrows clenched in his jaws and bow in his hands, firing projectiles at the bluecoats. His short bow protruded from the outstretched neck of his mustang. The renegade Indians snatched bloody wigs in mid-flight and dismembered the soldiers' bodies, strewing their parts among the dead horses, and in some cases, lobbing off their heads.

Wood Duck rode through the bodies of his enemy, his horse snapping at the dead men like a rabid dog. The rest of the outlaw gang members went from soldier to soldier, grabbing them by the hair and using their blades to slice around the skulls of both the dead and the living. A multitude of screams filled the air, mixing with the metallic smell of blood and the sulfuric odor of gunpowder.

Hooves pounded out of the smoke and dust as a few of the dead soldiers' horses escaped, limping and bloody, screaming as they raced for safety and away from all the noise. Some looked like pincushions with arrows jutting from their bodies as they clattered out of sight. Sunlight glittered off naked, wet, hairless skulls as animals squealed and groaned.

When darkness fell, Wood Duck and his men lost interest, and they turned away and headed for their camp nearby. On the killing field, something moved under a horse's neck and a soldier's headless body. Two men rose from the mountain of dead and scrambled for the tree line and into the forest. They looked like two shadows from a distance as they raced under the little moonlight there.

In the distance, they could see the light of the large campfire from the outlaw gang as they drank and played dice like it was just another day. They ducked into the brush as Captain Sutton glanced at the sky, making a dead reckoning, and they set off for Yellowstone Valley. Once there, if they survived, they would turn for Fort Boise and safety.

"If we keep going downhill, we should reach the valley floor eventually," Dallas whispered. "I can use the constellations to direct us in the right direction."

Sergeant Money replied, "I can hardly believe we've lost twenty-two men in the blink of an eye. They hit us like an earthquake. I hope we didn't leave anyone back there that's alive."

The cavalrymen turned and ran until their lungs burned. They assumed if nobody saw them, nobody would notice them that night. They knew the following day, the band of killers would pick through the dead and check for valuables and recover their weapons, shot, and powder the cavalry might still have. Nobody shot the horses out of mercy for the helpless animals. Those who escaped ran for their lives and didn't look back.

Their fists pumped like steam engine pistons as the captain and sergeant pushed themselves to their limits and then some more. They knew if they stopped, there was a chance they would be followed, so it was possible the killers could catch up, especially mounted on fast horses. They hoped against all hope they weren't seen as they escaped. Now, they had to find someplace safe to spend the next day sleeping so they could travel at night. They had to run for the rest of the day to ensure they were as far as possible from the skirmish and the dangerous threat.

When the stitches in their sides from running became unbearable, they finally stopped as they tried to gobble up enough air, but still, they felt dizzy, and their mouths were as dry as deserts. Fortunately, there was water found in abundance everywhere. The soldiers refreshed themselves as they crossed creeks and streams.

"At least we've still got our pistols," Captain Sutton said, "so we can defend ourselves. I hate losing my rifle and scope. It might have come in handy in the next days."

"I still can't believe we couldn't hold our ground," Penny said, shaking his bloody head and wiping sweat from his brow before it stung his eyes. Both men panted like broken bellows and held their sides.

"They rolled over us like a herd of buffalo, leaving no one standing," Sergeant Money said. "Who the hell were they, anyway? I'm not even sure how many hit us.

It was chaos and mayhem from start to finish." He rubbed the knot on his head and winced.

"All I know is that we must try to get back to Fort Boise before the same bunch of renegades find us again," the captain said. "If we stay here alone, we have no chance at all. We must evade them until we can reach safety. I'm afraid that all the way back is three weeks' distance. That is a long way for two men on foot against expert horsemen on healthy, strong animals." What he said sounded foreboding, even to himself.

"You ain't wrong there, Captain, sir." Penny cachinnated like a loon. His stern façade broke for a moment, but he caught himself and slapped his hand over his mouth. His eyes pleaded for pardon from his boss.

Narrow Escape

"Do you hear the thunder?" Dallas asked, wide-eyed. "If we get a bad storm, the temperatures might drop. It's spring, but I've heard up here anything goes. It can snow pretty much any time of year."

"It sounds like distant cannon fire to me," the sergeant replied, blinking, and looking at a pale blue sky. He rubbed a two-week beard growth with the back of his hand and frowned.

In the distance, cumulonimbus crowded the far western sky, making it dark and ominous, unlike where they stood. They could see precipitation fall far away like a thick curtain, but it swung wide of the men fleeing for their lives. Still, the sky rumbled as heat lightning flashed while it slowly traveled parallel to the soldiers.

"I feel like I should have died with my men," Sergeant Money whispered. A single tear cut a white path down his dirty cheek. He blinked his eyes, cleared his throat, and bucked up to the pain in his soul. The captain held his ground, and although clearly shaken, he didn't let it affect his judgment, and he maintained a stonelike, chiseled face. For him, even though he only had one soldier left, the sergeant was still his responsibility. Sutton intended to try to get him home safely.

The captain also felt like he should have died with his men. They had all been in their charge. Both men felt the heavy weight of their commands with death on their shoulders. It took their breath away when the images suddenly flashed in their minds.

"What are we gonna say or report when we get back to Fort Boise—if we get back, that is?" Money asked. "I doubt I'll have it in me to write down everything that happened. I know I'll have nightmares for years to come, if not forever. I've fought some bloody battles in my times, but those Indians were butchers. I've seen a lot of tribes and the way they dress, but I ain't ever seen any warriors all fancied up like them."

"Don't worry, Sergeant," the captain said, hoping he sounded confident. "I'll take care of everything. The men were my responsibility, and all you did was follow orders. If anyone is to blame here, it's me."

"Did you see that White man in the bunch of outlaws, or was I seein' things?" Money asked, clearly puzzled. His frown deepened.

"The only face that stuck in my mind was the one who I took as the leader," Captain Sutton replied.

The sergeant stood blinking like he was having difficulty putting the captain's words together to make any sense. He was suffering from something like shellshock. Penny still couldn't understand how so many men died so fast, and it left his mind spinning out of control.

"You know, Captain, the one who charged us so recklessly and murdered our men before our very eyes until I got knocked unconscious—I'll never forget that man's evil face—the red, white, and blue stripes down his wrinkled brow—the small, slanted eyes on a prominent Indian nose. What stood out was the gleam of delight in his eyes as he killed. I saw him taking deep breaths like he was smelling the blood of his victims so he could cherish it in his memories later. For me, he was the only one that stood out that I can remember. Everything else is a blur. I've never seen an Indian with a gray, braided chin beard like him."

The captain suddenly remembered something. His sergeant could see it in his face. He blinked and flinched like the image he was seeing in his mind's eye was real. He felt the threat and the raw fear again, just like during the attack.

"His sky-blue eyes—that was what was the oddest about him. I've never seen an Indian with eyes like that. Otherwise, it was all barrels and arrows, Sergeant."

"To be honest, I didn't even see ya go down, Captain," Money said. "I hardly had time to think, not alone look at faces and count the enemy. I was doin' all I could to survive a second or two more. I truly believed we were done for. All I saw were black gun barrels and pointed arrows and spears, just like you. There was no time to linger. I only got two wild shots off with my rifles. By the time I got 'em raised, one in each arm, they were already too close, and my shots got rushed. I might have put a couple of bullet holes in the ground between them and us or maybe shot a horse, but that's about it."

The sergeant paused for a minute while he gathered his thoughts. A deep shudder racked his body, and he fought back his emotions. He knew he had to hold it together before his superior officer. Gritting his teeth, he took a deep breath and continued.

"We were all pretty much a failure at returning fire. Most of our men hardly got more than one shot off, and some didn't even fire their weapons. They not only caught us by surprise but also rushed us so fast, we didn't have time to react. I doubt we could have taken those Indians with forty veteran Indian fighters like you and me. I've never seen such killing skills before bar none. Not even the Comanche in Texas were as hard as them. But, without a doubt, these fellas beat 'em, hands down."

"Don't feel disappointed in your skills, Penny," the captain said. "You did the same as us all, including me. So many men fell at once I could hardly tell what was happening—especially once the air filled with arrows and gun smoke. I believe that was what saved you and me. It was too late to check us all once it was done, body by body in the dark. I'm sure that's what they'll do tomorrow. I wonder if they will notice two missing men."

"I figure they'll know the captain and sergeant are missing once they have a look. They won't find your epaulets or my three stripes, and they know danged well a patrol won't be way out here without a captain or at least a lieutenant, and all patrols have sergeants."

"I wonder if they'll track us down," Sutton pondered. "It would seem like a lot of fuss for too little consequence. I think we've seen the last of those hostiles."

"I beg to differ with ya, Captain. Those men seemed like they were in some sports game instead of having a battle. They were all too eager and reckless for their own good. Either they're so confident they don't believe anyone can kill 'em, or they're caught up in the game of murderin' their fellow man. I've met veteran soldiers who grew a taste for killing after a year or two of fighting on the frontier. That was the same look these boys had in their eyes."

The following day, Sergeant Penny Money saw three streams of smoke rise into the air as soon as he rolled up his bedroll and stood. The sun hung at the world's edge at that early hour, so he used the flat of his hand to shade his eyes from the bright rays. He squinted into the distance as he blinked his eyes.

"Lookee over there, Captain. I could swear I see smoke. I hope it ain't a forest fire. The way our luck's runnin', I don't cross out anything. If it is a fire, it'll chase all the wild animals our way, and there's bound to be bears and lions among 'em." Paranoia sat perched on the sergeant's shoulder and whispered in his ear.

"That's no forest fire, or we would smell it and not only see it. I hope it isn't more of the same," Captain Sutton replied in a whisper. Despite seeing no one, they felt that somebody was listening to every word they said.

Both were injured, but their wounds weren't life-threatening. The cavalrymen had deep gashes in their heads. The sergeant's was from a tomahawk and the captain's from a war club—it was Wood Duck who swung it, too. Both lacerations and slight concussions had saved their lives because halfway through the battle, both were out cold as dead bodies fell on top of them, hiding them from their raving mad enemies.

Still, they had seen enough to know they were doomed. Lucky for them, the outlaw war party hadn't looked under the large horses' necks or soldiers' bodies, where both men lay. This saved them from being scalped and murdered. The outlaws mainly seemed to enjoy taking men's hair while they were still alive. They did this while on horseback, and Dallas and Penny had seen it firsthand and couldn't forget the sight, no matter how hard they tried.

Initially, they weren't quite sure they weren't seeing things out of desperation. But after a good look with the captain's spyglass, he confirmed that smoke was coming from what looked like three fires below them. It was anybody's guess if they were hostile or friendly, though.

So far, they hadn't seen any amicable faces since they left Fort Boise, and even there, people looked at them suspiciously. The United States Army did not have a stellar reputation, due to its previous actions against the Native Americans.

They both wished they had never come, despite their orders from Washington. Once again, good, loyal soldiers died because of some decision made from a politician back in the capital when the gentlemen giving the orders had never traveled west of Indiana themselves. But, with the rumors of innocent prospectors murdered in the hundreds, it was a political triumph to respond with all the fury of hell's fire.

The captain wondered how many of these supposed stellar Americans were really murderers and thieves. He had lived and fought on the Great Plains, protecting buffalo hunters long enough that most men this far west were of questionable nature.

If they made it back, they would have to inform their superiors and families of what had happened. Of course, they would exclude all the gruesome details except for in the formal report. The captain wondered in the back of his mind if he would get busted back to sergeant and Money to private. He believed he would be satisfied enough if they made it home in one piece.

Living another day was their current focus, which was more than enough in the middle of the wilderness. At this point, their situation was desperate and probably about to get worse. Hopefully, the smoke wasn't from an enemy Indian stronghold. Then they would be done for sure.

At this point, they had no choice but to follow the black trails in the sky and hope for the best. They knew it would take a minor miracle since they hadn't seen a hint of friendly men, whether Red, Black, or White.

Only two soldiers had escaped Wood Duck's fury, but they left twenty-two hairless heads and broken bodies behind. Many of them dismembered, but the renegade war party appeared to have tired from their killing frenzy and returned to their camp to drink and brag. Both men remembered their horses falling beneath them as lances and arrows filled their mounts' sides. They would never forget the sound of wailing animals and shrieking men.

A half day from the killing fields, Sutton and Money ran into a family of four. What they were doing in the mountains, the soldiers couldn't say. Their tongues swelled and eyes popped wide as rough hemp rope creaked. They all four swung in the wind. One was black and charred, his flesh drawn tight, and his eyeballs had cooked in his sockets. The remains of three pack mules were hacked to pieces, and the goods stolen or strewn across hell and half an acre. Wolves waited in the distance as buzzards perched above their heads.

The smell of vacated and bloated bodies overwhelmed them and covered all other smells. They put their bandanas over their noses to help block the offensive odor, but it was still only bearable. They wondered if these same few men had killed all those prospectors, but then the captain knew it was impossible. Still, they had gone through two dozen veteran soldiers like a hot knife through warm butter. Ultimately, they believed this family had fallen to the same fate as their men. The violence was extreme and much of it unnecessary, as they were probably already dead.

Both soldiers had lost their rifles in the initial chaos but still had their brace of pistols in their belts. The defeat had come so swiftly they hadn't had time to draw after they emptied their rifles. The tides of the battle had turned in a matter of two or three seconds. The assault was so swift and deadly that they tumbled over like bowling pins. Horses screamed as soldiers ululated while the men in their charge died.

"And here I thought we'd come out West for our health and better air," Sergeant Money huffed. "Hell, we're lucky to be breathin' at all."

The fleeing soldiers had no supplies and were without horses, so they had to travel on foot. Still, they couldn't keep up the pace without food. Water in the Rockies was readily available, but they didn't dare use their guns to kill any wild game, even if they were only squirrels, for fear someone heard them. So, they ate the abundant berries, salsify, rose hips, alfalfa, and dandelions to appease their appetites.

They could see for fifteen miles when they crested the summit at sunset. A sizable lake stood in the distance, and creeks and streams crisscrossed everywhere. As the sun dropped under the jagged rim of the Rocky Mountains, it blushed rose, reflecting on their faces. Then, it was suddenly dark, like a blanket had fallen over the land. Tiny dots of light pulsated in the heavens more than four light years away.

As the two cavalry soldiers descended the mountains and valleys in the dark with a sliver of moon, they held their hands out before them as their hazy gray shadows contorted over broken terrain. They walked like wolves into the dark and then slept like dogs during the day in the thick, soft grass.

As they passed a lake, it shimmered, its edges rimmed with great stands of trees and tightly bunched bushes of a hundred shades of green.

The sergeant spat with a dry mouth as they waited outside the buck-and-row fence. Finally, a man walked out onto the porch. At first, he didn't notice the strangers—they stood silently and hardly moved as their eyes spread wide with concern.

Would these men try to kill them, too? Were they honest, or were they more men of reckless blood like most they had seen back in Fort Boise? Questions bombarded their brains as they tensely waited.

New Encounters

When two more strangers appeared at the north gate, Rusty spat into the dirt and shook his head. Angus sat beside him as he grumbled and ground his teeth. Marshal Walker moved his hand to his pistol grip and wrapped his fingers around the smooth, worn wood.

"Just what we needed. More dad-gummed people," Rusty Steel growled. "You boys better get out here and bring your guns with ya! These two fellas are armed and may be dangerous. Will, it appears that you've got some of your folks out here. As they look to be cavalry soldiers, you had best take care of 'em. But beware. Just because they're dressed like US Army don't mean they ain't thieves in disguise. Lately, I question everything I see."

In moments, all nine members stood on the porch with pistols or rifles in their hands. Dahteste had an arrow strung in her bow as she slightly tensed the weapon. Nobody took anything for granted anymore. Times had become very dangerous. Since the thing with the newspaper article about the fake gold strike in the mountains, nothing had been the same. Evil people had come to the Rockies, and even the Indians were on the defensive. Nobody knew what would befall them next.

Will pushed Levi aside, saying, “I’ve got this, boys. They look like cavalry, all right.” Still, he put his hand behind his back where he had a third pistol. He was too far away for the strangers to hear the metallic click of the hammer.

Boot heels pounded across the porch, and they stepped into the compound yard. Soft grass smashed underfoot, leaving footprints as Forrester walked toward the gate. The two soldiers in front of him appeared as though they were ready to bolt or go for their guns, and Will wasn’t sure which one it was.

“Gentlemen, state your business,” Forrester called out in a neutral voice, and his face gave nothing away. He stopped halfway to ensure it wasn’t a trap, in case more men were waiting beyond the tree line, prepared to strike.

“I’m Captain Dallas Sutton, and this is Sergeant Penny Money of the United States Cavalry. We were attacked a distance away, and twenty-two of my men perished. If you want, we will lay down our guns.”

“All right,” Will replied as he blinked in wonder. Déjà vu hit him square in the face like freezing water. “Just make it real slow, like cold molasses. I’m afraid that we’re all on edge around here.”

Back on the porch, his wife, Betty, had to remind herself to breathe as her shoulders bunched and the tension rose. Her white-knuckled fist wrapped around her Tennessee rifle. The men’s hands neared their weapons and prepared for the worst. Long shadows stood beside the strangers as the sun dropped near the jagged horizon. In an hour, it would vanish over the world's end, and night would capture the light, shooing it away. Then, things would be even more dangerous outside the cabin walls.

Everything else seemed normal as birds chirped in the Engelmann spruces and Rocky Mountain Douglas firs. Woodpeckers hammered on ponderosa pine trunks. Cicadas chattered in the background as bees buzzed in the air. Spring was in full bloom in the mountains, but there were problems among its inhabitants. Their livelihood and way of life appeared threatened on all sides, endangering their very existence, so they no longer took anything for granted. It seemed their future in the Rocky Mountains hung on a thread.

"Step away from your guns and come into the compound, and we can talk," Captain Forrester warned the men. "Beware, my friends over there on the porch have nervous trigger fingers lately, so I would avoid any sudden movements."

The blood drained from the soldiers' faces as they wondered if they were stepping into more trouble. The Easterners in the compound didn't seem much friendlier than the hostile Indians, and their hands were full of weapons. At least they hadn't killed them—not yet, anyway. Suddenly, their numbers swelled. Their shouldered rifles carefully took beads on the trespassers.

"I'm going to put my hand into my jacket pocket, and I don't have any more guns or a knife. My only weapon is my saber, and I won't near it with my hand. I only want to show my formal documentation and my commission to captain from West Point. Maybe that will convince you that we are friendly. I truly hope you welcome honest men."

"I'm afraid we've had a lot of trouble lately, and we don't welcome *anyone* at the moment," Forrester said. When he heard where the captain had studied, Will's mind spun around and around, racing a million miles an hour, but he put on a calm façade. "We got attacked more than once recently and expect more trouble, so be forewarned."

The sergeant looked like he was just about to bust. Forrester didn't know if he was angry for not being respected as soon as they identified themselves or if he was just about to turn and run. The buckskin-clad mountain man slipped his finger into the trigger guard but kept it behind his back. He tensed himself as he prepared to bring his gun into play.

"Come closer," Will said, but his gut feeling suddenly told him the officer was telling the truth. What put him off balance was that the same thing happened to him not two years ago, which was why he abandoned everything to become a mountain man with his best friend, Levi Johnson. But, at the moment, he saw no advantage in telling a current army officer his personal past. It could even endanger him and his friend.

What was dead and buried was best left that way. Later, if they proved themselves to be honest men, he may reconsider, but at the moment, the less they knew about him, the better, and he knew his friends would keep tight lips. Now, they were all in this together.

Will studied the papers as his brow furrowed. Then, they finally nodded and returned them to the owner. He looked at the pair from head to toe and noted they were covered in blood stains, which apparently weren't theirs. Other streaks ran down their faces that came from wounds on their heads. Forrester tried to piece the puzzle together quickly but didn't have enough information yet.

The soldiers stood stunned and blinking with puzzled faces. They couldn't quite grasp what they were looking at—were these men dangerous, too? Or were they friendly Easterners in the end? They both knew it could go either way. They held their breaths, waiting for the mountain man to speak.

"Grab your pistols and come on in," Forrester said. "My name is Will, and I live here with my wife and friends. We're beaver trappers and work in the Rockies all year round. I see you found out quick just how dangerous it can get in the mountains."

The officer shook his head and said, "I've never seen anything similar to what I've seen up here in a few days. It's hard to believe anybody could survive long in such an environment."

"Do you have any idea of what kind of Indians were that attacked your patrol, or were they White men?" Forrester asked. "We've had trouble with both lately."

"I've been fighting Indians on the frontier for the last couple of years, so I'm fairly well versed in the tribes," Captain Sutton replied. "In my opinion, based on their clothing, I'd say they were renegades—a bunch of outlaws from different tribes. But they hit us so hard and fast that we hardly had time to engage. I've never seen anything like it. Especially the man, I believe, who is the gang leader. He's the only face I could identify."

"I saw a White man among them, too," Sergeant Money said. "At least, I think I did."

By then, they were standing beside the porch, and everybody was all ears. Rusty pushed his way to the front and approached the injured officer. His eyes narrowed as he considered the men before him. They looked hardened from battle but were as out of their environment as a couple of fish in a sandbox.

"Virgil here will have a look at your wounds," Rusty said as he jutted his chin at the only brown man in the bunch. "If you don't care for 'em fast, they could get infected, and then you'll have a much more serious problem. Our friend is as good a doctor as you'll find here in the wilderness. I can go as far as sayin' he has performed miracles in the past, and I've seen it with my own eyes. Once you're both tended to and fed, we can talk about what happened and who did it. We'll have to figure out who it was."

The soldiers both required a few stitches, but other than that, they were only banged up. Lovejoy gave them a potion he mixed in water in a tin cup and made each one drink up. Their faces wrinkled and mouths soured as they swallowed the foul liquid.

"If he don't cure ya of what ails ya, he'll poison ye so you don't suffer none." Rusty laughed. "I think Virgil makes us swallow that stuff every time we get sick just to be ornery. Come along; Angus has some vittles cookin' on the stove. Once you have some grub in your bellies, you'll feel better, and we can have that little talk I mentioned before. I'm sorry, but we can't put it off until tomorrow. If I'm not mistaken, you've just run into the most dangerous man I've ever known."

Marshal Walker stood behind Rusty, so he didn't

miss a word said. Steel shot him a dirty look so he would have some patience with the battered soldiers. If Steel was right, they would have just escaped a living hell.

In the back of the cabin, on the cookstove, sizzled and spat unidentified strips of flesh. Angus brought the two strangers bowls of beans with meat on the bottom. They wiped the broth from their ceramic plates with charred tortillas.

The smell of coffee overwhelmed the two visitors. Steam rolled off hot biscuits with honey. Grease dripped off large slabs of bacon, which the men devoured in seconds using their hands to eat. They didn't even notice the knives and forks. They were too hungry even to cut up the meat. They tore into it with their teeth like starving dogs. When they finished, Angus poured a splash of whiskey into their tin cups and refilled them with more steaming coffee. Now, they were ready for that talk.

"What kind of Indians were they?" Will asked. He couldn't help but notice the cavalry uniforms and the captain's saber. As of yet, he hadn't noticed anything suspicious about Sutton.

"The leader was tall, and his hair hung to his shoulders," Captain Sutton said. "He was a big man with a painted face."

"It was the worst thing I've seen in my entire life," the sergeant said.

Rusty shook his head and spat dryly. Betty sat with an old musket, wide-eyed as she watched them. Of course, Mrs. Forrester knew of her husband's dark past and the expedition he lost nearly to the last man. She wasn't about to let them take her husband away and back to the army to stand trial. She would kill them both first. After their meal, the soldiers silently sat by the fire as they listened to the night in the wilderness. It was different from the Great Plains.

"So, whatcha gotta say?" Rusty asked as the marshal sat beside him. His stare was hard and unfriendly, but Steel smiled to ease the tension.

"The renegade outlaws sat on the ridge as they pointed their guns our way and jabbered in an unknown tongue," Sergeant Money said. "They appeared so suddenly and attacked with such furiousness we were dumbfounded for a second, and then it was too late."

"It seemed like no sooner did we see them, they were charging right on top of us, and we had little time to react," the captain said.

"Now you've gone and done it," Joseph said. "If they're followin' y'all, and I reckon they are, you've just led them to us."

"Don't fret," Rusty said as he shot the marshal another dirty look. "If they're here in the mountains, they were already coming anyway. Now they'll just get here sooner. I'd say they're lookin' for the marshal and me. I'm Rusty Steel, and this is Kansas Marshal Joseph Walker."

"Who do you mean by *they*?" Captain Sutton asked. "You say you know who attacked us, so tell me his name. He killed all our men, and I intend to get revenge."

The sergeant's face drained and left a pallor. He unconsciously shook his head no, as his eyes spread, making the whites twice as large. He felt the hackles rise on his neck but remained silent so he wouldn't tarnish his honor before his captain.

That night in the cold stables, the cavalry men lay with their knees drawn up under buffalo blankets. The coyotes called out all night, and then, at dawn, the roosters began to crow, waking the soldiers. Hens scratched and pecked at worms in the ground.

IDENTIFICATION

FLIES DRAWN TO THE HORSES AND MULES BEGAN TO LAND on their half-asleep faces, trying to walk into their mouths, ears, and noses. Loose pieces of straw tickled the hair on their upper lips. Outside, roosters welcomed the sun with cock-a-doodle-doos. The light from the orange orb spilled onto the stable floor through a small glass window, making a square light on the ground.

Finally, Dallas waved his hand before his face, making the flies buzz in circles before returning. He pushed himself onto his elbows and blinked the sleep from his eyes. They stirred in beds of hay like nesting rats. That was when it all returned to him like the hot kiss of a swift fist.

Rusty stood peeing by the corral's split-rail fence just as the sun blushed orange on the mountainous horizon. Steam rose from the puddle in the crisp dawn air.

As soon as the soldiers walked outside, Steel said, "Morning, young men. I hope the hay was soft and the blanket warm enough. Sorry about makin' y'all sleep outside like that, but these days, a man has to tread cautiously. Once we get to know each other better, maybe it'll be a different situation. For that, time will tell."

"Good morning, Mr. Steel," the captain said, and the sergeant saluted silently, allowing his commander to take charge.

"Why, I ain't a mister nor a soldier." The mountain man laughed. "You just call me Rusty, and we'll get along fine. In the wilderness, there's no rank or order. We're all no more than human beings around here."

"We don't mind sleeping in the stables," Dallas replied. "Anything is better than sleeping out in the forest without cover or knowledge of our environment."

"I figure that's where you made your first mistake, Captain Dallas." Rusty chuckled. "Most folks come here thinkin' they're prepared when they ain't. So, don't believe you boys are the only ones. Of late, it happens all the time."

The aging mountain man studied the cavalrymen, not missing any detail of their dress or behavior. He even studied the way they walked. For Rusty, an animal was an animal, whether human or wild game. They all had a track and smell distinct from the rest. He noted it down and stashed it away in his memory so he could draw it out again at any time.

"Come on over to my cabin." Rusty grinned. "Angus will be cookin' up some grub in a few minutes. You might as well break bread with us while you're here. Then we can talk a little more about Wood Duck. I figure we'll all be meetin' up with that old devil again real soon."

By the time the strangers settled in, the long table on the porch was fully seated. Tin pie pans and ceramic bowls sat before each person. Everybody had their own spoon on a string around their necks. Even the captain and sergeant had one somewhere on their person. Everybody needed tools to eat.

Once they were done and sipping their morning java, Rusty began with the questions. They wanted to find out everything they could about Wood Duck before confronting him face-to-face. After what he left on the pike in their yard, they knew it was only a question of time.

"Did you remember anything else after a good night's sleep?" Rusty asked.

Curious eyes stared at the newcomers. Some were openly hostile, like Dahteste, and others friendly, like Rusty. Still, he kept an eye on the officer in case he did something strange. Most encounters with military men in the Rockies hadn't turned out well. Ex-Captain Will Forrester was the only exception, and when he first arrived, it took them time to warm up to him, even though he came with Levi Johnson.

"There was one thing that slipped my mind," Dallas said. "I remember this Wood Duck fellow had strings of red beads around his neck. A few dozen more hung from his saddle horn. It is a strange thing to remember, but I can see those blood-colored beads as clear as day: that and those sky-blue eyes. Nothing seemed to fit together right with that man. He seems to be the worst of both races from which he came. You did say he was a half-White man, didn't you?"

"It's quite common for Indians to wear colorful beads, both men and women," Will Forrester said. "The Spanish brought so many to trade with the locals that piles still lie around. Some folks say they come from a place called Italy, wherever that is—a place where they fire their ceramics inside special ovens with extremely high temperatures and glaze the outside. That's what makes them so pretty. The local natives fire their ceramics out in the open or in shallow pits."

"I would normally agree with you," Dallas said, "but whoever it was that killed that family of four hung red bead necklaces around their necks along with the hemp rope. They looked like the same ones as Wood Duck wore. I was just wondering if it was a calling card or something similar."

"Ya don't say?" Marshal Walker huffed. "We found the same type of necklaces on some of the folks that outlaw gang of renegades killed across Kansas. It's his calling card, all right. Now I know the man you ran into was one and the same. I chased that rascal and his gang for two months before my posse members got tired of the chase and went home to their families. That's one outlaw gang you don't want to take on all on your lonesome."

The tone in the room got more serious with every ticking minute. As the sun rose into the sky, the compound members remained in their seats. They even put off their daily chores. Important issues were discussed that would affect them all if the infamous outlaw found their cabins tucked away high in the mountains. Weapons lay scattered across the tabletop. Men and women cleaned their pistols and rifles as they chatted and dug deeper into the unlikely subject.

"Who would have thought Wood Duck would come all the way up here to hunt us down, Joseph?" Rusty said. "He's a determined rascal; I'll give 'em that much."

"So, you say you studied in West Point, didn't you?"

Forrester asked when his curiosity finally got the best of him. Betty dug her fingernails into his arm and squeezed. She didn't want him to be friendly with a man who could possibly ruin his life. That is, if they could get out of the mountains alive. If it came to it, she would kill them both herself. Betty Forrester still had her rifle leaned against the table by her side, and Levi sat beside her. But he was just the opposite. For a man who had been lung shot and almost died recently, he seemed unhealthily interested.

The more the two military officers talked, the more nervous Betty got. She slipped her finger into her pistol's trigger guard as she laid her thumb on the hammer. The second gun was in her lap under the table, pointing at Captain Sutton. It was primed and ready to fire. If the officer said the wrong thing, she intended to shoot him dead. Nobody would take her man away from her, come hell or high water.

"I get the feeling you know me, don't you?" Will asked.

"Oh, I know you, all right," the captain replied, then he frowned.

Maybe he had just said the wrong thing and put their lives in danger. He, too, had to remember not to trust anybody in the wilderness. If these men were suspicious of everything that walked, it stood to reason that he should be, too.

"I'd know that face in a crowded saloon. You were on the front pages of the newspaper across New York state and probably much farther," Sutton said, although now he regretted bringing up the complex subject. Now that he thought about it, things that happened to Captain

Forrester weren't all that different from what happened to him and his patrol.

"It was said that you and an entire expedition vanished," Dallas whispered like it was a secret that was to be safeguarded. "Of course, there were rumors after that, but I didn't believe any of them. I was in the same class as you, Captain Forrester. You always seemed too focused on your studies to pay much attention to the other cadets. But now I see that none of what I heard was true. What happened to you and your men—you know, the expedition? They said you, your soldier, and a few scientists set out from Fort Scott, Kansas, just a way from Fort Leavenworth, and vanished in the vast West."

"What else did you hear?" Will asked. He tried to appear disinterested, but his eagerness to learn more about the repercussions of his destiny betrayed his greed for more news from home.

"The newspapers said that the entire expedition vanished, and a Comanche war party murdered some scientists," Dallas said. "Is that about right?"

"That sizes it up, all right," the recuperating mountain man said. "My name is Levi Johnson, and I was the scout hired by the army to find new places to build forts for Captain Forrester. We were both there, and as the running battle with the Comanche ensued, pretty much everybody else died."

"There were a few of my surviving soldiers who wanted to turn around and try to make it back home, but from what I heard, they never arrived," Will said. "Hopefully some of them found a new life somewhere out West and didn't fall to more hostiles. Western Kansas was full of deadly Comanche a couple of years back."

"Wood Duck had a Comanche father and a White mother," Joseph said. "That's why he's got blue eyes."

"I even knew his mother once upon a time, long ago," Rusty said. "I tried to save her from her husband and the tribe that held her. I even managed to spirit her away, but she ran off. She disappeared into the night the first chance she got. She probably felt more Comanche than a White woman at that point and ran back for her home and family."

Revenge

Massive six-foot wings whooshed over cold, stiffening bodies as delicate finger-boned talons gripped, digging deep into the bloated skin. Their wrinkled faces, bald heads, and ruffled neck feathers followed bloody beaks as the vultures ripped at the soft underbelly of their dinner. From their wings up, they were covered in claret.

The sound of clopping hooves from nine horses became harder to hear as they distanced themselves from their last killing field. They had found a single trapper on his own and Wood Duck had captured him, then he gave him to his men to play their games of life and death. The leader had his eyes set on bigger and more satisfying targets, and the captain and sergeant would only be the start. Only fools would believe the famous outlaw would miss the patrol leaders among the dead. Any simpleton knew there would be an officer and a sergeant among a patrol of two dozen.

Wood Duck liked it better this way. He loved the hunt, especially when they were US Cavalry soldiers.

What better way to get the fluids running before moving toward their main targets, Walker and Steel? They had both started something he felt he should have finished long ago. He was going to be patient and enjoy the next few days.

The gang leader wondered what the two officers were doing in the mountains with such a small patrol. Apparently, they had no idea of the actual number of Indians that lived in the Yellowstone Valley and beyond. If they had come with two hundred riders, it wouldn't have been enough anyway if the other tribes got involved. As they were only two, and Wood Duck was tracking them, the other tribes, who surely knew precisely where they were, ignored their trespassers to avoid the apparent danger. Nobody wanted to be captured by the most famous torturer of all time.

The band of renegades was known by all the tribes down to every single member. He was the boogieman who they scared their children with when they were naughty. If they wanted to climb the mountain and kill Crow Indians, that was more than fine with them—especially their most hated enemy, The Blackfoot Nation.

Two days prior, one of the members of the outlaw gang was shot by a Crow warrior as they tried to take his life. Two more Indians quickly died, but one went for his pistol in the struggle. The bullet busted the bones in the outlaw's forearm, leaving his hand useless. As they chased the soldiers anew, they had to stop, or the winged gang member would probably die.

Bisa had tied a tourniquet just below his elbow. Despite their evil nature, all nine men had ridden together for decades and always had each other's backs

—at least until then. It had been that way from the beginning and now had become an instinctive reflex. The gang members always came first.

When the Navajo Indian outlaw Bisahalani from Utah pulled off his buckskin shirt, it first stuck to the skin. When he ripped it from the wound, yellow puss ran down his arm and dripped off his fingers. It was swollen to the size of his thigh and looked like it would explode if poked with the tip of a blade. Its color was a deep purple and fiery red. Little worms wiggled around the open wound, making it appear to be a living thing foreign to his body. Bisa growled in anger as he picked maggots from his festering skin.

The wounded Indian outlaw lay his arm on a tree stump and screamed, "Go ahead and do it! Do it now, or I'll rot in hell!" He didn't yell in pain but in raw anger. He was furious. One of the Crow Indians they tried to capture shot him in the arm at point-blank range. "Cut it off before it kills me! I'll just have to get along with one hand."

All the while, Wood Duck sat silently, watching and listening to what they did and said. The edges of his mouth curled into a tiny smile. It went unnoticed by the others. Everybody was staring at Bisa and his festering appendage. The gang leader wiggled his fingers before he wrapped them around a wooden handle.

The long machete-sized knife flashed, and in the blink of an eye, Bisa's arm dropped to the ground, rolled five feet, and came to a stop—the fingers seeming to wiggle even though they were detached from his body. The one-armed man looked at his appendage in shocking wonder and spread wide eyes. His mouth instantly went dry like desert sand.

Wuyi scooped up a metal pot full of orange, glowing coals from the open fire. The bucket full of fire made his face glow. "Stick your stump in here, and it'll sear it close to stop the bleeding. Quick now, Bisa, before you pass out."

The stump soaked with blood hissed when it hit the fiery cinders. Smoke rose with the stink of burning flesh. Wood Duck stuck a piece of wood between Bisa's teeth as he bit down, nearly breaking it in two. His eyes crawled back into his head, and he passed out.

"That looks like that's taken care of," Wood Duck said as he slapped his hands together, marking he was done. "But we'll have to wait here for a couple of days until Bisa gets his second wind. He's big and strong, so he should hold up, but he won't be able to ride for a spell."

"Just as long as we don't have to wait too long," Luke Dawson said. The boss immediately shot him a dirty look, and Dawson shut his mouth like a steel trap. They could hear his teeth chomp together like rocks on stone.

"What, and let the bluecoats get away?" Shilah, the Navajo Indian from Colorado, spat. "We nearly have them in our grasp. It would be foolish to let them slip away when we are so close to capturing them. Let Bisa wait here on his own while we capture the bluecoats. It was his fault he got shot anyway. He should have seen the Crow had a pistol hidden under his buckskin shirt. After we capture them, we can bring them back here to torture." He put his hands on his knees and started to get up.

The outlaw gang leader took this outburst as a sign of disrespect and didn't tolerate his gang members giving him orders or sassing back. The backhand came so fast that the Navajo Indian didn't see it until the last fraction of a second before it nailed him square in the nose. Wood Duck used his massive fist as a hammer, and Shilah's face was like an anvil. Bone cracked, and his eyes crossed as he joined Bisa on the ground, and now both were out cold.

The gang leader spat a brown stream across Shilah's colorful outfit and said, "Next time, you'll know to hold your tongue. When he wakes up, remind him what I said."

Wood Duck rocked back and forth on his heels as he locked eyes with his men, one by one. He raised an eyebrow in question to see if there were any more challenges, but there were none. Little lessons like this were essential for a leader to execute occasionally, or his men might forget who the real boss was.

"As soon as Bisa can ride, we'll chase the soldiers down, and then we'll go and visit that old fool Rusty Steel and that murderin' Marshal Walker. We'll teach that lawman to chase us with a posse. I aim to kill 'em both with my bare hands. Y'all can have to rest to do with what ya want. I wanna look 'em in the eyes as they die." A stormy violence lay under his dangerous voice.

"Yes, sir, boss," Luke replied with a strangely odd grin. It was forced and seemed to imply something other than delight or pleasure.

Fear lay behind it, deep and hidden, just as with the other members of the renegade gang. He, too, feared their leader just like they did that very first day they met. Of course, they were violent men in their own rights, but their boss was a special kind of evil human, and they had never seen an equal. He was one of a kind.

Wood Duck's confidence and commanding character were what they blindly followed from the start. Still, they felt that vibrant electrical energy emitting from his body. It worked like a magnet for dangerous men. They seemed to feed off his power. The more he grew, the more they, too, developed with him, both in skills and reputation. They had bounties on their heads in a dozen states across America and even in a few places in Mexico.

Despite the fact they had hefty rewards on their heads, no outlaw recovery agents were interested, even though the posters said dead or alive. Years ago, before he made a reputation, some had tried. But the renegade outlaw leader tortured them, leaving their bodies in the middle of towns to be explicitly discovered to warn their enemies.

There were no borders for Wood Duck and his men, and if someone claimed there were, they showed them their guns. None of them ever hesitated an instant to pull and shoot someone if they stood in their way or had something they wanted. When the boss target practiced in Mexico, he used living beings. Those were the places they wanted him for murder, but no Marshales Mexicanas came to arrest them. Nobody had the stones.

Home Defenses

Levi Johnson held a pistol in each hand as he sat in the corner of the cabin near the cook stove. Dahteste, his Crow wife, kneeled on a bearskin rug at his feet, worry and concern etched across her face. Everybody in Angus's cabin, even the women, was armed to the teeth. The table was covered in weapons, black powder, and patches. Extra gun parts and bow strings lay ready if needed. A bucket full of arrows stood beside the timber door.

The cabin was shuttered long ago, and the heavy four-inch-thick timber door had double two-by-fours across the inside, locking it tight as a drum. It would take a shot of a cannonball to take it down. The thickness made it hard to set alite, too. Gun slats were cut into the door and window shutter, top and bottom. There was space for five shooters simultaneously.

All eleven of them could take turns firing their weapons and retire instantly, replaced by another five clan members with loaded weapons. That left others to repair any damaged guns and prepare the rifles for another shot. Everything was set up to work like a fine Swiss watch. That way, they could provide a hard defense from a frontal attack, which was the only way to approach the cabin dug into the side of a hill and covered in dirt and sod. It was nearly impossible to burn them out, and if they didn't want to leave, it would be nearly beyond the bounds of possibility to force them to go.

They also had an ample enough supply of food and smoked game meat in the storage basement to last them for months, along with lots of black powder and ammunition. Fresh water constantly trickled from a hollow cane, dripping into a wooden bucket in the back of the cabin sourced from an underground spring. The only thing they couldn't fit in was an unlimited supply of firewood.

Still, a cord was stacked right beside the only door outside. That was their only weak spot, but they had stocked enough wood in the dry cellar to cover a few days in case of an emergency. Plus, it was springtime, and they used a fraction of that in summer. The occupants of the largest cabin in the compound were ready for war.

"Do you really think Wood Duck and his warriors will try to attack us in here at night?" Captain Sutton asked. He wore his cavalry cap cocked over one eye. "It seems an impossible task. This place is built like a little fortress."

"It has proven a safe refuge, time and again." Angus smiled. "We built one cabin to ward off the evils that wander into the wilderness. Still, I doubt we've had a wickeder man heading for our doorsteps. Time will tell if the cabin passes that test. That villain is as intelligent as he is skilled."

"I reckon old Wood Duck be part wolf," Rusty pondered. "Ain't that right, Dog?" He stared at his big black furry canine like he expected him to reply. "He hunts in the dark like wolves, so we've gotta be ready, night and day. If he's as close as I think he is, I reckon he'll come snooping around here to play first. This is all a big game to him and his people. They take pleasure in torturing folks mentally first, then physically later. Then, to finish, they take their lives. It's rare to run into anybody that escaped that devil."

"You escaped him, didn't you, Rusty?" Levi asked. "And you were chasin' him, Marshal."

"We were chasin' 'em all right when they weren't chasin' us," Joseph said as his eyes narrowed. "With some outlaws, it's hard to know who's followin' who."

Furs stretched on frames hung on the cabin walls, and dried garlic, chili peppers, and colorful Indian corn hung from the ceiling. Shelves were filled with pots, pans, cups, and bowls. A smoked leg of ham hung over the cookstove in the corner. Shadows flickered on the walls from flames in the fireplace.

Heat wavered across the room, making it cozy. The noise of nocturnal animals filled the night as coyotes continued their nightly choir. Eyes peered through gun slats and into the night. The full moon cast a silvery light, creating shadows where there were none before. A big-eyed great horned owl hooted, and its mate replied.

Men and women squinted into the darkness, searching for any sign of Wood Duck and his eight men. Each and every one was an evil monster in his own right.

Twigs cracked outside as heads tilted in the cabin, waiting for a following noise—maybe even gunfire. Will Forrester stood and fingered his empty sleeve. He wore a brace of pistols in his belt, both grips leaning toward the same side. Marshal Walker caressed his Henry rifle as he polished the wooden stock while Dahteste sharpened her knife.

Rusty Steel and Angus McFarlin sat on chairs as they stared out of the gun slats toward the compound entrance. Two rifles jutted from the holes cut into the wood. One was long and octagon-barreled, and the other had short double barrels. They believed Wood Duck would come from the same direction as the soldiers. He was sure the infamous outlaw was following the soldiers after they escaped his bloodbath. When Wood Duck found out they evaded his clutches, he would undoubtedly head for the compound. None of them had any uncertainty.

"Gold seekers headed west like some poison plague," Angus said, "and with them came their robbers and thieves—the ones who follow such men like a sickness. That was when the trouble all started a couple of months ago. I reckon it was from the day they shot and nearly killed Levi here. Bad luck seems to follow us like cats follow mice."

Betty put her hand in Will's hair and raked it back with her fingers.

The Compound

Wood Duck's men sat on blankets around the fire, drunk and half-naked as they snuffled and stirred, sucking their teeth like hairless apes. Their morning feed was bowls of pork and beans. The gang members sat by the firelight, eating with their fingers, and then they emptied the bowls by drinking the last like they were large cups. The gang members toweled up the grease with chunks of stale cornbread. Several men burped and farted, mixing the smell with beans and coffee.

Firelight reflected off Wood Duck's front gold teeth. In his hand, he carried a plaited rawhide quirt. He walked up and down, eyeing his men with his hands clasped behind his back as he tapped the whip on his shoulder. One of the gang members stumbled out of the cave and shuffled outside across dirt and to the campfire. The gang's dogs waited, loosely in their skins, like frames of canines in wrinkled hides. They growled and snapped until one of the gang members threw them a bone—any bone would do.

One of their prisoners tried to crawl away on his hands and knees because the renegades had skinned flesh off the bottoms of his feet. He screamed when Wood Duck lashed with the quirt on his naked back and bloody soles. The desperate sound made shivers run up a couple of the outlaws' backs, but then they smiled. Lucky for Crow warrior, the gang leader didn't use his bullwhip. Many men had died from his hidings as he stripped their bodies of skin, making their death all that much more painful.

The ground ran with blood in the gallons. More dead Crow lay brutally murdered and thrown into a ditch. From the camp in the distance, they could hear the moans of the dying somewhere in the forest nearby. Wood Duck's surviving Indian captives looked like skinned rats.

The renegades were a pack of black-eyed men with degenerate painted faces. They smoked hand-built cigarettes and cheroots as they brazenly eyed their surroundings. Wood Duck's men were a vicious-looking bunch of warriors mounted on unshod ponies. Some were smooth-faced, and others bearded, but one and all barbarous in their ways to anyone outside their tribe of nine.

They bore weapons of every characterization: heavy, large pistols and rifles—some long and others short with double barrels. Claymore-sized Bowie knives with bone handles flashed in their belts and boots.

Hobbled horses pulled on lush grass and slid their jaws while flicking their tails. Ornamental trappings made of human skin fashioned their bridles with blond and red woven hair in the manes and tails of the squat ponies. Some had crude symbols painted on their flanks and necks—arrows, triangles, and circles of various colors. Many also had handprints representing important warriors they had killed.

Some fresh and some dried ears were worn on pigging string necklaces around the outlaws' necks. The older ones were dehydrated to a dark gray like shriveled potato slices. When anyone neared, their wide-eyed horses showed their teeth like feral dogs. Some of the gang members at times fancied human flesh. They clearly had no boundaries. With no limits, Wood Duck and his gang became demons. They formed a heaping hoard of evilness devoted to only one man, and he was dedicated to one thing—hunting the living.

Wood Duck kept his cherished valuables in a soft kid-skin pouch. Inside were human teeth and dried round balls that looked like marbles.

He rocked back on his heels as he closely observed his inebriated men. This was when they spoke truths and conspired openly, mindless of what they said or who was listening. The gang leader was always looking for rebellious men, even though they had ridden together for decades. A good leader was ever aware when a challenge was about to come.

Bisa's arm was still painful, but his friends of questionable character felt no sympathy for their fellow man and continued toward their objective. He was alive, and that was all that mattered. His suffering was his problem, and when it came time to fight, they expected him to carry his weight just the same. On the afternoon of the third day after Wood Duck had amputated his arm with one swift slice of his massive knife, they saw a single trail of light gray smoke squirrel into the sky.

The one-armed outlaw swore as the heat bore down,

and his arm began to itch. He deadened the pain with a bottle of whiskey, which he generously gulped to stop the pulsating stump of his arm. Despite his injury, he held a pistol in his good hand along with the reins. They were approaching their destination, and now there was no room for error.

When they neared the house at dusk, Wood Duck observed chickens and goats roaming freely about the compound. A dozen horses raced around a sizable corral next to the stable. They neared the buck-and-rail fence, staying just out of sight in the shadows. The gang leader lifted his pistols and took aim.

The first three shots rang out, and an explosion of feathers and beaks appeared like magic. Three hens disappeared as the others scurried for safety. Only the dead fowls' feet lay on the ground twitching. Everything else was blown to smithereens. Another shot and a kid goat dropped suddenly as a pool of blood spread beneath it.

More gunshots rang out loud, and the large ceramic water vessel exploded on the porch, and bullets peppered the wall, sending splinters flying like tiny arrows. It was apparent the renegades were just playing games. For them, this was all sport, but for the people inside, it was as deadly as the devil who wanted to take their lives.

The outlaws did it all for entertainment. A haze of gun smoke drifted across the compound yard as horses squealed, racing around the corral even faster. The echoes of gunfire drifted away, and an eerie silence followed.

Wood Duck swung a rifle from the hip. He took a bead on a cat, silently sneaking up on its prey. He thumbed back the hammer with a click. The powerful explosion broke the silence again. The cat vanished in a puff of fur and whiskers, leaving nothing but empty skin. His shooting skills were excellent, and he proved it daily, so his men never forgot who was boss. He chuckled as he saw wide-spread eyeballs in the gun slats at the cabin door. He knew they were watching his every move.

"What is your life worth, Marshal Walker?" Wood Duck called out to those inside Rusty's cabin. "Or maybe I should ask what are your friend's lives worth *to you*? You too, Rusty Steel. I know you're both in there. Whatcha think, I'm a fool? And after I gave y'all such a nice present. I bet it was a heartwarming reunion you had with Rory Breaker." The evil laugh echoed across the small valley and bounced off the canyon walls. "For us, this is no more than a show of White buffoons, and tonight, you will provide our entertainment. Do you hear that, Marshal? Your time has come!"

Wood Duck's face suddenly clouded, and he began to grind his teeth. His mouth was no more than a brutal gash. The purple vein at his temple pulsed like a fuse. One of his men gasped like an asthmatic, but their leader's hard stare shut him up instantly. Nobody laughed at the boss or anything he did.

All that night, the Indian renegades took potshots at the turkeys, chickens, goats, and livestock in the yard. They didn't shoot the horses; they were too valuable, and the gang wanted them for themselves. They would take them after the people inside the cabin were all dead. That was why they had traveled so far and climbed the mountain. The horses were just a bonus.

The following day, the jagged peaks of the Rocky

Mountains turned blue in the dawn light. Birds flittered from limb to limb as the sun glared from the east and the pale moon silently vanished on the western horizon. The sunlight chased away the dark as heat wavered from the orange disk, dispersing the morning chill. With spring, it was getting warmer every day.

There was finally a sudden lull in the pistol fire, which dwindled until there was silence. Even the roosters refrained from crowing for fear of getting bullets for their noisy favor.

The lull in gunfire was worse than before. Each shot had spiked the tension, and then sudden silence doubled that. Wood Duck knew precisely what he was doing. He wanted to see wide, frantic eyes even before he began to torture them, one by one.

The Cabin

As the evening passed, the men and women in the cabin took turns peering out the gun slats into the night, making sure they would be ready when Wood Duck made his attack. They kept watch twenty-four hours a day, taking turns sleeping. Angus kept busy cooking for eleven people night and day. Orange coals warmed their backs, but they didn't stoke the fire that night, so it was dark inside the cabin, making it too hard to take a shot at a set of eyeballs peering into the dark.

"Why don't that devil come on and let's get this over with," Rusty grumbled. "He's makin' us wait on purpose, so we be more nervous when he does make his move."

"We've gotta be patient, just like Wood Duck," Levi whispered. Dahteste lay asleep, propped up on his side as he sat above her in the chair, watching for trouble out the hole in the shutters. "We have to wait until our opportunity arises; then we strike."

"And what kind of opportunity is that?" Marshal Walker asked.

"I'll let ya know when it dawns on me," Levi replied

with a troubled grin. "I doubt Wood Duck has much idea of how to break into here, either. I'd say we're at an impasse, but nobody will admit it. Let's just wait and see what the renegades are gonna do. We're nice and comfortable here in your cabin. We're a heck of a lot better in here than them out there."

Again, gunshots rang out sporadically as the villains shot the last of their livestock in the yard. More needless killing just for the sake of watching living things die. As a morning welcome, a cacophony of bullets slammed into the front of the log cabin, timber shutter, and door. The chairs and the table on the porch were full of bullet holes. Everything else was punctured or broken.

Rusty turned to the fire when the room began to fill with smoke. "Put it out before the room fills up, and we choke to death. That devil's blocked the chimney. It's a lucky thing it ain't winter, or we'd freeze to death. Close that flue, Will."

"I've already got the water hot, so I'll make up a kettle of coffee before we catch a chill," Angus said. "I didn't sleep at all last night, so I need to come to Java to keep me awake."

"Why, I never knew you snored when you were awake." Virgil laughed.

It was a nervous laugh and was contagious. Soon, they all were chuckling, which became a roar as they guffawed with hilarity.

"You hear how scared we are of ya, Wood Duck?" Rusty yelled as he bellowed with laughter until he got a stitch. He turned his eyes to Levi and said, "I always did think it was best to laugh in the face of danger. Now, hush for a spell and let me think. I'll come up with a plan of some sort or another. You just watch."

Everyone was living in Rusty and Angus's cabin for the siege. It was too dangerous to go outside. The other cabins were unguarded, although they had chained them up and used sledgehammers to cramp the steel links, but if the outlaws wanted to get in, that wouldn't stop them.

They didn't doubt Wood Duck's determination. He had come there to kill Walker and Steel, but now they would stay until they killed them all. Or, at least, Rusty believed that was their plan, although he still didn't know how they intended to do it, nor had he figured out how to go at outlaws.

Dog sat against Rusty's leg. He looked back over his shoulder and then back into the darkness as the hair on his back stood on end and he growled.

They sipped their coffees and munched on smoked ham and chunks of cornbread. The room was quiet as, most of the time, they were all focused on any noises outside. Marshal Walker and Rusty huddled by the door taking their turn and spoke in whispers. Levi watched as he sat by the cooking stove with Dahteste at his side. She stood guard over him like an Indian camp dog.

Now, the gunshots had ceased. Their animals were strewn across the yard—their bodies already beginning to bloat. The horses stood calmly and had simmered down after an exhausting night of nervous tension. Even the animals' patience was wearing thin. Something would have to happen soon, or their composure would falter, and somebody would decide to do something reckless.

Dahteste moved to the corner by the door, taking her turn keeping watch. Virgil stood by the shuttered window, resting the weight of the gun barrel in the gun slat. The Crow woman had her bow and an arrow in her hand, and another clamped between her teeth. Nobody saw her when she slipped her quiver of arrows over her shoulder and two pistols into her belt.

When she jumped up, she flung the two-by-fours off their cradle in one motion as she pushed the door open a crack and ran for the stables. She was a small woman anyway, and hunched over, she looked like an animal scurrying across the yard. Somebody behind her slammed the timber door shut with the doomed-like sound of a tomb.

"Whoa, whoa, whoa, slow down!" Rusty yelled at Levi. "You go out there and you're gonna get shot."

Sooner than she had expected, gunshots kicked up earth before her feet. They were leading their aim too much, but soon, they would adjust to her speed and shoot her dead, so she knew it was now or never. In one great leap, Dahteste flew over the split-rail fence of the corral. She disappeared into the small herd of horses and pushed her way to the back. The next thing they saw, she was on her mustang's back as she leaped the fence, racing up the north trail. The Crow camp was only a half-day's ride.

No sooner did she reach the gate and rode out, than she could hear Wood Duck shouting orders. Then, the pounding of horses' hooves followed a short distance behind. Her heels kicked her horse's flanks, and he shot off like a bullet with Dahteste riding on the far side, hidden behind the horse's back. She wanted to make a more challenging target as she fled for her life.

She wondered if Wood Duck knew there was a Crow stronghold five or six hours' ride north. At least she managed to break off part of the gang, making their numbers more manageable for her husband and the other mountain men. Now she knew she had to ride like she had never ridden before, or she too would die.

If anybody followed her, not knowing the Crow camp was there, they would fall into a trap. Either way, Wood Duck's days were numbered. All Dahteste had to do was make it to Chief Hachta and War Chief Wanata, and then she could organize a counterattack.

Crow Indians

Wood Duck and his men made camp on the windy plateau. The flames leaned downwind as the chains of fire raced through the kindling, lighting larger wood among the orange glowing coals. The outlaws' eyes looked ridged in the flickering light. One and all appeared evil. Yet, their leader was another step into darkness. He was the wickedest of them all.

The creek left a green corridor of trees along the banks below the higher mountains. There were a multitude of places for the renegade outlaw gang to hide, both night and day. They had packed food for a siege, and abundant water was available. Yet, they were all tired of waiting. The tactic they used on their enemies was working on them, and their tension spiked.

As the fire fled downwind, one of the outlaws began to chant. It was Bisa, and he started worrying because his arm began to smell. He could already tell the wounds were septic. His eyes were wild and angry. His face was iridescent in the moonglow as sweat ran down his forehead and neck. He was burning up.

Wood Duck's eyes shifted over the gang members. The one-armed man gibbered silently then raised his eyes to the leader and began to chant. It sounded like a death song. The gang leader's brow pleated like a porpoise.

A thunderclap and a frigid wind set the trees and bushes gnashing like forlorn beasts. They leaned into the wind. Wood Duck's eyes locked in cages of hot wires, red-rimmed. The stiff breeze flapped Bisa's empty sleeve.

Distant thunder quivered, and lightning slashed across the electric sky. The streaks of electricity were sucked away and replaced with blackness. Heavens full of foreboding clouds passed by.

The trappings of the Indian horses were fashioned out of human skin, and bridles were constructed of human hair. Teeth hung from their manes, ears, and tails like Christmas ornaments.

Long, wispy clouds glowed red, making the whole eastern horizon look like the world was burning as the sun breached the ridge sitting over the cabin.

"Now that we're here, we seem to be at a standoff," Wood Duck growled. "I didn't expect them to live in a fortress. We need to think up a plan to force them out."

"I've got just the trick to fix that, boss," Luke said. He flipped an orange stick in his hand. A wick protruded from one end. "You just let me take care of it. I stole this off the dead cavalry soldiers. They had a bag full, but we'll only need one."

Black-eyed renegade warriors with painted faces eyed the mountain man's cabin brazenly as their horses skittered and nervously shifted their hooves. They could barely see hazy white eyes peering through gun slats. Vicious-looking humans on unshod ponies prepared for revenge. Some were bearded and others smooth-faced, all clad in animal skins with silk and satin decorations but one and all barbarous and looking for a fight.

Many riders wore pigging string necklaces with scraps of dried human ears—some blackened by time. These men were wild and raw-looking, and they bared their teeth like rabid dogs. It was said that some ate human flesh. The horde of renegade rabble gigged their horses into a lunge for their attack. Hooves suddenly began to thunder as they closed the distance.

Seconds later, an explosion occurred, loud and with tremendous force. So much dust and gun smoke rose from the ruins that they couldn't see their targets. As they approached, bullets slammed into human flesh and horses. Still, the renegade Indians charged on. Only a hundred yards of compound separated the cabin from where they were mounted. Now Rusty Steel and Marshal Walker belonged to Wood Duck to do with what he wanted.

As the ponies squealed and the men screamed war cries, they raced toward their longtime enemies. Wood Duck and all knew the end was soon to come.

LEVI'S HEART jumped into his throat before he could even move. His wife had caught them so off guard that nobody was ready to stop her. She did the last thing anyone expected. Now, it was too late, and she was gone. Johnson swore under his breath. He gritted his teeth and wanted to hit something with his fist, but he knew he couldn't help anything.

Dahteste has sealed her fate. Johnson's heart thudded dangerously. All the nerves in his body went dead instantly. He forced the pain from his mind and focused on the task at hand. If they didn't win here, they would all die by Wood Duck's knife—even his Dahteste.

When the truth settled in, Steel's eyes spread. For the briefest of moments, everything froze like in a picture for Rusty. Levi screamed when he saw what was unfolding, but he was too late to stop his wife. She was suddenly out the door and gone. They heard gunshots follow in her footsteps.

The fiery disk rose with the color of steel. A teeth-clenched curse followed the marshal. The captain eyed Betty beside him. A rifle was strapped over his shoulder. He veered his eyes so she wouldn't see what was hidden there. Her features shined in the firelight warmly, but he maintained his stern face due to the situation. Still, his blood pumped through his body like steam through a locomotive. Now, the worst was to come.

Hostile eyes were watching them and were moving in for the attack. Then, there was a strange quiet. The mountain men peered into the inky blackness, straining their ears. The silence was suddenly broken, the sounds of vegetation moving followed by several muffled screams.

Rusty's dog sat in the corner, squatting loosely in his skin as he growled. He waited for his master to move, and they would attack as one.

Levi fired his scattergun, and a foot-long flame shot out of the end of the double barrels. There was too much smoke to see if he hit anything or not. He broke the double barrel open, pried out the spent hulls, and groped in his pockets for two fresh shells. His face glistened with sweat, and his shirt stuck to his back. Everything was happening too fast to mourn. If he survived, he would have time for that later.

With the suddenness of rain, the gunfire began to crack off the porch posts, logs, and roof. The barrage of bullets was even worse than before as a cacophony of projectiles whizzed through the air. Rocks, wood, and adobe clay chipped up around them as hot lead zipped around the cabin. The bullets clanged and peeyowed as chunks of led flew wild as the mountain men returned fire. Chaos and mayhem followed.

The blood pounding in Rusty's ears was as loud as thunder. These were his people, and he had to save them even if it cost him his life.

The smell of gunpowder. Just a whiff of it, then a cloud of smoke enveloped them. The way the explosion came made it impossible for anyone to prepare themselves. It was so powerful that it felt like it burst inside their heads, numbing their brains, and making them deaf.

The dynamite blast loosened the dirt, and the heavy timber door collapsed as a cloud of smoke grew like a mushroom. The musty hissing sound was like a chorus of rattlesnakes. Clouds of dust billowed over him like a wave.

That was when Crow war cries surrounded the entire compound. Clouds of arrows flew through the air with the suddenness of death. Then the warrior braves attacked with lances and war clubs, bashing in the skulls of their enemies. They pushed the renegades to the small creek two hundred yards from the compound fence.

Levi's heart red-zoned immediately. When they went out to check for survivors, there was only blood—not drops of it but streaks and smears forming in large dark pools.

Everybody listened to the lull in firing, which grew into total silence.

When they checked on the enemy, they found blood by the gallon. Men looked like pincushion dolls. Everybody chased the last man standing. Wood Duck raced before his enemies just out of reach, heading for the water.

When he reached the quick-flowing creek, the gang leader dove for safety. Wood Duck slid like one more predator beneath the ink-black water and out of sight. Mountain men and Crow warriors circled the creek to wait for the devil to resurface. They knew he could only hold his breath so long.

The other outlaws looked like skinned rats, full of holes and projectiles. They found Bisa a distance away as he leaned dead beside a tree. His empty sleeve fluttered in the breeze.

Some assumed Wood Duck had drowned and was dead, but others like Rusty and Joseph knew better than to believe anything they didn't see with their own eyes.

Will flicked wisps of hair out of his face with the backs of his fingers and glared. Betty came racing to his side, a brace of pistols still in her fists.

At the edge of the compound, Crow Chief Hachta's gaze was like a stone wall reflecting some primal part of his being. His woman war chief stood beside her leader;

then she rushed to her husband's arms. He was safe, and again, she had saved the day.

"Gold seekers and trespassers bleed West like itinerant degenerates," Angus spat. "That's what started all this mess. And now the Rendezvous is no more. I don't know if I can put up with more changes. Life is gettin' more complicated every season."

"I ain't seen a beatin' like that since somebody shoved a banana in my pants and let a monkey loose." Joseph laughed.

"Lay off, you're pontificating," Rusty spat.

"That's about as sincere as a two-dollar funeral, Marshal," Dennis hacked.

"Things can go to blazes in a handbasket," Levi said.

The sun sprayed orange rays of light.

Buffalo Herds

As they traveled down the mountain toward Yellowstone Valley, massive herds of bison covered the distance like a sea of brown, bushy fur. Bulls were heard bellowing in the mass of hair as they went through the freshly grown grass like a hundred thousand scythes, leaving bare stubs in their wake. When they finished, they shifted to their next grade and repeated the process. Occasionally, something would spook the herd, and they would instantly burst into motion and run like one giant beast, trampling every plant, tree, and living thing in their path.

Despite the fact they had heard the Rendezvous was canceled this year, they headed for the site of the last fur trading meet just the same. What else were they to do with their cold-water beaver pelts? Even if the market had crashed, the furs must be worth something. But if the rumors were true, they would have to find another profession because the top hat industry had collapsed.

When the party of mountain men and wives crossed

stretches of one or two hundred thousand buffalo, they rode high on the ridges to avoid being run over and flattened like a Mexican tortilla. Such a natural force demanded respect. Sixty million bison lived across the Great American Plains from French Canada to Texas. Their numbers appeared never-ending and impossible to kill to extinction.

Everybody was aware of the prize buffalo hides brought, but they were also aware that the tribes used these same animals for everything in their struggle to survive, from food to blankets to sewing needles. The Indians left nothing to go to waste. Without the buffalo, the Plains Indians wouldn't even exist. They looked like lumbering hirsute cows as they slowly grazed across the mountains and plains.

An eastern newspaper quoted one army officer as saying, 'Kill every buffalo you can! Every bison dead is an Indian gone.'

This remark struck a note with them all, and they begrudgingly let the bison they spied on live to graze another day. This sign of respect also satisfied the tribes on whose land they lived. They didn't take the food out of their fellow man's mouth unless it was a few for their use as food and blankets back in the cabins.

The buffalo hunters began trickling onto the plains, searching for the valuable skins and tongues. Some of the Easterners and Europeans that arrived did so with an entourage of wagons and servants with large tents and all the amenities from home in the big cities. All Indians and mountain men alike despised these men. They came to shoot for sport and left the bloated bodies on the valley floor to rot and for the coyotes and vultures to eat. All they came to do was see who could shoot the greatest number of the massive but dumb beasts as possible.

They heard the rumble of hundreds of thousands of hooves beating through the valley under the bright rays of the sun. Animal hair flew suspended in the air above the herd. Once one field was grazed to stubs, they moved to another, creating massive clouds of dust that could be seen for miles.

Eastern politicians in Washington said it would be impossible to civilize the Indian nations as long as the buffalo remained. The Secretary of Interior further explained that he would not seriously regret the total disappearance of the buffalo from the American western prairies and plains because it would hasten the Indians' dependence on products of the soil from their own labors.

With the buffalo gone, it would be easy to force the American Natives onto reservations. They saw the buffalo as being incompatible with their plans and the progress machine that currently raced across the North American continent.

Another argument eastern White men claimed was that the buffalo ate valuable grass that could be used to extend the cattle population, but only if the buffalo vanished.

A representative in the House said: 'There is no law that Congress can pass that will prevent the buffalo from disappearing before the march of civilization. There is no law which human hands can write, there is no law which a Congress of men can enact, that will stay the disappearance of these wild animals before civilization. They *eat* the grass. They trample upon the plains which our settlers desire to herd *their* cattle and *their* sheep. They destroy the pasture. They are as uncivilized as the Indians.'

These publications in the newspapers alarmed all mountain men and frontiersmen alike. When Washington used such words, they knew it was an end that was waiting to come, and it seemed to be much nearer than any had expected.

All day long, herds of shaggy buffalo darkened the entire horizon. When the party climbed high up a ridge to steer away from a possible stampede, they stopped and stared in wonder. As far as the eye could see, innumerable herds completely blackened the countryside. Every valley in the distance was shoulder-to-shoulder with buffalo.

"I've never seen anything like this," Betty Forrester said breathlessly.

"It's hard to imagine these mountains without buffalo," Will said. Tears welled in his eyes at the sheer beauty of what he beheld. The animals stretched for ten miles into the distance and were another five miles wide.

Late in the afternoon, they all stopped, hobbled their horses, and put them out to graze. The smell of frying pan biscuits filled the air in half an hour. They all crowded around the fire as the night chill set in. Days were already warm, but the mountain evenings were still chilly.

They set out guards, night and day, but they didn't expect any more trouble. With Wood Duck vanishing or possibly drowning in the quick-flowing stream and his men all confirmed dead, they felt they could let their guard down, at least a little. They had no idea of what lay ahead for them in the future. Uncertainty filled their minds with a hazy future still unknown to them.

"I've heard of herds that covered fifty square miles," Joseph said. The marshal saw a new business standing right before him. The possibilities appeared to be unlimited. "Some buffalo hunters claim they find herds two million strong. That must be somethin' to see."

"Nobody really understands the relationship the Indians have with the buffalo," Rusty said. Everybody sitting around the fire turned toward the mentor. "No one knows the bison like the Winnebago, Ho-Chunk, Lakota, Anishinaabe, Kiowa, Gros Ventre, Cheyenne, Shoshone Bannock—and the list goes on. I just can't remember 'em all right now." Rusty chuckled. "I reckon we're blessed to be the few to see such a spectacle. Who knows how long it will last? It never ceases to leave me spellbound and breathless at the sheer power in a single herd. The Indians have worshipped them for thousands of years."

"Well, I don't find the practice all that unusual," Joseph said. "For a poor man, a dollar or two a hide is considerable money. If you do the labor yourself, your only expense is gunpowder and bullets. Shooting a hundred animals in one session shouldn't be a problem. That's two hundred dollars for a single day's work. When did trappin' beaver get so easy? We have to skin' 'em, scrape 'em, and freeze 'em again to dry. Then we spend the whole winter curin' 'em to boot. All that for three or four dollars, tops, with twenty times the work. And you won't have your cabin stinking up everything with your winter hides."

"You would have somethin' contrary to say about it,

wouldn't ya, fool?" Rusty growled. The buffalo around them continued blowing and pawing at the ground.

After the fight with Wood Duck and his men, they all decided that they would all go down and see if news about the Rendezvous was true. They still found it hard to believe that a trappers' meet held for fifteen years would suddenly vanish. But news that came from the Crow Chief Hachta was seldom wrong.

Still, they had to sell their beaver pelts somewhere, and they hoped to find somebody at the fur trading meet to trade their furs. Too many trappers relied on the Rendezvous to just quit and walk away. They had to sell their beaver skins somewhere.

"What'll we do if there's nobody at the spot of the last Rendezvous when we get there?" Dahteste asked. "I don't think there is anywhere to barter our furs other than Fort Boise."

Only Levi Johnson shared the secret of what Dahteste did to the newspaper owner at the fort. She had crippled him for life in a way that only she and Levi knew. They thought better than to mention it, especially with Captain Sutton and Sergeant Money along for the ride. The two soldiers said they planned to return to the garrison and take new orders from there.

Nobody knew what was in store for them. They not only didn't save the four hundred prospectors but also lost twenty-two of their patrol in the process. But unlike Will Forrester, the captain felt it was his duty to make the full report. Everyone wondered how that would work out.

"What'll we do if there ain't nobody at the location of last year's Rendezvous?" Levi asked.

His lung was healing fine, but he was still out of

breath. The damaged lung was still on the mend, but Johnson wasn't willing to stay back at the cabin with his wife when the rest of the men and women in the compound had joined the men for the journey to Daniel, Wyoming, on the Green River. Since no location was indicated this year, all they could do was visit the site of the last Rendezvous, hoping that some trading company would take a chance and pick up their pelts at low prices.

"If there isn't anybody there to buy our furs, what are we going to do?" Will asked. "I'm sure other trappers will show, just like us, but I don't know about the American Fur Trading Company or their Canadian counterparts."

"When did you all begin to worry about the future like a bunch of old hens?" Virgil laughed. "You know it's a fool's game, frettin' over something that may not be as bad as you think. Even if it is, there's not a danged thing we can do about it and worryin' won't help. It is what it is." Lovejoy smiled at his own wisdom.

"He's right, ya know." Levi chuckled. "We never worried about what was gonna happen tomorrow, let alone what happens a week from now. That's not how Rusty taught us."

Betty leaned into Levi as they sat before the flickering flames that danced in the eyes of the trappers and wives. Dahteste appeared more nervous than the others, but nobody knew why. Only Levi Johnson guarded her secret of what she did to the man who started the whole gold strike chaos with his falsehoods in his newspaper. She had secretly taken revenge for what the journalist caused to happen to her husband. Restitution was taken on all those involved.

They uncinched the saddles and pulled them down, hobbling the rear leg to the foreleg. The horses pulled at lush green grass, sliding their jaws, and whisking their tails to shoo away flies.

While enjoying the fire and company, Angus made the day's last meal. Everybody waited anxiously for tonight's surprise. They smelled baked apples coming from a cast iron skillet. McFarlin generously covered them in honey and cinnamon, making mouths water.

Rusty Steel sat back against a stone and looked at his people one by one. Levi and Will had become mountain men, and the old mentor had little more to teach them. Johnson might even know more about the wilderness than his mentor at this point. This made the aging trapper smile. What better way to spend your last years than passing on everything you know to deserving young men?

His teachings would allow them to live in the mountains as long as he, Dennis, and Angus had. Time would tell, but they had a good start. They were every bit as much mountain men as Rusty, Angus, and Dennis, and they had a whole lifetime before them. Rusty was just glad he had in Levi the son he had always wanted. And they were just right for all the lessons he had bestowed on them. This knowledge made him a very happy man.

"These apples taste just fine." Rusty smiled. "I reckon you're the best frontiersman cook in the Rocky Mountains, Angus." Everybody around the fire nodded their agreement with full mouths.

McFarlin never tired of the compliments. The kind words made all the work of cooking for such a large clan enjoyable for him. A man never knew where valuable rewards would come from next.

Nobody spoke as they gobbled down the desert and more whiskey-laced coffee. A comfortable silence befell the close friends. Even the strangers enjoyed their company, but even they saw they weren't one of them. It would take the officers years to become frontiersmen if they ever did. In the army, out here on the most isolated part of the Indian frontier, they would learn little more than how to kill what the government called hostiles. But the mountain men saw that they were only trying to survive, just like every other human who lived in the wilderness.

"Ain't life grand?" Rusty grinned so wide you could see his wisdom teeth. "Sittin' around a hot fire in the middle of the forest, living hand-in-hand with Mother Nature. We must be the luckiest people on Earth."

When the moon rose, it looked like a giant pumpkin, and stars twinkled behind it millions of years away. When a shower of falling stars raced for the earth's atmosphere, all eleven took a moment to make a wish. They all hoped for more time together like they had now.

The clan was now complete, and in a few days, the two members who didn't belong would be on their way to Fort Boise to make their report and probably face the music. They were the only ones worried about the future. But they hadn't had Rusty Steel to teach them the way of the Indians, wild animals, and the forest.

"There are all kinds of truths in this world of ours, here in the dense forests," Angus whispered, like if they talked too loudly, the spell would be broken.

"And many of those are yet to be spoken, my friends," Rusty added. "I reckon the biggest one is everything is *impermanent*. Nothing will last forever, not even us. But our friendship will always remain."

"Phenomena free from the duality of apprehender and apprehended," Virgil added. "We can't fully understand life until we understand death. Once you eliminate the impossible, whatever remains, no matter how improbable, must be the truth."

"I have come to have my own truths," Levi said in a low, respectful voice. "Make it easy, make it quick, when possible, show rather than tell and respond to emotion, love, and beauty. Those simple things changed my life, and all of you were responsible for my lesson in how to live, especially my mentor. I thank you all kindly from the depths of my heart." He kissed his petite Crow wife on the top of her head, and she closed her eyes and smiled. She, too, was as happy as she had ever been.

"You forgot one," Marshal Walker added. "Make it look good, whatever you do."

They all looked at their friend, the Kansas marshal. Although he had spent most of his life fighting outlaws and Indians and living the life of a mountain man, he still didn't completely understand.

Rusty made a pistol's finger and thumb and aimed it at the marshal and said, "Bang, bang."

Levi and Dahteste watched as the fireflies glowed yellow at some point in the night only to flash somewhere else. It was like a concert of tiny lights in the black of the night.

Virgil was reading the Bible, moving his finger under the words.

The red-skinned beauty's coal-black eyes sparkled with mischief as her long, full hair hung below her waist. As the breeze rose, her hair lifted in the wind like pages of a book. Dahteste pushed a wisp of hair out of her eyes and gave Levi a hopeful smile.

The following day, God's paintbrush colored the sky shades of pink as the red disk hid over the horizon.

Grasshoppers clung to his pants legs before they jumped to the next plant and the sun was already high and hot in the morning sky.

Captain Forrester had the brim of his hat slapped up like the men of the Seventh Cavalry.

The morning fire lashed its tails over orange coals as the smoke vanished a few feet above, disappearing with the wind.

The Last Rendezvous

Levi Johnson Mountain Man Scout 18

This book is dedicated to my readers without whom I would be no more than a scribbler and not the author you have created.

"Life is short. Break the rules. Forgive quickly. Kiss slowly. Love truly. Laugh uncontrollably. Never regret anything that makes you smile."

Mark Twain

The Arrival

Even though the Indian gossip said there wouldn't be a Rendezvous that summer, all the mountain men from the compound and two of their wives still traveled down the winding trail to see for themselves. Even Dennis and Angus, who claimed they wouldn't go, were too curious to stay home.

It was something they found too difficult to believe to be true. They wondered what they would do with their furs and hides if it were factual. The previous year, there were five to six hundred visitors, many of whom stayed the entire two weeks.

Thousands of pelts changed hands for money, gold, and supplies. The fur traders brought rolling trading posts on large oxen-drawn wagons, so they made money coming and going all day and night long. It was a significant business that seemed to have vanished like steam on sun-warmed glass.

Rusty and Levi led the party from the compound, but the happy faces from the previous years vanished like smoke through a keyhole when they got a look at the old fur traders' site. That summer, many of the curious mountain men in the Rockies traveled to the location of the previous Rendezvous. When Rusty and Levi got there, they saw dozens of confused frontiersmen.

Some hadn't heard the news of the event's cancellation due to the lack of demand for cold-water pelts. There were parts of the Rockies where men trapped that were so remote, they passed the entire year without seeing a single soul. The trappers' meet was their only time to socialize. At this point, nobody knew what to do with their hides and furs. The closest trading post was in Fort Boise, a three-week ride from the compound. For many, even that was too civilized, but they would have to buy their supplies somewhere.

"Whatcha think we ought to do, Rusty?" Levi asked. "Maybe we should keep on goin' and sell 'em for what we can in Fort Boise. There's not much use of takin' 'em back up the mountain, is there? We gotta get rid of 'em somehow for any price we can. That or hang onto 'em, hopin' the market somehow turns around."

"From the looks of things, it don't appear there will be anymore trappers' meets." Dennis huffed. "There ain't even a tent saloon to get a bottle of labeled whiskey. All I see is more folks like us."

"We've still got to buy supplies from somewhere," Virgil said as his brown hand pulled on a few chin whiskers. "Even if we don't sell the pelts right now, we still need coffee, tea, sugar, and a bunch of other goods, or Angus won't have anything to cook with. How would you like to spend a whole winter without a drop of coffee? We're even out of store-bought liquor; that's how low our supplies are. Remember, we've been feedin' extra mouths of late and have been goin' through our food stock like honey badgers, especially the java and spirits. We don't have enough to get through half the winter, and we still have mules loaded with skins. I reckon this is what's called a conundrum."

"I believe this leaves us all in a predicament," Will Forrester said as Betty pulled up her horse by his side. "I don't see the prices coming back up. Fashion in the big cities is fickle, to say the least. What was one year's rave is the next year's trash. We better get rid of everything we have as quickly as possible. Or else, we'll be waiting in a line five miles long."

Levi looked back at his Crow wife, Dahteste, and they locked eyes. At first, she shook her head, but after a moment, she shrugged, gestured with open hands, and said, "Why not?"

The woman war chief obviously wasn't afraid whether Perry Weston, the owner of the *Les Boise* newspaper, had survived her knife. As she had said, White men thought all Indian women looked alike—especially men who lingered in the shadows following clouds of patchouli oil from spoiled doves.

Life in the wilderness threw constant dangers at those who lived there, and she knew a person had to deal with one at a time. What they needed to do first was find someplace to sell the furs, regardless of where it was. They couldn't let all winter's work be for nothing. She would have to suffer the danger for the good of them all.

"If we have to go, I'm well enough to make the ride if that's what you're worried about, Rusty." Levi smiled, and it reached his eyes. "Lately, you've been peckin' around me like an old hen, but I promise I can keep up. I feel better every day."

As wagon wheels whirled by, churning up dust at Daniel, Wyoming, the family of mountain men and their wives watched in wonder. There were no big tents, hawkers, fortune tellers, or men with elixir cure-alls. There wasn't even a sharpshooter contest, much to Rusty's disappointment.

None of the fur trading companies of the previous years were present, nor were their supplies of goods to trade for recently valuable beaver pelts. Hundreds of people hadn't materialized as many expected, and the Indians were nowhere to be found. It was as though they were better informed than the trappers.

A dust devil whirled through the middle of it all, giving the impression of something like a ghost town. The fifty or so men they saw were half of questionable character and came to prey on those with valuables.

In this case, beaver pelts would do even if they were worth a fraction of what they were the previous year. It was still free money for a thief, so they kept their eyes and ears sharp.

"How are we gonna make a living if there's no Rendezvous anymore and nobody wants beaver furs? That's our livelihood, for Pete's sake," Angus grumbled.

Rusty stood stupefied at the reality standing before him. "Yep, I reckon we'll have to head for Fort Boise. Maybe we'll ride to the plains while the weather is still good and hunt buffalo. Bison hides are still worth money, ain't they?"

"And join that bunch of fools that stand on hills shootin' dumb, helpless animals all day?" Dennis asked.

"I doubt I'm built for killin' innocent beasts like that. It's a turkey shoot."

"What it is, is a living, like it or not," Rusty growled. "If you're so clever, why don't you tell us what we're gonna do to make money if not hunt buffalo? Don't go all quiet on me now. Come on, let's hear what Angus has to say."

"Now's your chance to jump in with me and help me guide that wagon train across the Oregon Trail," Marshal Walker said with hopeful eyes. Since he lost Rory Banks, he knew finding reliable help on such short notice would be hard.

"Now you're talkin' nonsense, Joseph," Rusty replied. "You'll have to get someone else to replace Rory. We've gotta keep our eye on the target, get rid of these pelts, and prepare ourselves for a summer of huntin' buffs. There're a lot of mouths to feed in our little square of mountain. Preparing for next winter comes before everything else. But first things first. I agree with Levi; we should get rid of the pelts first before they're worth less money than they are now. The first trappers to unload their winter's catch will get the best price. If Levi is up to it, I think we shouldn't linger. I reckon we've been fired from our beaver trappin' job and need to get supplies and get after them buffalo."

"But we just spent the winter preparing for the summer," Joseph grumbled. "When are we gonna get a rest?"

"You won't be getting much rest in the next year if you plan on taking two hundred wagons across The South Pass and onward to Oregon City," Will said. "I've seen enough expeditions gone wrong. The only way to travel is with veteran frontiersmen like yourself. Otherwise, you'll be looking at a doomed journey. Mark my words, I've been through it already."

Two weeks later, nine mountain people rode into Fort Boise. Horses' hooves clopped on the hard ground. Outside the fort stood at least a hundred tents. Campfires dotted the area outside. Big doors stood open at the fort's entrance.

Carriages, wagons, and horses stood beside stores or slanted along buildings, loading and unloading cargo. A British flag with the letters H.B.C.—Hudson's Bay Company—fluttered over the turret in the corner. It sat on the east bank of the Snake River, only ten miles from its mouth.

A massive wagon train circled on the outskirts of the fort, and hundreds of people, if not thousands, cooked and worked around dozens of campfires. They had just crossed the long and dusty journey over the Snake River Plains. A few trappers made their camps on the other side, but there were fewer than expected. Maybe they *had* arrived first. Still, they all assembled at Chance Wesson's Chief Idaho trading post. This was where all travelers refilled their supplies for the journey west or east.

The outside walls were thick and durable, made from adobe clay. Blockhouses emerged from all four corners and were defenses against hostile Indian attacks. The fort was formidable and appeared impossible to breach without a cannon and an army.

This building made it possible to maintain the trading post year-round. The tall watchtowers stood high above the other buildings on each corner. Army guards with guns were visible on the turrets.

"It looks like you might be too late, Joseph," Rusty said as he eyed the circled wagons and all the people milling around. "Why don't you go over and ask them where they come from and where they're headin'?" Rusty couldn't help but chuckle. Even though he stifled his laughter, the marshal felt the dig.

The big gates at the entrance opened onto the river, which was dotted day and night with fishermen.

As they passed towering gates, they saw numerous small buildings one story high. They built them along all four sides. These were living quarters, storage, and small shops providing services like a farrier, saddle makers, a doctor's office, and a few other tradesmen. The trading post was the most prominent building in the courtyard.

"Maybe you should have your gunshot wound looked at by a real doctor," Virgil said. "I can patch a man up, but I don't claim to be a physician, not by a long shot."

"Why would I need a school-taught doctor when I've got you, Virgil?" Levi replied. "You're Rocky Mountain's best. I'd prefer natural healin' than taking medicine when I don't know quite what it is."

When the trappers party from Rusty's Mountain pulled up before the trading post, a merry, fat old gentleman fifty-some years old greeted them. He and his servants beseeched the newcomers to the fort with kindness.

The frontiersmen were dirty and smelly from the hard ride. Saddles creaked when they dismounted. Trail dust filled every wrinkle in their skin and clothing. They brushed off their clothes with their hats.

"Howdy, gentlemen. My name is Francis Payette. I see you've come to sell your pelts. You *have* heard about the fall from fashion of beaver top hats, haven't you? It seemed to happen from one day to the next. Let my men take care of your horses. You must be tired and hungry, too."

Soon, the travelers found themselves heading toward a diner. Soldiers filled several tables on the porch, and residents occupied the interior. Faces turned and inspected the strangers. Then again, new people came and went from Fort Boise daily. Mountain men weren't new to the fort, so a glance sufficed.

"Thank ya kindly," Rusty said. "I reckon we should introduce ourselves before we have a proper meal. It's been three weeks since we've eaten anything besides dried jerky and beans. Levi Johnson and I are in charge of tracking for the bunch."

"I must admit, I'm famished," Levi said.

"When aren't you hungry?" Will snickered.

Dahteste clutched his arm as she shot wary glances across the room full of White men. Some of the suits frowned when they saw the Indian enter the small restaurant, but when they got sight of Levi and the captain, they diverted their stares.

"Come on, follow me," Francis said as he waddled to the back. Boards creaked under his weight.

As soon as Francis entered the hall, several servants jumped to action and seated the new guests around a long wooden table.

Levi's wife's eyes constantly studied the faces, memorizing all the White people eating and passing their time over coffee or tea. She heard Americans talking, but there were British, too, who were more challenging to understand. Of course, she recognized the French trappers for their sing-song language, but she grasped nothing they said.

The Black men and women helping Francis treated him more like an owner than a boss. They tended to his every beck and call. Dahteste noticed they always looked at the floor and rarely made eye contact with their master. There were slaves in many of the Indian camps, too, so she understood immediately who they were and how their owner treated them.

"We have proper milk cows brought from Ohio," Francis said proudly. "You won't believe how good the butter is."

They were served salmon made in every way possible: broiled, fried, boiled, and baked. Steam rose from large loaves of warm bread fresh from a proper oven. Steam rose from corn on the cob and mashed potatoes.

People stopped and greeted Francis with a "Bonjour," like most Canadians. Each time somebody stopped by the table, he stood and shook hands.

"Do you know where those wagons outside the fort come from?" Marshal Walker asked as his brow furrowed. "It looks like a sizable wagon train."

"Why, of course, I do," Francis replied. "There's little that happens around here that I don't hear about. They all come from Independence, Missouri. At least, that's where they started the wagon train. Three hundred wagons, carriages, and buggies are waitin' to make the cross—along with cattle, sheep, goats, and even a drift of pigs. It'll be the third train to stop here for supplies this spring and summer. The progress machine is heading westward, and soon, locomotives will cut the time in half. If this keeps up, we'll have lots of commerce trading with all those who must resupply. I believe this is just the start."

"The Oregon Trail?" Joseph mumbled, frowning. He was seeing his plans go up in smoke before his face.

The news was devastating for the marshal. He had planned on being the first to make the cross, only to find out three wagon trains had already done it. He instantly lost interest in his planned expedition, especially without Rory Breaker, his right-hand man. His dream was like a bubble, and when it burst, it disappeared.

Marshal Walker pushed it back into the corners of his mind. He wasn't the kind of man to dwell on missed opportunities when he could focus on something positive.

"I beg your pardon, Marshal?" Francis asked. "I didn't quite get that."

Everybody froze like ice was injected into their veins with a syringe as their heads craned toward the door. A small man limped into the diner with two military police at his sides. His angry eyes flashed over the room until they landed on the Crow Indian.

"That's the heathen that damaged me for life!" he cried out as he pointed his finger at Dahteste.

Levi wrapped his fingers around his guns and immediately stood between his wife and the soldiers.

"You touch my woman, and I'll kill ya where ya stand," Johnson growled. Nobody in the room doubted he would do it simply by the tone of his voice and his size. It all said he wasn't fooling.

He still hadn't recovered all his lost weight due to

the bullet hole in his left lung. Still, he towered over the soldiers. Rusty popped up out of his chair with fire in his eyes.

"How do you know you have the right person?" Levi asked, nearly growling. His voice was full of danger. He slipped his finger into the trigger guard as he rested his thumb on the hammer.

Suddenly, they heard boots hammering on the timber porch. Tables screeched as they pushed them aside, and chairs toppled over. Twenty more soldiers burst into the diner to back up the men arresting Dahteste. Rusty and Levi stood down, or they would be the ones shot where they stood. Their arms went limp with their pistols still in their hands.

"Take that woman into custody," the lieutenant ordered crisply. He was obviously used to giving orders and having them carried out promptly. He impatiently tapped his leg with his riding crop. "If anybody interferes, arrest them, too. I won't have disorderly conduct in my fort."

The Fort Boise lieutenant nodded to the sergeant and saluted the cavalry officer sitting with the mountain men at the table. But he was all business and turned with the prisoner and stormed away. Two guards remained outside the door on the porch just in case the frontiersmen started trouble. Each had a primed rifle in their fists. The looks on their faces said they weren't fooling around.

They all saw Dahteste scratch, kick, and bite as they relieved her of her weapons. She cringed at what she saw when she locked eyes with the tabloid owner, Perry Weston. Of course, in the past, the journalist was an avid womanizer, spending his free time with ladies of the night and women of questionable employment.

So, when Dahteste had removed his stones with the flick of a knife, he swore he would get even with her if he ever saw her again. Today, he had seen her out his office window when she rode in. His day had finally come, and he rushed to the door as he headed for the lieutenant's office.

"Everybody comes by Fort Boise at some time," Weston whispered. "I knew it was just a matter of time."

"What did you say, sir?" the lieutenant asked.

"Nothing," he grumbled. "I want to see that heathen hanged by tomorrow noon. Do you understand?"

The officer nodded without a word. He knew if the newspaperman wanted, he could invent another falsehood and ruin his life in the blink of an eye. If Mr. Weston was bold enough to invent and publish an article about a fake gold strike in the Rocky Mountains, he was capable of doing anything.

Levi stood at the window as he watched the soldiers drag Dahteste down the street. His mind began to churn, looking for a way to get her out. He kicked himself because he knew better than to bring her into the fort after what she did to the journalist. Sure, he had it coming, but just the same, now they had a much bigger problem than selling their furs.

Fort Boise

The ancient bell was sea-green with age. It hung from double poles between adobe dolmens. Twelve gongs said it was midday. The sun glared down on the courtyard, bleaching everything with light. A hot breeze fluttered curtains in the locals' windows and pushed dust across the ground. All the houses in the fort faced the courtyard. The walls towered so high that all that was visible was the sky. White clouds shaped like animals floated across a light blue background.

Mountain bluebirds fluttered from porch to porch, enjoying the shade. A gaggle of white ducks waddled across the courtyard like they owned the place. The stone buildings lined the street using the back of the fort's scarps as walls. Chimneys made of rock protruded from shingled roofs. Heavy timber framed the windows and doors. Two tall wooden gates were the only way in or out. Armed army guards stood on either side.

Rusty sat on the diner porch, tapping his fingers on the tabletop, deep in thought. Joseph, Virgil, Will, and Angus sat across from Steel as Levi paced the floor.

Wood planks groaned under Beaver's feet, and his face glistened with sweat—his eyes etched with concern.

"Would you sit *down* for a minute," Rusty growled. "I can't think until you stop fidgetin', so be still for a spell while I try to figure this out. Whatcha say, Marshal? Is there any legal way to get Dahteste out of jail?"

"The Indian Territories ain't in a Kansas marshal's jurisdiction," Joseph replied. "Only the Indian Agency and the army have any weight here. Even when I worked as an Indian fighter, I was on the Army payroll. I figure these soldiers way out here can do pretty much whatever they want and not worry about repercussions. The law's not very clear except on White man's land. The Indians have no rights at all. They ain't even considered American citizens, and they were here before us. It's funny how that worked out, ain't it?"

"Funny for a White fella but not for a Red or Black man," Virgil replied. "I'm lucky I'm free and not a slave. You have no idea what it's like to be on the other side of White. I was there for most of my life."

"I reckon if Dahteste is my wife, then she's American too, dagnabbit," Levi said as he finally sat. "I knew I shouldn't have brought her, but she said White men think all Indian women look alike."

"I doubt the army puts much stock Eastern men marryin' Indian women anyway," Joseph said. He looked at Levi, concerned.

"When were you gonna tell us about what she did to the scribbler?" Rusty asked. "I've never known you to keep secrets from me—especially when it affects us all. You weren't thinkin' straight on that one, pilgrim."

Levi frowned and nodded, but he didn't have words. How could they have been so naive as to think the man who she maimed wouldn't recognize her? He realized now that it wouldn't be a face any man quickly forgot. A small shudder ran through his body at the thought of such a thing happening to him.

A waiter scrambled out the door onto the porch with a large coffee kettle in his mitt-covered hand. It was obviously piping hot; brown bubbles burst and steam rolled out the spout. The table went quiet when the stranger neared, but he was oblivious to any conversations. The diner was understaffed, and the server ran, stumbling to keep up. Grumpy customers growled and barked as he rushed for the kitchen. A big, shaggy black dog sat at Rusty's feet. It opened one eye, looked around and went back to sleep.

"We don't have time to worry about what we should have been told or not," the marshal said. "They plan to hang Levi's wife tomorrow at noon. That doesn't give us much time. It rubs me wrong, but I don't see a legal way out of this. I ain't never broken the law in my life, but I reckon there's a first time for everything. I sure as heck ain't gonna take the first wagon train to Oregon City after somebody else has already done it. What the hell? After this, maybe I'll become an outlaw."

"Stop talkin' nonsense," Rusty retorted. "Don't we get a trial, Joseph?"

"This is the Army and not the Supreme Court," the marshal said, "and Dahteste ain't an important politician—she's an Indian. Our only hope is to get a word with the commanding officer. I'm sure that lieutenant ain't the boss. I reckon as a United States Marshal, I might be able to persuade my way into a meeting with the highest-ranking officer at this post or at least the second in command. I can give it a try anyway."

"Hopefully, that lieutenant's not the commander's assistant," Angus said. "He doesn't look like an easy tree to bend."

"Did you see the look in that journalist's eyes when he saw Dahteste?" Levi asked. "He looked plumb crazy to me."

"Yeah, and how would you feel if somebody cut off your stones?" Marshal Walker asked. "I doubt you'd take it kindly."

"She was only getting even for me." Levi huffed as he sighed, his shoulders drooping. He looked like a beaten dog. "This Perry Weston of the *Les Boise* newspaper was the one who invented the lie about gold in the Rockies. And how much trouble did that start, and how many lives did it cost? That should be enough to have *him* locked up. It ain't no more than a monthly rag anyway."

"I'm afraid that ain't true," Marshal Walker said. "The Constitution of this here United States gives each man the right to say what he danged well pleases. Sometimes, the law is a double-edged knife, though. It all depends on what side you're on. I figure Indians are always on the wrong side when it comes to White folks."

Will Forrester pushed his cavalry hat back on his head, removing his eyes from the brim's shadows. His empty sleeve festooned in the breeze. "I guess I'm your only real chance, Levi. Remember, I was a West Point captain before I became a mountain man. The commanding officer will be officially obliged to see me if I tell him who I really am. It would be his duty, and he couldn't refuse."

"Do you really wanna go there, pard?" Levi asked as concern filled his eyes. "That would be another problem to deal with. If this captain is anything like his lieutenant, they might lock you up, too. Considerin' how your expedition went, they may even throw away the key. They weren't there like we were, so they might not understand the which of why you just walked off like ya did. Some things you have to live to understand."

"Boy, that girl really did open a can of worms when she cut his nuts off, didn't she?" Rusty chuckled. He couldn't keep a straight face. "And you say this fella is a womanizer, too? Maybe we can snoop around and find out how many friends this fella has here. He might be easier to topple over than we think."

Chills shot up their spines, and hackles sprouted on their necks as hammers drove sixteen-penny nails into the soft pine two-by-fours. Their eyes were drawn to the center of the courtyard where men had just begun to build the gallows. It looked like they were planning to have the hanging on time. The blood drained from Levi's face as the carpenters continued to saw and hammer.

"They better not touch a hair on her head," Levi growled as he fingered the pistol in his belt. "If they do, I'll kill 'em."

"Instead of planning to kill folks, why don't you focus on savin' somebody, namely, your wife," Rusty scolded. "If you'd have brought this to me from the start, I'd have steered you in the right direction. You messed up, Beaver. Yes, sir, this time, you really screwed the pooch."

"Leave the young man alone, Rusty," Marshal Walker spat. "If I remember right, you got yourself into a mess or two back when I first knew ya years ago. You were a handful, you were. We all make mistakes. Hopefully, you've learned from it, son."

Angus grabbed a bottle from the middle of the table and poured a half glass of whiskey into his dented tin cup. He topped it up with coffee as the aroma filled the air. They waved their hands before their faces as flies buzzed around their heads. People, horses, and wagons passed as they dropped off and collected cargo. The absence of animal skins was noticeable.

"There used to be a time when you came here of a summer an' there would be pelts stacked to the rafters, and now, the only ones I see are ours," Rusty said. "We best tend to business before we run out of money. We still have to sell those hides and furs. Angus and Virgil can come with me and have a talk with the owner of the tradin' post. Captain, you, Levi, and Joseph figure out how you go about makin' a meeting with the boss of this place. I reckon they're gonna find out who you are anyway. Remember, we brought those army boys with us, and given a little time, they'll all be as thick as thieves with the other officers. As soon as we arrived, they disappeared. The army is just another tribe, so, in the end, they'll all stick together."

Cups and glasses covered the table, but only three remained. The mountain men sat in an uncomfortable silence. A dust devil appeared in the courtyard's center like an ominous prediction. It raced across the ground but disappeared right before it reached the gallows. The carpenters stopped and stared.

One man tested the trapdoor. It slammed open with a bang, making them all jump nervously. The feeling was something between dread and excitement for the builders. They knew what they were constructing and the outcome of their skills. They were building a theater for the last moments of a person's life—a platform where death would be a public exhibition.

"So, whatta we do now?" the marshal asked.

"I suppose we should all go and see the commanding officer," Captain Forrester said. "Levi, because he's the condemned's husband, Joseph, because you're a US Marshal. And, of course, me—a failure and deserter of the United States Cavalry."

As Will said it, things started to sink in. Of course, when he didn't return to the fort in Kansas, in the army's eyes, he was probably considered a deserter, even if he had been an honored officer from an important military family back in New York. He was far from home now, and the fort authority would have the last word. What they went through with the Comanche back in Kansas would change any man.

The loss of his expedition of important scientists and soldiers was more than the captain could bear. That was why he didn't return to what would have probably been a court-martial. When the Fort Boise commander discovered who he was, he could end up shot. He doubted they bothered with things like military hearings so far away from civilization. He looked for a moment at the gallows and wondered if he would be joining Dahteste at the rope party.

The Stockade

According to the US Constitution, people incarcerated should be protected against cruel and unusual punishment. Prisoners should receive life's basic necessities, such as food, shelter, and medical care. But in the West, the dangerous and sometimes brutal conditions violated the country's laws, and nobody seemed to care.

Especially if the individual locked up was an Indian —a woman, no less—even when White, without the rights of a man. They gave them the label of enemy combatants to rationalize this harsh treatment. This allowed swift punishment without a trial. All enemies of the State were guilty, regardless of what they might claim or do. Most were sent directly to the gallows, although the wayward soldiers stood before firing squads. It was a messier end, but it guaranteed a painless death. With hangings, without an expert, things could quickly go awry.

Moisture from the humidity dripped from the ceiling of the dank, dark cell. Beads of water rolled down the old stone and adobe walls. Dahteste imagined being locked in such a room for months, and it neared her toward panic. At least she would be spared that indignity and would be hanged the following day.

Standing on her steel bunk, stretching to her tiptoes, she could see over the bottom of the windowsill. Mrs. Johnson peered at the half-built wooden structure. The builders finished the platform, and she heard them testing the trapdoor, loudly banging several times until they had their adjustments correct.

Every beat of the pounding hammer meant another nail in her coffin. She knew the end was close at hand, but she had her death song prepared and was aware of how they expected her to act. Indian gossip raced across the wilderness like wildfire, so the news of her demise would reach far and wide in only a matter of weeks or, at most, months.

She wasn't as confident as she had always thought she would be. Dahteste watched as her hands trembled. This wasn't how she expected to die. As a war chief, she had played out her demise in her mind's eye many times, but always in battle. She had imagined a proud and rebellious end—not to be some spectacle for White people to batter with rotten tomatoes and apples and cheer as she passed.

Dahteste was to be disgraced by one and all. Hopefully, no Crow spies would be present. Yet the world would eventually know all the gruesome details just the same. All she could do was try to put on the best act she knew how because her confidence seemed to be hiding for the day, and paranoia was its replacement.

When the Crow war chief entered the block of ten cells, most of them were teeming with Indian men, although there were a few army soldiers locked up, too. She could only imagine what a White man had to do to get jailed alongside a dozen Native Americans accused of injustices against the United States. All the Indians were really doing was protecting their families and property. There were no hearings, courts, judges, or juries for them. The commanding officer would decide Dahteste's fate, and she wasn't expecting mercy.

When two soldiers rattled a skeleton key in the lock and pulled back the steel bars, rusty hinges squeaked. The room was little more than an oxidized cage for wild animals, and they treated inmates accordingly. The building was squalid, dark, and rife with sickness, especially among the those who had little defense against white men's diseases. Despite the heavy steel trapping them inside, they also wore irons to further dissuade them from attempted escapes. Or perhaps it was simply more torture.

When Dahteste turned toward the screeching door, her chains clanked and jingled when she jumped from the bed to the bare stone floor. The added restraints guaranteed there would be no rebellious prisoners. The building appeared impenetrable.

In the back of her mind, she screamed for her husband *not* to try to save her. It would guarantee his death, too. If they would lock up their own privates, corporals, and sergeants, she could only imagine what they might do to a man who chose the life of an Indian over that of a White man, especially if he went as far as marrying a Crow woman.

She could only hope that Levi, Will, and Rusty Steel would walk away; seeing interference or the possibility of rescue was impossible. They might all end up swinging in the breeze by the neck if they did anything rash. She knew how Levi was and only hoped his best friend and his mentor would dissuade him from acting crazy. Dahteste felt hopeless when she looked back on their little time together, yet she wouldn't trade it for anything in the world.

Of course, she had seen the stocks in the middle of the courtyard. For now, they remained empty. She wondered if they would lock her in the pillory, too. The wooden device was erected on a metal framework and attached to a post, with holes for securing the head and hands. They used it to humiliate and hold their prisoners still for public whipping and were placed on a platform to increase visibility. They often used open punishment to deter further violations of the law or even a dose of special retribution on the way to the gallows to hang.

This little show on the newly erected scaffold provided more entertainment for the expected spectators. Dahteste had heard about hangings in White men's towns. It was a public exhibition of humiliation and death. She wondered why people liked to see each other suffer. She had no doubt she would draw a large crowd. She had heard of few women hanged, but she knew she would be an exception for her sins.

For a moment, she let regret chew at her stomach like mice. She almost wished she hadn't done what she did to the newspaperman. One side of her mind told her she had done something stupid, and the other cheered her on for more. Now, she wondered which side would win the tug-of-war: her peaceful side or the violent one.

The Crow woman believed when the time came for

her punishment, it would be in more forms than just a noose over a trapdoor. She knew what would come first. Dahteste could see the cruel hunger in the soldiers' eyes as they craned their necks to ensure the coast was clear before they closed the steel door behind them and had their way with the Indian woman.

As they tore away her clothes, she refused to scream for help or fight but lay as limp as a ragdoll. This frustrated her torturers more, so they beat her until she was unconscious. Blood pooled under her head and thighs as her breath came shallow and fast. The cruel soldiers ducked back out the way they came without being noticed.

Only the other prisoners saw what happened, but they were too afraid to talk or, in the case of the Indians, wouldn't be listened to. Wide, white eyes stared at the heap of torn buckskins and long black hair on the floor. Her breathing was only *just* visible. They had beaten her within an inch of her life. For a moment, the Indian woman stirred. Her head spun so hard she teetered as she tried to sit up, and vomit rose to her mouth. Her eyes crawled back into her head, and she fell on her face. Blood ran from her nose and mouth, forming a puddle.

The captive Indians became angrier by the minute, but after the initial shock, the soldiers looked on as if it were an everyday occurrence. Despite their incarceration, they appeared to dislike their fellow inmates as much as Lieutenant Willas. A person's skin color meant as much inside the Fort Boise stockade as outside.

The day passed, and nobody came to check on the new prisoner. Dahteste continued to lie in her own blood, unconscious. Inmates mumbled among themselves, trying not to be overheard. Snickers ripped through the soldiers as warrior braves swore under their breaths.

One Crow Indian sat quietly in the corner just out of her sight, but he could see her well enough. Wanata saw the entire thing but knew he couldn't say a word. Still, he memorized the soldiers' faces, burning them into his memory. If only he, too, weren't supposed to hang from the gallows the next day.

Maybe he could kill one guard or both before he was gunned down. That was preferable to dying as a spectacle for people who hated you. He wondered where her husband, Levi Johnson, was. If he was nearby, there was going to be trouble. Both men were to be reckoned with, especially if Rusty Steel was with him.

Wanata locked his jaw, grinding his teeth as his eyes filled with hate and violence. The other Indians locked up with him saw his gaze and moved away, giving him all the space they could in the small jail cell. He fumed silently, but it was easy to tell his mind was churning a hundred miles an hour. He knew he couldn't save either one of them, but they could go out in style, killing their enemy and the men who blemished Dahteste for life.

Murmurs rumbled through the cells all along the block. Only the white prisoners were quiet as they looked on with questioning eyes. The soldiers didn't know one Indian from another, let alone who belonged to which tribe. But among the Indians, everybody knew from which tribe a warrior came, and all of them had heard of the Crow hunter. He was the chief provider in the stronghold high in the mountains.

Wanata's eyes shifted from Shoshone, Nez Percé,

Blackfoot, and Arapaho Indians. Most of them were arrested for resisting arrest. None had dared bear arms against the army. The chiefs forbade it because they knew it would open a hornets' nest. Even though they were often enemies outside the jail, they all had one common enemy: the United States Army and the officers of Fort Boise.

The Commander

The officer frowned as he stared out the window at the gallows. It was already half-built. The commander wondered who it was for this time. He heard Lieutenant Phil Willas say an Indian had injured an essential member of the fort's community. Lately, he had his doubts about his second in command. Why hadn't he come to his superior officer with this information? He had heard about Weston and believed there was something fishy about his actions.

The missing soldiers hadn't gone unnoticed by the commander during Reveille. It appeared his first officer had put more of his men in the stockade. He suspected most of the claimed infractions were unfounded, but it was yet to be proven. During his short time as fort commander, he noted irregularities in all aspects of his first officer's life and duty. He suspected there was much more there than he had seen so far.

Maybe I should investigate this, Benson thought. *It's one thing locking up Indians, which Washington encourages, but it was an entirely different matter when US Army soldiers were imprisoned for unknown crimes. The protocol of such actions demanded the commander be informed first.*

Benson wondered if his first officer believed he was stupid because he was young. The captain thought he would let the lieutenant think whatever he wanted, at least for the time being or until he could dig deeper into a few suspicious actions he had noticed.

When he acquired all his evidence, he would drop the hammer on a man who forgot what being a soldier was. He planned to send him away just like he regularly sent his soldiers to the stockade. But he would be sent to the federal prison, Fort Leavenworth in Kansas.

Captain Robert Benson suspected Willas's behavior meant more than infractions of military laws and maybe even the Constitution, if not the Almighty. If he weren't in the Indian Territories, he would probably be considered guilty of murder. But in the wilderness, the laws were different, and judgment often fell on the shoulders of the army.

The officer knew Willas was as shifty as a politician and was always hanging around the newspaperman man, who was publicly proven to be a liar. The officer found it absurd that Fort Boise had a tabloid rag anyway. Then again, in the future, they might all be surprised because the wagon trains were proof that the civilization machine was moving west and in high gear.

Three wagon masters had sat before him bartering for supplies during the last weeks. Over a thousand White Americans and immigrants from across the globe accompanied each train of wagons across the western United States. Some came from the big cities back east and others had just gotten off ships from Europe, but none of them had the experience it took to survive in the wilderness alone.

Washington put more pressure on the army daily to address Indian affairs. It appeared they were desperate and would do anything to reach their objective, and there were no limits to their private war. They wanted all the land between the East Coast of New York and the West Coast in California and Oregon.

Their ultimate goal was the total annihilation or captivity of the Indian nations across America. This was supposed to be only known by a chosen few. Still, gossip was rampant everywhere in North America, from the hundreds of Indian tribes to the politicians in Washington, DC Of course, they expected the army to be at their every beck and call. They appointed hand-picked officers who they believed they could shape and form to fit their plans.

Captain Benson came from the best military school in the United States, West Point. He had graduated with honors only a few years prior. He had volunteered for the Indian Territories, hoping to seek adventure, but he had been stuck inside Fort Boise for months and hadn't seen anything but Lieutenant Willas's hangings and the few apparently tame Indians that frequented the compound.

He yearned for action on the frontier, but his veteran first officer insisted it was too risky for the leaders of the small garrison of soldiers to venture out into the wilderness rife with hostiles. Willas claimed that the men would be lost if something happened to their leaders and probably all perish before replacements could arrive.

Sergeant Jack Walton accompanied any patrols that

the lieutenant sent out. He was a short, middle-aged, no-nonsense man with a gut that hung over his belt. Yet he could beat any soldier in the garrison in any way they wanted to fight.

The captain recognized a competent noncommissioned officer when he saw one. He also got a glimpse of his cruel nature once when he saw anger flash in his eyes—it also spelled trouble. He was a killer, and that was what he ate, slept, and drank daily.

Captain Benson heard footsteps coming down the hall. Shadows of boot heels showed under the captain's door, and three knocks immediately followed.

"It's open!" the fort commander roared.

His aide craned his head around the door and said, "Lieutenant Willas is here to see you, sir. Can I show him in?"

"All right, I'll see him," Benson replied. He put on a friendly face and hid his revulsion. There was something dirty about his first officer, yet he couldn't quite put his finger on what it was.

Heels hammered the stone floor, and a tall, middle-aged officer entered. His coal-black handlebar mustache was twisted and waxed on the ends. He looked down on the commanding officer and smiled like he was his best friend.

"Don't get up, Captain," Willas said. "Mind if I make myself a drink?"

The captain stood and saluted without a word. He stared at his first officer, feigning boredom. The lieutenant awkwardly returned the gesture as his face turned red with sudden anger, but he bit his tongue, and the smile quickly returned. Still, Benson saw it, but he acted like he didn't. He wanted to keep Phil in the dark.

"Sit down, Willas," Captain Benson said. "So, what brings you here, Lieutenant? Is there anything happening that I should know about?"

"Of course not," Willas lied. "Just another routine day."

"Since when are hanging days routine?" Benson asked as his eyes narrowed. "Who is the condemned, and when did you plan to tell me? It's not for today, is it?" He tapped his finger on his desk, annoying his first officer even more.

Willas was having difficulty hiding his hatred for his boss. But he swallowed his pride and straightened his blue jacket, flicking off invisible lint.

"Why, I didn't know you wanted me to notify you of every Indian we have to hang for being an enemy combatant." The first officer smiled, but it didn't reach his eyes. "Our stockade is full of the usual—Shoshone, Bannock, and Nez Percé. Oh, and the Crow woman I plan to hang tomorrow."

"You're planning to hang a *woman* without telling your superior officer?" Benson barked. "How dare you, Lieutenant!"

Willas started to jump from his chair angrily, but the look in the captain's eyes changed his mind. He quickly sat back down, took a deep breath, and slowly blew it out, attempting to calm down.

"Why, I was planning to tell you right now, sir." He said "sir" almost sarcastically.

"Well, I'm all ears. You have my undivided attention, Willas. You might as well tell me why you have a half dozen of my soldiers in the brig, too. Later today, you can give me your full report on paper, but for now, give me the principal details."

"The soldiers got caught stealing whiskey from the company stocks," Willas said. "I gave each of them ninety days."

"So, we have six men out of action because they got drunk on the cook's whiskey?" the captain asked. "Take them out of jail immediately and give them ten lashes on the stockade where everybody can see. That's a harsh enough punishment, and they will recover quicker than ninety days in jail. Putting our men in prison costs the government money for room and board, not to mention the loss of labor."

The first officer was fuming by now and stood abruptly and saluted, turning to go.

"Sit down, Willas!" Benson roared. He stood six feet tall, an inch taller than the officer, and the young man was still fibered with muscle, unlike the lazy lieutenant. "You'll go when I dismiss you, mister. Do you understand? I have the feeling that you have gone astray, sir. And what about this Indian woman you plan to execute? What did she do, and why haven't I heard about it before now?"

"She tried to kill one of the most important members of our community," Willas spat, now unable to restrain himself. "The owner of the *Les Boise* newspaper, Perry Weston. He's a fine man, and I can vouch for him myself."

"Do you consider that liar one of the peers of our community and your close friend?" Benson asked, raising an eyebrow. "I heard about the falsehoods he published in his tabloid about the gold strike in the Rocky Mountains."

"Nobody proved there wasn't gold in the mountains," Willas retorted.

"Nobody proved there was either, did they?" Benson asked. "Nobody found those gold nuggets he said you could pick up off the ground. That's about as big a lie as I've ever heard. You know it was nothing but a bag of untruths to make his newspaper famous and bring more settlers to the area so he could make up more lies and try to manipulate and deceive the people. What did the Indian woman do to Mr. Weston that was so bad? I've seen him walking the streets like he was king. Why is he so important here in Boise? Come on, speak up. I haven't got all day."

Perry Weston

Lieutenant Willas sat in a plush chair before the newspaperman's large walnut desk. The furniture was ordered specially from the East Coast. A grandfather clock stood in the corner. It struck the hour and chimed seven times. The officer twirled the tip of his waxed mustache.

Perry had high ambitions and expectations for the future in the West. He dreamed of one day having the most-read newspaper in the vast areas known as the Indian Plains and the Rocky Mountains.

The sun's rays spilled through the window onto the floor, leaving squares of white light. The open crack ruffled the curtains, allowing fresh air into the stuffy room. The journalist's face twisted into a permanent snarl. Ever since the Indian woman removed his manhood, he had a high, squeaky voice. The army officer had to bite his tongue and try not to make a snide comment or laugh. Perry sounded like a falsetto.

Before the incident, Weston had always bragged about his sexual exploits. He saw himself as a lady's man, despite the fact only prostitutes tolerated him, and that was only because of his money. They made him pay dearly for his twisted desires. But all that was in the past, and the only craving remaining was revenge.

Perry no longer frequented the soiled doves in the town saloon or the starving Indian women waiting outside of the fort, ready to exchange food for pleasure. As Weston came from a wealthy family, he had money to do with what he pleased and felt privileged, above all those in and around Fort Boise, especially in such a primitive place as the American wilderness. He thought he had no equals.

"Has the captain asked about the gallows yet?" Perry asked, angry. "Why don't you convince him to go out and chase Indians? Maybe he'll get killed, and you'll become the fort commander. I doubt Benson would last two or three patrols before an Indian had his scalp. Maybe you should send him out without Sergeant Walton. Jack is ornery enough to bring him back alive, even if he got shot with a few arrows. We need someone less competent. How about your corporal? You know, the one that works in the stockade, I think they call him Dickie. Let the captain have his wish—all these frontier commanders who volunteer dream of power and fame. I doubt your new boss is any different. We could let his ignorance kill him, and nobody would ever know."

"I've stopped my boss from venturing out where it's dangerous until now," Willas replied as he carefully eyed the scribbler. "If he goes out, I might be expected to follow, which is not on my list of desires for the future." He stifled a snicker. "I have no intention of mingling with Indians anywhere other than where I'm in command. The captain can continue to think he's the one running the fort. He has no idea what's going on. How dare Washington send me an officer so young. I can't take orders from a man with no experience and half my age."

"They should have never passed you over after the last commander committed suicide," Perry said. "At least this one chose to come here, unlike the others who were sent here as punishment for some dark, unmentioned deed. The fools in Washington don't know what's happening west of Indiana. All they know is what we tell them."

The lieutenant smiled and nodded. He was careful what he said to the journalist. Perry had a nasty habit of destroying those he didn't like or who offended him, just like he planned to do with the Crow woman. Willas didn't care what happened to the Indian, but he was aware she was married to a White man. So, he couldn't discount his future involvement. Especially as this Easterner lived in the mountains and supposedly with wild Indians.

He wasn't sure who her spouse was, but apparently, everybody had heard of his friend, the famed frontiersman Rusty Steel. They said he could be a dangerous man when crossed. Then again, he wouldn't bother an army officer. If there was trouble, which he doubted, the woman's husband would go directly for the scribbler, which would be what he deserved. Plus, the first officer represented the United States Army, and nobody dared defy the government—especially a few ignorant mountain men.

"Here's what I promised you for the favor," Perry said as he pushed a yellow envelope across his desk, keeping his hand on it. "You know, the mess with the

Indian woman. Let's keep this as quiet as possible, but I still want a front-row seat at the hanging." After locking eyes with Willas, he sat back and removed his hand.

The Army officer opened the flap, fanned dollar bills, and nodded. He reminded himself to count the bribe later. It would be an insult to do so in front of the journalist, but he didn't trust him with a dime, much less than with a hundred dollars. Months before, he had made a mental note to make sure Weston didn't cheat him again. The newspaperman had a habit of short-changing his agreements.

Weston never stole so much that it deserved a reprimand, but enough to see he was beyond frugal and had to fiddle every transaction. But with his little but influential newspaper behind him, nobody dared complain, although the lieutenant was sure he would go too far one day and maybe even find himself swinging in the breeze at the end of a noose. The thought made the officer smile, but it was fine—he didn't have to hide it. The scribbler assumed he was grinning because of the money.

"Thank you very much," Willas said. "I needed some extra cash. Now, if you don't mind, if you don't have any more business, I'll be on my way, sir."

"Hold on just a minute, Lieutenant," Perry Weston said. "You still haven't answered my first question." He drummed his fingers on his desk impatiently and raised his eyebrow.

"And what was that?" Willas asked, playing ignorant. "I'm afraid I don't remember."

Perry gave him a snide look, saying he didn't believe him for a minute. "You know, has the captain asked about the new gallows? I know you talk to him daily, so don't pussyfoot around." His frown deepened.

"I mentioned it to him in passing," Willas said like he was bored with the issue. "You know he doesn't put up a fuss if we hang Indians when Sergeant Walton catches them after they've engaged violently. I must admit, the boss was a little upset that the condemned is a woman. But I told him she attacked and permanently damaged a role model citizen and a man of many peers."

Perry smiled; he liked nothing more than being complimented, but still, he was wary of the lieutenant. A higher bidder could do the same if he could bribe him. He knew the relationship they had wasn't about friendship; it was about money. And for now, Perry Weston had plenty, and Phil Willas wanted every penny he could graft.

The journalist didn't know it, but Willas wasn't the only hungry wolf. More creatures of prey waited at his door as they watched him carefully. When he printed the sensational lie about the gold strike, he made many enemies, but most feared he might invent a lie about them, publish it, and ruin their lives. More than one man would like to see Perry's demise—maybe even the first officer.

Weston scratched a match across the bottom of expensive soles, sparking it to life. The room smelled of sulfur mixed with kerosene as he fed the flame to the lantern on his desk. Light spilled from the window onto the ground outside in yellow squares. He opened the newspaper. It had come in the last cargo shipment. It was the *New York Sun* Sunday special and was only a month old. Perry licked his finger as he turned the page.

He raised his eyebrows and saw that there it was. His article made it to the second page. Next time, he was determined to write a story worthy of a first-page publication in one of the best newspapers in America. Despite the clamor claiming his gold strike was a lie, the story continued to gain steam. Soon, it would work its way into the headlines nationwide. Then people would come in hordes, governments would be established, and he would use his newspaper to manipulate them all.

Willas made his way down the walled street toward the double gates. At night, they were closed, and only a tiny timber door was open at the bottom. From the fort's safety, he saw dozens of campfires; beyond that, a watchman walked by with a lantern, calling the hour softly for the other soldiers.

The varnished doors along the courtyard wall were set so close they might have been closets. There was limited space in the fort, and everybody did their best with what they had. At the top of the towers, the forms of the guards looked like they were excavated from the bog. The occasional glint of metal flashed off a torch's flame.

Phil Willas looked down the square to the other end, where it was dark. The courtyard was nearly empty. His garrison of soldiers would be finishing their last meal of the day. The few horses present shied and sidestepped. There was something in the air that told him trouble was coming. Maybe not for him, but the business with the Indian woman had paranoia whispering in his ear. He brushed it off, recognizing it for what it was—fear.

A few miles to the south, lightning flashed soundlessly as the wind moaned, pushing the storm away. Willows swayed on the river's edge as water rippled across the surface. Bullfrogs croaked their nightly choir as owls left their nests for their nocturnal hunt. As the sun fell off the end of the world, darkness crept across the land like a black curtain. Moments later, a pumpkin moon reflected off the river's surface, casting the fort in a yellow glow.

The lieutenant rubbed his red-rimmed eyes with the heels of his hands and then tried to penetrate the arriving darkness outside. He squinted his eyes, but to no effect.

"Give me that lantern, Private," the first officer growled. The soldier passed it to him without a word.

"Stand at attention when I address you!" Willas spat, his voice full of superiority.

Standing ramrod straight, the soldier snapped a salute and said, "My apologies, sir. It won't happen again."

As soon as Willas stepped into the night, fear began to creep into his pores, under his skin, and filled his soul with dread. He had made the plan weeks ago but had not yet sealed the deal with the would-be perpetrators.

Initially, he planned to use local Indians to execute the murder. Then he heard about a renegade, half White and half Comanche. This Indian seemed to be precisely what he needed from what he was told.

It was the only way to kill the captain and have no repercussions. He held out the lamp before him. The yellow circle followed as he walked. The directions to where they were to meet arrived that morning in the form of an Indian woman begging on in the plaza.

She instantly knew who he was. As he recklessly stumbled through the night, Willas saw an isolated teepee in the distance. The buffalo hide tent glowed like a lamp. A dark figure moved inside.

A dried cowhide hung for a door. The teepee was dark, and images without definition wavered. The small dwelling smelled of wood smoke and human sweat. The infamous Indian swept a clawed hand through his hair as he watched the officer in his fancy uniform. He ducked into the ratty tent. The confines smelled rank, and the man was bathless. Black ropy braids of hair hung to his chest beside a braided beard.

Flakes of dried mud fell from the lieutenant's shiny black boots. The inside of the tent was dark and smelled of earth. Orange coals from a small fire reflected in the Indian's eyes and provided just enough light to see as he watched the White man over the dying flames.

Of course, Willas didn't dare share his secret with Perry Weston. Then, the newspaperman would have too much leverage. He would be an accomplice too dangerous to tell. Although the officer did feel it was a sad loss of opportunity to make serious money, he could never trust anyone with the secret. He would take it to the grave. At least he would if everything worked out.

To kill the Fort Boise commander was no small feat. There would be repercussions, but if they pointed toward the hostile Indians, he couldn't care less. Even that would be a win for the first lieutenant. More soldiers would be sent to the string of frontier forts to reinforce the line. More troops would mean more power for Willas and added power would mean more bribes and money.

With the arrival of new troops, they would run thin of officers, and he believed his time would come. Once he was commander of Fort Boise, nobody would make him leave. Then, he would control everything.

The Indian leaned forward, showing his colorfully painted face. Willis wondered why all the getup. Indians' vanity never ceased to amaze him. They never seemed to pass up an opportunity to show off and paint themselves up.

"Sit," the gruff voice said. He pointed to a spot before him across from the fire.

The lieutenant left the lamp beside the teepee flap. When he sat, only the flames separated them. He locked eyes with the infamous renegade and instantly felt the danger ooze from the pores of the man's skin. Willas suddenly wondered if he had gotten himself into something he shouldn't have.

"I'm Lieutenant Willas," he said, proffering his hand, not as sure of himself as before. The Indian ignored the gesture. The first officer had to break off eye contact; the Indian's stare made him too nervous. "And you are...you know, the man I was meant to see?"

"They call me Wood Duck," the aging Indian whispered as if he said it too loud, something terrible would happen.

"Excellent, Mr. Duck." Willas grinned, feeling relieved. This man didn't seem to be as frightening as he was told. "Here's your money as we agreed."

"Leave it on the ground," Wood Duck whispered even lighter, making Willas lean in close. The old Indian knew he could kill him any time he wanted.

The renegade outlaw leaned close and inhaled lungfuls of air. It was as if he were a wild animal and was memorizing the smell for a future hunt.

"You're sure you know who to...shoot?" Willas said.

"I know all I need to know," Wood Duck replied curtly. "Go, before I decide to kill *you*."

Willas ran through the teepee flap like a bullet out of a pistol, racing for the fort. His arms pumped like steam engine pistons as his boots hammered the ground. He didn't dare look back nor slow down until he arrived at the guarded gates. He gulped air as his head spun. Now, he wondered exactly who he hired to kill his boss and whether Wood Duck might come back and kill him, too.

The Saloon

When Lieutenant Willas walked into the saloon, most of the patrons went quiet, and all the mountain men craned their heads to see who it was. Frowns and angry eyes filled the mountain men's table, but the rest of the room went on like nothing happened. His wasn't a strange face—everybody knew who he was. Rusty's dog opened one eye and sniffed the air, and hackles rose on his back. The old mountain man patted his head.

Levi went to jump to his feet, but Rusty grabbed his arm and shot him a dirty look. Levi tried to jerk it away, but his mentor dug his claws into his arm.

"Don't start nothin' that we can't finish, Beaver," Rusty whispered. "He's got a bunch of soldiers behind 'im just down the street. This ain't over yet, though. We've still got all night and tomorrow mornin'. A lot can happen from now to then."

"I wonder how Captain Forrester and Marshal Walker are gettin' along," Virgil whispered. "Maybe it's just as well the lieutenant is here and not in the barracks. Should we try to keep 'im here? This all seems mighty risky for the captain, but we've gotta do whatever it takes to save Dahteste. We've gotta step up."

"Even if she did cut that fool's gonads off"—Angus grinned—"she's got spunk, I'll say that much for 'er. Mind you, she must have the worst timing of anyone I've ever met."

Smoke hovered a foot from the ceiling as men played poker for whatever they possessed. Guns, gold nuggets, and paper bills filled the kitty. Gold watches and silver spurs lay on the pile. Expressionless faces looked at their cards, never giving their opponents a hint of what's in their hands—winner takes all, and losers walk away with nothing. Patchouli oil floated on puffs of air, mixing with the smell of freshly perked coffee. Behind the pleasant aromas lingered the scent of sweaty men.

Spittoons littered the floor as lamp light reflected off the polished brass. A cracked mirror ran twenty feet down the back of the simple timber bar, reflecting all types of hats. Bottles of labeled whiskey and brandy stood beside corked jugs of corn liquor. The only army man in the cantina stood at the bar and seemed oblivious to those surrounding him. He acted as though he were alone. An old man swept the clay floor in the back of the saloon with a straw broom.

Virgil winked at Rusty as he stood, shuffled to the bar, and asked, "How about another bottle of whiskey, pilgrim? I'm afraid we're fresh out." He initially ignored the soldier.

The first lieutenant eyed Virgil with suspicion. "What's a Black man doing on the frontier and Indian Territories, especially in my fort?"

Virgil smiled as mischief danced in his eyes. "The

same thing those other mountain men are doin', Officer. We're trappers, and we live with the Indians. And here I thought this fort belonged to the United States, not a lieutenant."

"What do you mean, you live with the Indians?" Willas asked, surprised. "I didn't know White men lived with the local tribes. Of course, the fort belongs to the United States. Are you trying to get smart with me, boy?"

"A simple man like me ain't gonna get smart with an intelligent man like you. No, sir, I ain't. But that goes to show you how much you don't know about your environment." Virgil grinned wider. "Half of the fellas at my table have lived with Flathead or Crow Indians at one time or another. They even speak the language. That's what's called knowing your surroundings. Why, the older fella can track a fly across a herd of cattle, and the big fella can wrestle them down."

Virgil doled coins onto the bar. The barman filled a dented cup. Lovejoy took the whiskey, drained it, and set the cup down again, raising his eyebrows. Large tallow candles provided light in the back. Yellow circles flickered on the poker tables. Johnson counted the remaining coins. There was a tense silence at the bar. The mountain men looked like mud effigies.

Lieutenant Willas acted like he didn't know who the frontiersmen were, but one of his soldiers had already pointed them out.

I wonder which one's the squaw's husband, Willas thought. He tried to eye the men without them noticing, but they caught him every time.

Rusty shook his rueful head and sipped his drink

and murmured as he stood on the other side of the lieutenant.

"And what are you here for, mister?" Willas asked, looking down his nose at the aging mountain man.

"I'm here for a good time," Rusty replied, "but not a long time. Now, I reckon I don't know."

"We've still gotta sell our beaver pelts and buffalo hides," Virgil added. "This here is the head of our clan."

"And you're in the clan with the White people?" the officer asked, surprised.

"In the wilderness, there's no color," Rusty added, "not when it comes to my friends. Just stupid and smart, and if ya ain't the clever one, you're probably dead or soon to be."

Levi balled his massive fist and lambasted the table a dozen times, matching the timing with the thunderclap outside as the wind set their teeth gnashing. Everybody turned and looked at the giant man's face and then to the window as the lightning lit up the courtyard as though it were daylight.

Now I know who the squaw's husband is, Willas thought.

Levi's eyes lay dark and tunneled in a haunted face as he stared through the army officer. His face clouded as his blood began to boil and sweat beaded on his forehead. His mentor could see what was coming—Rusty thrust his chin, clucking with his tongue. He shooed Levi away with the backs of his hands.

"Let's go outside and have a breath of fresh air, Beaver," Rusty said. "Mind me now, or you'll be sorry, mark my words."

Rusty pushed his student through the bat-wing doors. They swooshed as the men stepped onto the porch. Soldiers sat and drank at the corner tables and looked at the frontiersmen suspiciously.

"We're outnumbered here, and if we make a mistake now, you're never gonna see your wife again," Rusty whispered. "Keep your head and don't ruin the only chance you've got of getting Dahteste out of jail. You've gotta trust Will. For now, it's the only option we've got. Curb your temper, Levi. If you kill that man, it won't do any of us any good, including your wife. As it is, we have a chance, even if it is small. We've gotten out of tighter spots than this. Whatcha say, pard?"

Levi's mentor could see him struggle with his demons. The detention of his Crow wife was tearing him apart. Johnson blamed himself for allowing her to come to Fort Boise in the first place, knowing it could be risky. But, at the time, he was the only one who knew, and for some reason, he didn't think it would be such a big thing, and they would easily go unperceived. In the end, he was wrong.

"Are you ready to go back in there and let us have dinner without tryin' to kill somebody?" Rusty asked, frowning, but it didn't reach his eyes. They were full of concern. "We've gotta wait until Will and Joseph come back anyway. Virgil thinks it'll be better if we keep the lieutenant busy, and I agree. Come on, let's get somethin' to eat. Remember you're still on the mend and need to regain a little more weight."

Levi pursed his mouth and shrugged his broad shoulders. "All right, boss. I'll mind my manners, but if I find out that soldier has anything to do with locking Dahteste up besides doing his duty, he's mine."

"Go on along now and order two of whatever you

want," Rusty said. "I'm gonna snoop around this soldier to see if he don't give somethin' away in passing."

Virgil stared into his whiskey as he swirled the golden liquid before he tossed back yet another glass. He still stood at the bar beside the officer.

"Are you trying to get drunk, mister?" the lieutenant asked. "If you get disorderly in my fort, you'll wish you'd never come."

"There ya go again." Virgil chuckled. "Do you own any other properties in the area? The Indians around here say no man owns the land. Their wise men believe it is the land that owns the people."

"That's a foolish thought," Willas said. "Why are you so well-spoken, you know, for a Black man?"

"My old owner allowed me to attend a sort of school," Virgil remembered. "He said a man lost too much in life unless he could read. Well, I've been reading my way across the West ever since. He was kind enough to free me while I still had some prime years to enjoy. But just in case some folks didn't believe my story and wanted to string me up, I headed for the frontiers."

"I must admit I haven't seen many coloreds so far," Willas said. "Most people here in the fort can hardly afford to buy a horse, let alone a slave."

The way he said it told the whole story to Virgil Lovejoy. He had been around slave owners to know he was standing beside one right then. Maybe they were back East with his family, but he instantly knew which side of the fence he was on.

While Virgil kept the lieutenant busy, Rusty spied a Crow Indian standing in the shadows beside the door.

"Don't mind me, boys," Rusty said. "I'm just gonna pop outside and take a leak." He pushed his way out the door again, but this time, he turned left and stepped off the porch and into the shadows of two buildings.

"Sho'daache Kahee," the Crow hunter said. "I have news from my people."

Rusty grabbed his arm and dragged him deeper into the gloom. "Talk to me in Crow so these fools don't understand."

"Our camp spies saw the lieutenant meet privately with a warrior you know," the Indian said. "Somebody spotted Wood Duck a few hours ago, and the gossip said he would meet with an army officer. They plan to kill the White chief."

"Wood Duck," Rusty repeated the words in hardly a whisper. "I knew he didn't drown like everybody wanted to believe. Until we have his head in our hands, we know he's still alive. Run off now before those soldiers see us together. It might go hard on ya bein' seen with the likes of me."

Crow Spies

When the large Indian presented himself to the stockade guard, he acted humble and didn't make eye contact. He claimed to have a brother locked up and wanted to say goodbye. The guard, one of the men who raped and beat Dahteste, was usually ornery and treated Indians like sub-human beings. But there was something he felt that was more dangerous about this Indian that made him uncomfortable, so he ushered him to the cell for fear of denying him his wish.

The guard knew he didn't want to anger this Indian for some reason. The sheer size of the man made him nervous. He couldn't imagine what he was capable of if crossed.

"Stand aside, you bunch of heathens," Dickie Bennet growled. He pulled his flintlock pistol and drew back the hammer. "Any of y'all get out of line, you'll be gut shot before you can make it out the door." He turned to the frightening Indian. "Do you see your kin?"

Tatanka nodded, and they ushered him inside. The

heavy barred door closed behind him with a bang, and the lock clunked like an ancient clock.

"Give me a shout when you're done." Dickie laughed, feeling braver with the steel bars between the Crow and him. Still, he felt there was something unusual about the Indian—as though there was some strange danger just under the surface, and he was afraid to wake it up.

What would one little visit matter anyway, as long as the boss don't know? Bennet thought.

His inherent fear of Indians was something that Dickie had been able to hide so far. He volunteered to do guard duty for fear of striking out with a patrol into the wilderness. He wasn't even an out-of-doors type of man. He preferred to sleep on mattresses in the bunkhouse rather rough on the ground, not to mention the danger that lay just outside of Fort Boise.

Of course, he wasn't afraid of the Indian woman, and they gave her a what-for that she would never forget. Some of the braves, especially ones like this big fellow, gave him pause, but he figured if they let them in the gate, he wouldn't be too dangerous even though he appeared as though he was.

Bennet's metal-plated boot heels shot sparks each time he dragged his feet. He liked the noise it made on the stone floor. Dickie resumed his position on the chair by the stockade's entrance, uncocking his gun and stuffing it into his belt. Leaning back, he pushed his hat down over his eyes and dozed in the shade of the brim.

Of eight Indians, plus the visitor, only two huddled together, and the rest respectfully waited in the other corner, almost timid. They all knew who the visitor was. He came from Crow Chief Hachta's stronghold. They tried to act like they weren't eavesdropping, but each one was straining their ears to catch a word or two.

"I don't know if I can break you out," Tatanka whispered. "When I heard, I had to come and see if it was possible. Now that I'm here, I don't see how. Do you have any ideas?"

"I thought you were coming for Dahteste," Wanata replied. "The guard said they were going to hang me at first, but now the fort's chief seems to have changed his mind, and they're only going to give me twenty lashes with a whip. They want to hang me on the wooden post in the courtyard to shame me while they cut my back to pieces. But I can survive that and ten lashes more if I must." The Crow hunter jutted out his chin in defiance.

"Wait a moment," Tatanka said, blinking, puzzled. "What did you say about Dahteste?"

Wanata craned his head toward the apparently empty cell across the hall. Tatanka's eyes followed his friend's. At first, he didn't see her, but as he looked harder, he saw a woman curled up like a snail. Her face was so bruised and swollen he barely recognized her. One eye was swollen shut, and her clothing was torn to shreds. Dark bruises covered her petite body, and blood matted her hair.

Tatanka's face suddenly changed into a mask, and his eyes seemed to stare right through the stockade wall and on for a thousand yards. The only sign of reaction was small downward curls at the edges of his lips.

"Does Levi Johnson and Rusty Steel know about this atrocity?" Tatanka asked. "Hachta knows nothing of this back in the stronghold on the mountain."

"What brought you here, brother?" Wanata asked. "I didn't hear you were coming to the edge of civilization."

"The Rendezvous got abandoned, and nobody attended. I have been going to the trappers' meet for fifteen years, and this was the first season I've seen the Canadian fur companies miss. I wonder what happened. This is the closest trading post, so I came here to buy coffee, black powder, and medicine for the tribe. Then, when I arrived, I heard from Indians outside the fort that you were inside. Why did the bluecoats arrest you?

"When they spoke to me, I didn't understand them, so I walked away," Wanata said. "If they don't know how to speak to me in Crow, they should not expect me to listen to some language I can't understand. The White bluecoats must have found it offensive when I turned my back on them, but I had nothing more to say. In the end, they claimed they arrested me for resisting arrest. Does that make any sense?

"I heard Rusty and Levi were there when a dozen soldiers took her," Wanata said. "I didn't get to speak with Dahteste. She was only here for a short time before they raped her and beat her and left her unconscious. She appeared near death but now seems to be breathing better, but it is still touch and go."

"I better find Rusty Steel," Tatanka whispered. "He will know what to do. I don't know how things work in the White man's world, but Chief Hachta will want us to stop their plans. They won't keep a Crow warrior in jail."

"They canceled the Rendezvous because the men back East in the big cities and across the great water stopped wearing beaver hats," Wanata said. "It is amazing how such a small change can have so much effect on so many lives. I wonder what they will wear if they don't wear a hat? I came here because I had nowhere to sell my furs, either. Now they have stolen them, and I have nothing. Luckily, I have my life and will still be here tomorrow."

"Is that all?" Tatanka asked.

"She is supposed to hang tomorrow," Wanata said, indicating Dahteste. "They already built the gallows."

"Guard, me ready!" Tatanka barked in broken English. "Time I go." He looked back at his old friend and said in Crow, "I will be waiting for you nearby. I camp far away from the fort. There are too many prying eyes."

Dickie reluctantly pushed back his hat and stood as he looped the keyring around his finger, making the metal jingle. He flicked them into his palm. His eyes ran across the Indians in cell number three.

He gave them the scariest look he could muster, but it didn't appear to frighten anyone. He wondered if they were angry because he and Ned Nebraska raped the young girl. Maybe they should have done it in private.

"Stand back, all of ya!" He pulled his gun again and waved it around recklessly, but this time, it wasn't cocked. He didn't appear to feel so threatened, nor did the Indians seem scared.

Tatanka stepped out as soon as the squeaky door opened. He nodded to the guard, and they locked eyes for the briefest of moments. A tremble ran through Dickie's body, and the hair on the back of his neck stood on end. Metal scraped the stone floor behind the war chief with every step Bennet took. The warrior took a mental note to cut off his feet before he killed him.

The Indian vanished, mixing in with the hundred

people or so milling around the square, including soldiers on guard at the turrets.

He ducked into the first shadows so he could watch the fort's movements and peoples' habits without being spied on. He settled down for the wait. Tatanka knew if he stayed in one place long enough, he was bound to see Rusty Steel and Levi Johnson.

Horses trotted from one end of the large courtyard to the other. Kids used sticks to roll tin wheels across the flat ground as they churned up small clouds of dust. The mid-summer sun continued to bleach the land before it, making long shadows as the orange disk neared the horizon.

Tomorrow would be another day, and then at noon, the hanging would come. Tatanka had nowhere else to go, so he sat there all night. He dozed against the towering wall with one eye open.

Captain Benson

Will rummaged through his saddlebags and pulled out a leather wrap. Inside were his treasures from his time as an officer in the United States Army. He picked up his graduation certificate and read *West Point* as he ran his fingers over the letters. He slipped the document into his buckskin shirt and one-handedly strapped on the wide belt holding his saber. The ex-captain's black boots were highly polished. The yellow stripe on his army-issue pants stood out against a blue background.

The mountain men made their camp upriver at the edge of the fort. Dozens of wickiups and teepees dotted the ground around the walls. Angus went through the supplies to see what they needed from the trading post. Until they sold the furs, he didn't want to spend any more money on expensive restaurants. None of them liked living cooped up like in a henhouse. They preferred the out of doors and sleeping under the stars.

The west flashed pale streaks of light, changing shades near the earth. A deeper run of red the color of blood seeped up from the ground as the sun fell off the end of the world. A vicious snarl of flies made the horses sidestep and truculent. Ripples of the Snake River flowed on the water's edge—tinged silver by a moon shimmering low on the horizon.

The hobbled horses pulled at grass and slid their jaws beside the mountain men's camp; they blew and nickered. Somewhere in the coming darkness, coyotes sang. They went silent when wolves answered.

It certainly seemed like another lifetime, but it wasn't ancient history. Will was sure there were plenty of military people who would still remember who he was and what happened to the patrol from Kansas. He wondered what kind of captain he could expect way out on the wilderness frontiers.

He wondered if they wasted many valuable officers in such faraway places. He had heard the frontier forts were where they sent wayward soldiers for punishment. What was worse than to be deprived of all your civilized worldly goods and be dropped into the middle of the wilderness? They forced them to live in a place with no more than the slightest signs of civilization—a place most officers would despise.

The bartender said the last captain killed himself after being banished from his detachment back east. He knew the new commander was young, but that was as much as he wished to share. The whole town waited to see how the new military leader panned out. Many had expected Lieutenant Willas to take charge, but Washington had other plans. Maybe the resonance of his betrayals had reached the bosses back East.

Levi and Will walked through the small Indian campsites that dotted outside the fort. Most of them were there for their safety from attacks from other tribes. Others were there to spy for their chiefs. Some stayed near the gates, like widows with small children looking for a handout from the soldiers.

They walked around the circled wagons. When they found an opening, they crossed toward the other side. Music from a fiddle and washboard joined in when a woman began singing. Soon, a group of people were clapping as they sang along. These were the people who wanted to populate Oregon City and farther north to new frontiers. This was the third wagon train to take the Oregon Trail, and seeing it up close made the marshal's blood pump through his veins like a train.

"I told ya it was a good idea," Joseph said as he looked around. His eyes sparked with excitement. "I just wasn't quick enough. Hadn't I run off with you boys to the mountains, we could have been first."

As they walked through the fort's gates, the smell of charcoal filled the air. Indian men sat against the tall walls as White children played in the dust at dusk. The West Point cadet's empty sleeve fluttered in the breeze. They carried no pistols because they hoped to meet with the current captain. Any sign of aggression could stop their intent by the posted guards. They had to present themselves as friendly visitors. For all pretenses, they were there for no more than a neighborly visit.

A short walk across the plaza brought them to the barracks. Boot heels hammered the packed earth until they came to a stop at the entrance. Two guards stared at the approaching men with boredom. Neither one had chosen to come to the Indian Frontiers, and all they wanted to do was go home.

A squat sergeant with a bald head pushed his way to the entrance and asked, "Can I help you gentlemen with something?" He sounded friendly but hard; angry eyes betrayed him.

Sergeant Walton raised an eyebrow in question. He noticed the buckskin-clad blond's empty sleeve and an officer's saber against military-issue britches and black boots. His face went from angry to puzzled. He didn't know how to treat the man before him. Was he an officer like his weapon and dress insinuated, or was he a thief or maybe even a murderer come to take the captain's life?

"I'm United States Army Captain Will Forrester out of Fort Scott, Kansas," Will stated, "and I would like to see the fort commander, please."

"And may I ask what this is all about?" Walton asked, still suspicious.

"No, you may not," Captain Forrester replied curtly. "If you tell the captain who I am, it should suffice. If not, bring him to the door."

"But, you're armed," Sergeant Walton said. "Your weapon must stay here...sir." Jack felt like he was in uncharted waters but was still suspicious. A lot of the people in the wilderness claimed to be something or somebody they weren't, and he didn't plan to lose another boss.

"You want my saber? I am afraid *that* I cannot allow. As you can see, we didn't bring our pistols to a peaceful meeting. Do you need anything else, mister? If I remember right, a captain ranks higher than a sergeant. Am I right or wrong?"

"I'll be right back." Sergeant Walton saluted the long-haired officer, mumbling and shaking his head, retreating into the building. He wondered how the captain had lost his arm.

Marshal Walker sat on the bench under the window and said, "Take a load off, Will. If I know officers, they'll make us wait. Especially if we ain't Army."

"But that's probably part of the problem," Will replied. "I suppose I still am in the army, and the government may want me. Only a couple of years or so have passed since my scientific expedition was wiped off the face of the earth by the Comanche. I even lost a famous geologist. The government sent me to find new locations for military forts across the uncharted frontier to protect the soon-to-arrive settlers. I'm afraid I didn't get far enough to see uncharted land."

Much sooner than expected, they heard boots storm the hallway inside. For a moment, Joseph and Will wondered if leaving their weapons behind was a mistake.

The sergeant's belly arrived first. After that came the officer's orderly and, finally, a man in a starched white shirt and leather suspenders—he was slipping them over his shoulders. He smiled so wide Will could see his tonsils.

"William!" Captain Benson said, obviously happy. "What a pleasant surprise. You *do* remember me, don't you? Bob Benson, I was in your class at West Point."

"Of course, I remember you, Bob." Will tried to hide his sigh of relief. "How did you get posted way out here? This is my friend Marshal Joseph Walker from Kansas. I thought they sent officers here for punishment. If I remember correctly, you were near the top of our class."

"Let these gentlemen by, Sergeant. They are my guests. Bring them to my room, Orderly. See that we have glasses and brandy." Bob turned his head and asked, "Are you hungry, Will? Anything you want, ask for it. If I remember right, you were at the top of the class, too, but higher than me."

The sergeant led them to the captain's quarters and stood beside the door, gesturing with his hand to enter. "Please be seated, Captain Forrester." Walton saluted, then said to Joseph, "Marshal, sir." He curtly made an about-face and returned to his quarters after sending both guards to return to their posts.

Captain Forrester sat and leaned back and folded his one arm across his lap. Marshal Walker leaned forward with his hands on his knees like he was ready to spring. Benson sat and smiled, apparently happy.

"Finally, I have someone to talk to," Bob said. "I thought you were dead for the longest time, then we heard you survived the Comanche attack. Some even said you were adopted by the Indians. I can hardly imagine Will Forrester sleeping in a teepee."

Marshal Walker politely stifled a snicker with his fist and said, "I reckon what you heard wasn't too far from the truth, was it, Captain? The fellas he lives with are as wild as any Indians I've ever met."

"I've been going crazy with boredom here, and you walk right in from the wilderness and save my sanity." Benson grinned. "Tell me all about your adventures. It's good to see you, Captain."

"You've got no idea how happy I am to find you here, Bob," Will said. "You are just the man I need right now."

Benson said. "Here, let me pour us a drink." He held up the crystal and said, "To West Point."

Half-filled glasses appeared as if by magic. They rattled a toast, and Will sipped the high-quality brandy, but the marshal tossed it back in one gulp.

"What are you doing here, Will?" Bob asked. "Why

didn't you come back to Fort Smith? I was there a few months ago before I got my final posting here in Fort Boise. They said nobody had seen you for years. This is about as far into Indian territory we have a defense built."

"After losing so many men, I figured I'd be court-martialed as soon as I returned," Will replied. "I'd had enough failures for one year. I partnered up with Levi Johnson, who is my business partner and friend. Have you ever heard of him?"

"I haven't been around for long enough to know much of anybody," Benson replied. "My first officer keeps telling me the brass doesn't go out on patrols, so I've been cooped up here for weeks on end. He seems to keep most of his information to himself. Especially about who he hangs or not. I'm not quite sure whose side he's on these days. As far as you being in trouble back East, I doubt they even remember. So much has happened since you left. Washington has fallen into chaos over Indian affairs. I know for a fact your old friends don't think less of you. We've heard gossip about your heroics. I doubt you lost that arm in a romance with a lady."

"I appreciate the candor, Bob," Will said, ignoring the comment on his missing arm as usual. He acted like he didn't notice the loss and got on with life, living with what he had and ignoring what he didn't. "I came here for a reason. I had no idea who the fort commander was. I've already met your first officer, and I wasn't impressed. He seemed to me like one of those upcoming officers with an agenda."

"I can't disagree with you there," Bob replied. "I'm afraid I didn't trust my first officer the moment we met. I had a little spat with him a couple of hours ago."

"That must have been right before he entered the saloon and met Rusty and Virgil," Marshal Walker said. "He seemed to be preoccupied with something. He kept saying that this was his fort—something I've never heard a lieutenant claim before."

"His fort, ah-ha," Bob replied. "I trust this man less every day."

"What was your earlier meeting about with Lieutenant Willas, if you don't mind my asking?" Will said.

"Why, I suppose it won't be an offense if I tell a fellow officer," Bob said, then he turned to Joseph and frowned. "This will be strictly off the record. Do you understand, Marshal? Every little bit of news in this town seems to make its way to Perry Weston's newspaper. That scribbler is the scourge of Fort Boise. I heard he published a lie about gold in the Rockies and got away with it. When I asked him about it, he challenged me to disprove it. I'm still thinking about how to answer. You'll know the man if you hear him. He squeaks like a mouse when he talks."

Will gave the marshal a knowing look and said, "The journalist is who we're here to talk to you about. Him and your first officer."

"We think the scribbler and your lieutenant are in cahoots," Marshal Walker added. "That's why he was with the soldiers when they nabbed the Indian woman. He's the same man who invented the lies about the gold strike up our way. He caused a lot of trouble and cost folks a passel of lives, and here he lives like he never did a thing wrong. Such is the power of the wealthy and connected."

Court-Martial

"Why are you so worried, Lieutenant?" Captain Benson asked. "If this woman is guilty of something, why not bring it out for everyone to see? I have the hearing arranged for nine o'clock, along with twelve community members as jurors. We can let them decide if she deserves to hang or not. It would be a blemish were a woman's hanging be in the fort's records."

"She's as guilty as sin, and she's an Indian. Who's going to care if she lives or dies?" Willas replied flippantly. "I think it'll be embarrassing for my friend, Perry. We don't want to offend a man with so much power. He could print something that could ruin your career, Captain."

"That sounds like a threat to me, Willas," Captain Benson spat. "If I were you, I'd be careful what I say, or you may be the next one on trial, but yours will be a court-martial, and there will be no jury—only me to serve justice."

"I, of course, have no favorites, sir," Willas said

soothingly, changing his tone of voice. "Have your trial, but remember, I have planned your first patrol for the day after tomorrow. You wanted to see the wilderness and rub shoulders with the local Indians, didn't you? I have arranged for Sergeant Walton to take you on his next excursion into the wilderness, where you'll see buffalo and wild Indians. Exactly what you came here for."

"So, you're not going with us?" Benson asked, feigning surprise.

"Somebody must stay and take care of the fort." Willas laughed. "We can't leave it to a couple of corporals, can we?"

"No, but we can leave Sergeant Walton to take command," Benson said. "I'm sure he's capable enough."

"That sounds risky to me, Captain," Willas said as his heart sank. He'd never been out on patrol and didn't want to start now. He liked his cushy life in the fort, especially with the graft he received in nearly every shape and form.

"Get your mind straight, soldier," Captain Benson said. "You're in the army, and I believe my lieutenants should all be combat veterans. How do you expect to know what's happening if you're not in the field? I'm sure you can't believe your friend. Every time he opens his mouth, it's more lies. I'd be ashamed to call that scoundrel an acquaintance, let alone more."

"That's because you don't know him yet, sir," Willas cooed. "You couldn't imagine what he could do for you as the commander of Fort Boise."

"Are you suggesting bribes?" Benson smiled greedily, but it didn't reach his eyes. He acted as though he was going to take the bait. He wanted to see how far Willas would go.

"It's simple, really," Willas said. "We rub Perry's back, and he rubs ours and the money will start to flow."

The captain stared right through the lieutenant, but he wasn't smiling anymore. A look of realization crossed his face, and he just confirmed he smelled a rat, and it was standing before him.

"Make sure your friend Perry Weston attends the trial and ensure he's not late, or you will be responsible. Is that clear, Willas? Now get out of my sight. Every dog has their day."

"But, Captain, Perry is a fine man, and he can change your life forever like he has mine," Willas pleaded, saying more than he intended but pushing on just the same. "At least meet with him and give him a chance. He has more money than you've ever dreamed of."

"I believe we have come to a moral quandary, Lieutenant," Benson said calmly. The young officer didn't fluster as easily as Willas expected. "That will be all for now. Remember to be punctual in the morning. Every minute you and your friend are late will cost you twenty dollars."

"But that's preposterous!" Willas shouted, forgetting his place. "How dare you fine me in *my* fort!"

Benson remembered how Captain Forrester said Willas referred to Fort Boise as his.

"So, you do claim that Fort Boise is yours," Benson growled. "I have heard this claim from others. Have you lost your mind, man? The fort doesn't belong to you any more than it belongs to me, and I'm in charge—or maybe you've forgotten that small detail. What I believe is that you've been using the courtyard and its businesses to scheme and make money on the side. How many store owners give you graft monthly? Are you taking bribes from everybody in the fort?"

Willas felt his bravado shrink like a mushroom in the sunlight. He cleared his throat to object, and his mouth moved, but no sound came out. He didn't have a foot to stand on, and his future suddenly appeared dim. He stammered to find something to say, but his mind went blank.

Lieutenant Willas briskly stood, pushing the chair with the back of his knees as it clattered to the floor. He stiffly saluted the captain, made an about-face, and walked out of his boss's quarters.

Phil could hear his footsteps echo on the hall walls. Now, they sounded like the walkway to the gallows. If he didn't stop things now, he would be the one to hang or at least spend a long time in a federal prison somewhere back in Kansas.

The day after next, he would have his chance. Despite Willas's hatred for the wilderness, he would have to go this once to ensure Wood Duck had his opportunity. The thought crossed his mind that the notorious Indian outlaw might turn against him, but he knew the key to every man's heart was money, and everybody had their price. At least Phil thought so. The fact that some people were completely honest never crossed his mind.

"How'd it go, boss?" Dickie Bennet whispered. "I bet you told 'im, didn't cha?"

"Who does he think he is, anyway?" Ned Nebraska

added. "There's only one leader here, and that's you, ain't that right, Phil?"

Willas walked by the guards but didn't hear them. He was lost in his thoughts, trying to figure out how to stop the trial the next day and hang the woman before they could stop him. Then, they would sweep the problem under the rug. Nobody cared about a dead Indian, anyway. It was the living ones who caused all the issues.

The following day would take care of itself. Sure, his dependable Sergeant Jack Walton wouldn't be with them to keep them out of danger, but he believed one venture into the unknown shouldn't be too dear a risk. After Benson was gone, he and Weston could return to business as usual. And he would take over command no matter what anybody said. There was more than one way to go about a problem.

The lieutenant made a beeline for the small newspaper office and his friend, Perry Weston. Despite Willas' arrogance, he often sought his only friend's wisdom. There was seldom a problem that the scribbler couldn't solve or fix. He might even know how to postpone the trial indefinitely.

He spied someone peeking out the curtains as he approached the newspaperman's tiny abode. The first officer sensed Perry already knew more than he suspected. He never did say why the Indian woman singled him out and attacked him for no apparent reason right there in the fort. All he told the first officer was he wanted to see her hang and claimed she mutilated him.

Although Weston didn't go into details, Doc Black let a

few secrets slip when they him bought enough liquor. He was a frugal man, but he loved to drink, making him as malleable as lead. After a few whiskeys, he happily gave all his information on the fort's citizens' ailments, from a bad heart to bone spurs on someone's feet. The fact that Weston got castrated by the Indian woman Dahteste, he told with great detail and seemed to enjoy talking about Weston's ill fate. Everybody in town knew why he had the voice of a young child. It was only he who thought it was still a secret.

Willas always suspected it was a small affair gone astray. It was known to all that Weston fancied Indian women and the soiled doves at the local saloon. Some wayward ladies had to leave town because he suddenly and unexpectedly stopped paying their way to continue living in this faraway place. One moment he was interested in women and the next, he wasn't, due to Dahteste's actions.

He made a fist and went to knock, but Perry opened the door just enough for the lieutenant to squeeze by. The journalist looked up and down the courtyard.

"Quick, let me close the door," Perry whispered. "Didn't you hear who the mountain men in town are? Rusty Steel is among those ruffians. He's known across the Rockies."

"Why would you worry about the mountain men?" Willas asked. "They have no authority here in Fort Boise. I'm the last word as far as the law, not some crazy fool who made a name for himself living with heathens. I've heard of Rusty Steel, too. Everybody has, but you're a newspaperman. You know most of what they say about such sorts are lies and fabrication."

Phil knew one of the mountain men was the Indian woman's husband, but he didn't expect trouble from them with forty men at his disposal in the garrison. He would have to be crazy to take on the United States Army. He decided not to mention this fact to Perry, who was excited as it was. He knew the next bit of news would be unwelcome, too.

"Don't give it a second thought," his friend Phil said, smiling. "By the way, we must be in court tomorrow morning. Orders from the new captain."

"Court?" Perry asked, perplexed. "A trial for who?"

"Why, for the Indian woman you accused of attacking you," Willas replied. He suddenly realized he liked putting a small fire under the arrogant newspaperman's bottom. Maybe he had a better grip on him than he thought. "I am sure it will all be no more than a formality. Don't worry; all you must do is *tell the truth*. If you have a problem with *that*, I'll speak for you. All you need is to sit back while I work as your attorney." The insinuation about the truth went right over the scribbler's head.

"My lawyer?" Perry asked. "Who's on trial here anyway? The Indian woman or me?"

"Why do you worry so much?" the first lieutenant asked. "We still control this fort. Give me a few more days, and I doubt our captain will be around much longer. I believe he is about to grow a dislike for the wilderness."

Willas gave the scribbler a sly smile, but even then, he realized he had disclosed too much. If the newspaperman put together the death of the captain and the promotion of his first lieutenant to his position, he might turn about and blackmail him. Phil knew better than to tell everything to Weston. He would bite the very hand that fed him. The officer was aware if cornered, Weston would act like a rat and turn and attack anybody within reach.

Perry got up from his large desk and stood with his back to the wall beside the curtains. He slowly pulled back the material and peeked out the window. Paranoia sat on his shoulder, and it weighed a ton.

Levi Johnson

"Did Wanata say if they did anything else other than beat Dahteste?" Levi asked as blood rushed through his veins at lightning speed—his breath was short and fast, and a purple vein throbbed on his forehead like a fuse. His fists were so tight his fingernails dug into his palms, making them bleed.

Tatanka's silence said more than a thousand words. Sorrow filled his eyes as he shared the pain with his White friend. After living with the Crow people, they accepted Levi as an equal and, in some cases, considered him braver than many despite his young age.

They were all aware he had learned everything he knew from Rusty Steel, and even Chief Hachta honored *him*. They were blood brothers, after all.

Gritting his teeth, Levi couldn't find the words. Will patted him on the back and mumbled soothing nothings in his ear. But the captain was almost as affected as his best friend. Fury, for vengeance, etched his face as though chiseled in stone.

"Mind your manners now, young men," Rusty said

in a soothing voice. "Losing your tempers and shooting off without a plan will do nothin' but get y'all kilt or hanged along with your wife. We need more information about this Perry Weston and maybe even Lieutenant Willas. How did that meetin' work out with the commanding officer, Will? Any luck?"

"Yes, sir," Will replied, sitting. He and the marshal had just returned from the barracks. "He seems to trust his first officer about as much as we do—not at all. But, as far as Dahteste's concerned, she'll have to stand trial. There's no way around it. Captain Benson did say he would allow a civilian jury to decide her fate, but maybe we can get some more dirt on Weston and Willas. If it weren't for Bob, the commander, Dahteste would hang tomorrow, trial or not. I doubt any other Indians have had a jury decide what happened to them. At least not in Fort Boise."

"That's cuttin' it a little close, ain't it?" Virgil asked. "The hangin' is planned for twelve noon." He held his finger under the words in his black Bible to avoid losing his place.

"The trial will be in the morning. I can't believe I brought her back here to this, and we were so happy," Levi said. "Now, I'm gonna kill Perry Weston for sure. There's no question about it. All this stops here." He turned his attention back to Tatanka and said, "Tell me everything Wanata said, word for word, and don't leave anything out. And you say you know who did it?"

"Are you talking about the captain of this fort, named Benson?" Wanata asked. "There is a plan to kill him, and this Lieutenant Willas has paid a half-breed renegade to do the job. It's all over the Indian gossip.

Whenever Wood Duck is about, everybody is concerned."

"You didn't answer my question, Tatanka," Levi retorted. He had to know everything that happened and exactly who did what. No matter how much it would hurt.

"It was the two White men who stood morning guard. They grabbed her a few minutes after the dozen soldiers locked her up. Wanata said he saw the whole thing. They beat her badly, but she was still alive. They did...things to her I don't feel comfortable talking about." The large warrior stared at the fire and spoke no more.

"These two will go first," Levi growled, ignoring his mentor. "They're gonna die for what they've done. There's no way I can let this go, never, ever. I'm sorry, Rusty, but I have to do this my way."

He didn't say a word as he turned to leave. Tombstones reflected in Levi's eyes.

"I'm going with you," Will Forrester called out.

"You can't," Levi said over his shoulder. "I won't allow it. What I'm going to do may have repercussions. I don't care if it's legal or not; both of these men must die."

"Because we're friends doesn't mean you get to tell me what I can and cannot do," Will said firmly. "I wasn't asking; I was telling you. You don't get to decide if I go or not. Maybe I'll go on my own and kill them before you can. Now, do you want me or not, because if you don't, I'll do this my way. I don't necessarily need your help. I consider Dahteste as family, too."

"Since when did you get so dad-gummed stubborn?" Levi asked. "Hangin' around Rusty is makin' you grumpy like 'im."

Levi turned to go but, to his displeasure, loose gravel ground under boots behind him as Will and Rusty followed him into the street. Joseph, Dennis, and Virgil joined and came running right behind them.

"If one of us is gonna get into trouble, the rest of us might as well tag along and get into Dutch too," Virgil said, slapping his Bible closed.

"Are ya *all* comin'?" Levi asked, exasperated. "Why don't we make it a party?"

The six-foot-seven Johnson ducked his head under branches as they immediately vanished into the forest. The sound of rustling leaves quickly disappeared. Everybody raced to keep up with Levi as he stormed for the stockade. Indians stopped what they were doing to stare. They could feel the danger and hoped it didn't touch them.

A wake of dust followed Johnson as he crossed the plaza and stomped onto the porch as the planks groaned under his weight.

He didn't mince words as they burst into the barracks entrance. The night guards were on and were oblivious to what Bennet and Nebraska had done. When the giant walked in, the men went for the guards' weapons, and they disarmed them before they could bring them to bear. Each man's feet kicked in the air as Johnson held them by the scruffs of their necks and began to shake both men like ragdolls.

Shaking the soldiers, Levi screamed, "Where are they? You know who I'm talkin' about. Those two no-good guards that work the stockade morning shift—where are their bunks? If you don't tell me, I'm gonna snap your necks like twigs." He roughly shook them again.

"Don't kill me," the private pleaded. "I don't wanna die."

The other guard gave up the information before Levi focused on him. "They rode out with Lieutenant Willas. Not more than half an hour ago. Please let us go. We didn't do nothin' to your wife, sir."

By then, Rusty and Joseph were behind him. Will ran for the captain's office as Virgil passed by the trading post and got provisions for a night. They were going to take chase, and nothing would stop them.

"Buffalo hunters, gold seekers, scalp collectors, and Indian fighters; all degenerates bleeding westward like a plague," Rusty spat. "The place is becomin' overrun by fools lookin' for somethin' that ain't here."

"You look as nervous as a burning cat," Will said as Captain Benson rode up. His orderly followed running before a string of horses. "Don't worry, sir, you're in good hands. Woe be to those who defy *us*."

They all climbed onto their saddles. The captain's pistols rested in scabbards mounted across the saddle horn's pommel riding at each knee. His long saber flashed moonlight off the blade. Despite his lack of hesitation and willingness to fight, the veterans could see how green he was, although they all knew he had good intentions.

Luckily, Will and Bob were old friends from back in New York. If not, Dahteste would already be lost. Still, some crimes are better tended to by the victims. Today, Johnson was going to get his revenge.

They rode out of the fort kicking up dust which quickly dispersed, getting lost in the endless landscape.

The moon stood high in the sky, casting a silvery glow across the valley, ridges, and mountains. It was so big it felt like they could reach out and touch it. The size made them feel small and unimportant. Levi locked his jaws and took the lead.

"Trackin' two soldiers is like following a herd of buffalo, Captain." Rusty chuckled. "They leave more track than hens in a chicken coop yard."

"I doubt they expect we're following them," Captain Benson said in a low voice. At night, it seemed like a sound carried a long distance, and a whisper sounded loud. The fort captain leerily looked around.

Rusty suddenly pulled to a stop and screeched like a bluebird, making Levi halt. The mentor motioned for everybody to gather around.

"I smell sweat and something else that smells like swamp water," Rusty mouthed. "The last time I noticed that smell was when we almost caught Wood Duck."

"Wood Duck?" Benson asked.

"Things just got a lot more dangerous," Joseph said. "The soldiers will be headin' to meet up with that devil. He'll kill 'em just as soon as look at 'em. Willas don't know where he's stuck his nose. He probably plans to kill Willas as soon as he gives up the money. The two guards were just unlucky."

Before they had time to catch up, the privates' riderless horses came out of the dust, flapping empty saddles, wild manes, and eyes white with fear. Private Nebraska lay on the ground feathered with arrows. A fringe of hair was visible below his scalped head; tonsured to the bone, he lay maimed and broken. The earth under the soldier was stained from urine and blood as flies clambered over a peeled, wigless skull.

When Dickie Bennet walked out of the trees with a knot on his head, he used his bandana to stifle the blood. He looked up and saw the mountain men and the captain. Bennet appeared puzzled and confused as he repeatedly blinked his eyes.

"The Indian said the lieutenant was supposed to come alone," Dickie said. He looked up and meekly saluted his captain. "Where's Nebraska? He scalped 'im where he stood, then shot 'im full of arrows. I should be dead, too, but he just hit me in the head with a war club and knocked me off my horse."

Another riderless horse came racing by with its eyes spread wide. Hooves hammered as it passed and ran wild into the night.

"Where's Lieutenant Willas?" Captain Benson asked. His eyes dared his soldier to lie.

Levi shucked his boot backward out of the stirrup and kicked Dickie in the chest, knocking him on his butt. Levi swung down, hooted, and pummeled the corporal like a wild ape—dark puddles formed under silver light.

"I'll finish up with you after the hearing tomorrow," Levi growled. "You better hope she don't hang or you're gonna follow her, but you won't be goin' to Heaven; you'll be goin' straight to Hell the hard way."

"Now, where's that Indian and your boss?" Rusty asked.

Dickie could see the violence in Rusty's eyes but couldn't decide who to fear more—the insane Indian or the wild mountain men? The captain concluded the confusion.

"Chase down Nebraska's horse, or you'll be walking back to the fort on your own, and as you now know, it may well cost you your life. He's dead there on the ground at your feet, fool," Captain Benson growled just loud enough to hear.

"Let's go get 'em," Levi said, looking at Captain Benson. "If you get a shot at that Indian, be my guest. If not, and he sees you first, you'll be the one to die. He's more dangerous than bein' locked in a cage with a bunch of honey badgers."

The rest of the men dropped off their horses, tied them to trees, and walked the rest of the way. It wouldn't do to have Wood Duck's ponies hear them nicker. They saw the flames glow through the trees and across the open clearing. They crawled the last hundred yards.

Behind Wood Duck were the scalps of slaughtered Indians flapping in the wind, drying on cords. Curing buffalo hides festooned at his side. He was tall for an Indian and wore his hair in braids to his shoulders and his chin beard to his chest. The renegade had a White mother. His Comanche father was a big man, too.

The fire's coals glowed orange in his eyes, making him look even eviler. Thick, juicy strips of elk meat on stripped branches sizzled and spat above the flickering fire. The flame's shadows danced on the trees at the edge of the clearing. The vicious-looking killer's unshod ponies grazed behind their master.

Wood Duck's fist locked around the shaft of his six-foot spear. Bats flew forth from their roosting in a cave across the valley. Buffalo moved along the skyline in scarves of dust under a silver moon. Wood Duck had a cluster of arrows in his jaws, and his shield was covered in pieces of broken mirrors, winking in the dark.

There were harnesses, fashioned from human skin, and bridles woven from men's hair. Teeth hung like decorations. He fingered his ear necklace as he cocked his head and listened to the wind. When men approached, his ponies bared their teeth like dogs.

Rocking back on his heels, Rusty pulled both triggers before anyone could speak. One round bounced off the mirrored shield, but the other perforated a lung. Bloody bubbles popped from Wood Duck's grinning mouth.

Lieutenant Willas spun on his heels with wild eyes. He had gone from one certain death to another in the huff of a single breath.

"You should know better than makin' deals with the Devil," Rusty said. "Now you're gonna come with us and see who says what in the trial."

Captain Benson grabbed the reins from his first officer and barked orders at the corporal. "Tie his hands, and if he gets away, shoot him. Do you understand, Bennet?"

Rusty walked over to the infamous outlaw. This was the third time he had run into him, and luckily, it would be the last. Wood Duck let out a long pneumatic sigh as he stared at the moon with sightless eyes. The mountain man mentor shook his head and spat a yard of brown juice across the renegade's paling face. A haze of gray-green gun smoke lay over the campsite.

Vultures circled between the earth and the heavenly globe, coming lower with each twitch of their wings. As soon as the party of humans left, they folded into a dive.

Fine fingerbones steadied the leather wings as a vulture walked across Wood Duck's corpse. Wrinkled and bare, vicious lips crimped into a ghastly smile. It leaned over, folding its wings, and drank his blood.

Painted ponies stood sulking in the first light. They

saw no birds in the sky, save buzzards. The following day, they saw clouds of dust lying across the earth for miles as herds of buffalo ran wild. They rode with their heads down, faceless under the shade of their hats. Coyotes were visible, howling all along the ridges.

When they entered the Fort Boise courtyard, dogs barking and faces parting curtains in lamp-lit windows accompanied them. The clatter of horses' hooves rode through the gate. They clopped through the plaza thronged with mules and wagons. All the dogs in town continued to complain, and as dawn came, roosters crowed their cock-a-doodle-doos.

Shadows of fort turrets lay long across the ground like thick pencil lines, and tall men on elongated horses.

DAHTESTE

LEVI JERKED HIS ARMS AND LEGS AS HE SLEPT, LIKE A dreaming dog chasing a cat. He tossed and turned, trying to push the nightmare from his mind. The naked feet of the dead woman jostled stiffly from side to side in the buckboard wagon as it pulled away from the gallows. Johnson whimpered like a puppy robbed of its mother.

It was early morning, and his companions watched and worried. They knew he was tormented but were beginning to realize how much.

While the mountain men got forty winks, the Indian camps around the fort came to life. Streams of smoke from different tribes began to rise all across the various campsites. The wagon train had noisily made its way onto the Oregon Trail and toward Oregon City and north. Of a thousand weary travelers, two hundred had died already. Some wandered off; others didn't pay attention and were left behind. The occasional daydreamer lost their scalp, never to be seen again.

Others got abducted as they tended to their personals. They were snatched up just beyond the light of the circled wagons. The wagon master always warned his people never to enter the dark, but a few others ignored his warning, and they, too, disappeared. Occasionally, they heard a scream at night but never found the remains the next day. Maybe they took the reckless travelers someplace where they could torture them slowly or perhaps turned them into slaves.

As Joseph eyed the rubble and trash that hundreds of wagons left behind, he began to have second thoughts about what he had intended to do with his old partner, Rory Breaker. Maybe it *was*, like Rusty said, a bad thing for those who lived in the wilderness. It was true that the dead lost along the way would pave the trail in human bones, and this was only the beginning. Most of them would make it, but many would remain somewhere along the trail. Maybe things had worked out in the end anyway.

The news of Wood Duck's demise was on everybody's lips. There was nothing the Indian gossip didn't catch—certainly not an event as important as the passing of a common enemy responsible for the loss of countless lives. He had been terrorizing people, regardless of race, across the plains for decades. The environment was festive for everyone but the mountain men who were responsible for his death.

They were still struggling to deal with the fact they had finally killed him. The part that stumped them the most was how they had stumbled on him and caught him off guard. Once again, Rusty Steel was all over the Indian gossip.

Across the dozens of flickering campfires, past the fort gates, and inside the stockade, they served bowls of beans and charred tortillas to the prisoners once a day. They rationed water to the drop. It was too much work carrying buckets from the well, so the guards cut the prisoners' consumption down to nearly nothing.

The imprisoned waiting for final judgment or execution sat cross-legged by candlelight, eating from their bowls with their fingers, toweling grease with stale, flat round bread. The only light came from two small barred windows not more than two feet wide and high. The soldiers kept them at the point of starvation and dehydration because it left them weak and helpless. They were less likely to resist and try to escape, even if some succumbed to their hunger or thirst and died. Unidentified pieces of rancid meat lay under the cold beans at the bottom of each bowl. White maggots wiggled on the surface.

The men who brought breakfast to the cell block were not the same guards as the day before. New faces stared with hatred at the Indian woman, and revenge flashed in their eyes. She was proving to be much more trouble than she was worth.

Willas had made grafting an everyday routine. Among the ranks, the soldiers were used to the extra money for a small item they usually couldn't afford. Most of them ran questionable errands for the first lieutenant. They knew they were probably committing crimes and perhaps on the fuzzy line of the law where it was hard to see what was right and what was wrong. But a few dollars at the end of the month meant a night out with a soiled dove or a dozen store-bought imported cigars. They used anything to break the monotony of living isolated, lost in the wilderness.

The first lieutenant took control of the fort right

under the previous commander's nose and used the soldiers as strong-arm men against the small shops inside the compound. Willas collected money extorted from the businesses as well as those living outside the tall adobe walls. No matter how little the amount, they denied safety to the people who didn't pay. When the Indians made their periodic attacks, they wouldn't be allowed entrance to the only safe place for hundreds of miles.

This corruption had festered and was now a deep infection with the ranks of the new commander, Benson, in its clutches. Now, the captain had to navigate dangerous waters carefully. He knew he had to weed out the crime now, or it would be too late, but Benson intended to follow his instincts and do everything with intentional plans that could only lead to success.

There appeared to be a small light of hope for the new fort leader, Captain Benson. He wasn't interested in money or bribes and was learning fast that what they initially showed him had little to do with what really stood outside the tall adobe walls. More importantly, what happened inside in secret?

A loud bang rang out, making the prisoners flinch—Dahteste jumped an inch from the floor. Everybody's nerves were as tight as guitar strings. The hangman had made the last adjustments to the gallows trapdoor.

Today, they would hold a trial, and more than Dahteste Johnson's life would be at stake. The first lieutenant already appeared to be destined to live in a Kansas federal prison. Only the formalities remained. Dickie Bennet's future was still to be determined. Would he pay for his sins on the courtyard square, or would the military court forgive him? Unlike Dahteste, Bennet was a soldier, and a favorable court-martial was his only chance. Usually, Indians weren't allowed as witnesses, but these conditions weren't normal.

Even if he beat the rap due to the lack of White witnesses and regained his freedom in the eyes of the army's laws, he knew that Levi Johnson would never let him escape, no matter what a judge and fort commander thought. When Johnson had told him he was going to kill him, Dickie believed every word he said.

The rusty lock clacked loudly like the gears of a broken clock. The female prisoner rose and shuffled barefoot out of her dingy cell and into the cellblock hall. A ringing church bell floated through the window with the limited morning light. Moisture accumulated on the ceiling and finally dripped down the walls.

A priest sat with his hands cupping a fat belly as dogs protested across town. From the chair across the hall, he carefully watched the prisoner. A knowing look filled his eyes. For him, like the hangman, their minds were already made up and were only waiting to get to work. The Indian woman should hang at noon regardless of whether or not the husband was friends with the new commander. The law was the law and couldn't be changed no matter who you were.

They watched the executioner dressed in black as he covertly passed the prisoner with his hands clasped behind his back. His wide-brimmed hat cast his eyes in shadows. The guards carried short shotguns with barrels so big your thumb fit.

Dogs lay in the shade under the wood-plank porch, loosely in their skins, their faces wrinkled. They snapped and bared their yellow teeth as they struggled for a safer place to wait.

Lifeforms shimmered in the heat as they walked across the courtyard to the mess hall where they would hold court. The gallows sat across the square. Spectators already filled the plaza shoulder to shoulder. The guards had to push their way through the crowd to keep the prisoners from being crushed. If the truth were known, nobody in town cared for Perry Weston. They all knew him for what he was. But, still, an Indian attacking one of their citizens had most of the crowd up in arms. If it happened to him, they believed it could happen to them, too.

The number of spectators continued to swell and began to become unruly. Soldiers shouted as they jostled along the tall adobe wall and into the courtyard. Many carried baskets of rotten fruit, and more than one chanted, "tarred and feathered."

To most of the spectators, it didn't matter who was to hang. The excitement of the carnival-like event brought them from near and far. In the wilderness, any excuse sufficed for a celebration—even a visit to the gallows on a sunny day. Some laid out blankets and had picnics while they waited, and little children gawked.

When the guards walked the barefoot woman in buckskins into the large mess hall, civilians sat on two rows of twelve chairs. Jurors waited as they assembled tables to accommodate the army prosecution and the witness of events before and after the alleged crime. The captain sat at a small square table alone. His pistol lay beside his hand, so he grabbed the barrel and hammered the grip on the table for lack of a mallet.

"Order in the court!" Captain Benson yelled over the

din of talking. "Keep your voices down back there, or I'll clear the mess hall."

Everybody in the room had a different opinion, and some were ready to fight. Sergeant Walton grabbed two privates by the ears and dragged them from the building. They yelped and struggled to keep up. When they got out the door, he gave each of them a swift kick in the butt, and they tumbled into the street.

"Take yourselves to the brig right now!" Jack Walton said. "If you ain't there when I get back, you better be dead or scalped by wild Indians because, with any less excuse, I'll kill ya myself."

He clapped the dust off his hands like they were dirty, turned his stocky body, and returned to the hearing. Eyes followed the sergeant, but he ignored everyone but his boss, Captain Benson. They exchanged looks, and Jack nodded, confirming he had his men under control. Tiny curls formed on Benson's lips, marking the slightest smile.

Sergeant Walton hadn't been happy with how things went with the last commander and his first lieutenant, but Jack only had three stripes on his shoulders and had always known his place in the military hierarchy. Right or wrong, he followed orders to the letter.

Besides that, he was rarely told what to do because Lieutenant Willas disliked going on dangerous patrols. Instead, the officer passed on any communication from headquarters, and the sergeant initiated whatever actions were deemed necessary.

Lieutenant Willas sat at a table alone. To his left and right were witnesses, both civilian and military. It appeared everybody in town had a bone to pick with Phil, especially the merchants who had been paying five percent of their earnings for permission to remain in business when they should be paying nothing at all. One small merchant who couldn't make the payments lost everything he and his wife had, forcing them to return to Kansas.

Somehow, the first lieutenant ended up owning the space. More evidence piled on the prosecutor's desk. Every merchant inside the adobe walls had denounced Willas as soon as they heard what happened.

Maybe now we'll have an honest officer to take charge, Sergeant Walton thought. *It'll be good to feel like I'm in the army again.*

Dahteste sat with rigid eyes in the bright mess hall. Large windows dotted each side. She bit her lip as she waited for her victim to appear. Everyone else was there and ready, but still no show from the scribbler. Captain Benson ignored his delay for the moment, but if Weston remained absent, he would order his arrest and take it from there. Bob was more interested in getting his soldiers in line than the local businessmen, especially as everybody despised Perry aside from his apparent partner, Willas.

Captain Benson spoke to Dahteste warmly and gestured with great expansiveness of spirit. He questioned her gently in nearly a whisper. The men and women at the hearing had to lean forward to hear what was said. Dahteste spoke even softer. Despite her bravery in battle, she was in a new situation and believed she knew how it would end.

Soon, she would walk toward the gallows as she sang her death song. Time began to race by as she clutched at hope. She knew Rusty Steel was full of surprises, but to be locked in a fort made it appear impossible to get out.

Still, the woman Crow war chief had no remorse for what she did. The false publication of a nonexistent gold strike almost cost her husband's life and did cost the lives of countless others. If she had to do it all over again, she would, if only to save other women from this wicked man. After the incident, Perry Weston had involuntarily seeped into the Indian gossip, and his misuse of native women outside the fort came to light, too. Still, as usual, his money saved him among the poor and his newspaper among the wealthy.

Little did Captain Benson know how corrupt the fort and its few influential residents were. There were evil men behind the scenes, from the first lieutenant down to Corporal Dickie Bennet. Willas had as much interest as Weston for the fort to grow into a town with time. Then, the graft would be much more substantial and truly change their lives.

Both men had partnered up from the beginning, seeing how their skills and positions could eventually lead them to control Fort Boise and all the government-granted money. The opportunities to make even more profits were endless. They even planned to tax the drovers who delivered their supplies. From their point of view, there were chances to make money from top to bottom.

Lieutenant Phil Willas knew the future would bear critical political positions, and with a town, the fort would be of imperative value to all the new settlers they hoped to see arrive. The larger the population, the more families with real money would venture west and stay after seeing all that Fort Boise had to offer.

Their three-year plan seemed utterly feasible, but only with Phil Willas in charge. For it to work, he had to be the fort commander. They believed then, between his connections and power and Perry's money and tabloid rag, they would control everything from the town sheriff to the mayor.

The captain cleared his throat, and the courtroom went silent. The acting judge was ready to bring his first lieutenant forward for prosecution. The soldiers sitting at the witness table regarded their commander with expressionless faces.

Dahteste stared at the jury with eyes as black as gun bores. When the captain called her to the stand, she rose and shuffled forward silently in her bare feet. Despite her haggard face, her eyes shone defiantly.

The prosecution sketched for the captain the problematic career of the first lieutenant. He used his hands with great dexterity to shape the varied wayward paths the accused had taken. Lieutenant Willas sat with his mouth agape as he tried to talk, but the words didn't come out. He felt as though his mouth was full of sand.

"That's the worst behavior of soldiers and citizens I've ever heard!" Captain Benson shouted when the prosecutor finished. "You, Corporal Bennet, should be grateful that I can't hang you because you raped and beat an *Indian* woman. A war chief, no less. What in the world were you thinking? And all this was done here in Fort Boise under my very nose. Take him away at once. I don't want to have to look at him for another minute."

Dickie looked from the floor to the captain as his eyes shot daggers of hate.

"You make me nauseous," Benson continued. "I know I can't hand you over to the executioner, but I can make you wish I had. I hereby sentence you to a hundred lashes on the stockade. I want to ensure everybody sees it and to hear what you did. Your crimes are to be repeated out loud for one and all to hear before the whipping. Be this a warning to any man who defies military or civilian law within these walls. As far as Private Nebraska goes, he got what he deserved. For the record, his sentence is the same as yours, Corporal."

"And regarding Lieutenant Willas?" the prosecution asked.

"I heard about your little agreement with a renegade by the name of Wood Duck, too, Willas. From the sound of it, you barely escaped with your life. I'm amazed that an educated man like you can go from one mistake to another without slowing down. Sometimes, you must stop digging your hole, sir. Now, I am afraid you have dug too deep."

The remaining guard sat stunned, blinking in disbelief. Dickie wiggled a finger in his ear to make sure he heard right. It started to sink in when he realized what Captain Benson had said about Private Nebraska. Now, he found himself headed for the stock and a hundred lashes. Bennet knew that if he survived, he would be reposted to an even more remote place—if that were possible—and they would strip Dickie of his rank.

The cotton eye of the moon squatted above their heads in broad daylight.

When Perry Weston busted in the door, he used the barrel of his gun to knock the guard to the floor. The look in his eyes was that of a madman. He aimed the pistol at the captain and slipped his finger into the trigger guard—the scribbler couldn't help it as a grin stretched across his face.

Captain Will Forrester watched as he helplessly went for his gun, but he was too late. He didn't have time to save his college friend, the captain.

The *BOOM* resonated through the closed room, vibrating the glass windows. Two behind Weston cracked and then shattered. Shards of glass covered the floor, crystal crushing underfoot. The pistol had blown up in Perry's hand, and his face was charred and full of powder burns. The scribbler's facial hair, eyelashes, and eyebrows instantly seared. Speckled blood covered his face. He looked at his fingerless hand, blinking in disbelief.

The sun glared readily through the gun smoke as the odor of cordite filled the air. The silence ended as the spectators roared, pointing fingers.

Joseph sat in the back, laughing silently at the situation.

Sergeant Walton

Captain Forrester raised his weapon, took a bead, and pulled the trigger. His pistol recoiled as fire and smoke followed the lead slug out of the barrel. Will's gun followed Perry's by a full second. Had Weston's gun not blown up in his own face, Captain Benson would be dead. Weston's shocked and seared face exploded in a puff of blood, mucus, and brains.

Patches of hair stuck to the windows. Smoke wafted from the captain's barrel. A second gun was suddenly in his hand. His empty sleeve fluttered in the breeze through the broken windows. Any assassination attempt on the fort's commander would be another stain on Forrester's record, and he was doing his best to make his past wrongs right. If he allowed his old friend Bob Benson to die in his presence, it would be unforgivable.

The shot caught the scribbler dead between the eyes, and his profile flattened. On his way down, teeth clattered to the floor staring up white like a disjointed smile.

In an instant, the threat vaporized. Everybody in the mess hall was stunned into silence. A woman suddenly screamed and broke the ice, and the room exploded into shouts and wild gesticulations. Blood pooled beneath the faceless body.

"ORDER! ORDER!" Captain Benson shouted. "Everybody *sit* down! Sergeant Walton, drag the body outside before he befouls the entire room. Come on, make it quick. Your presence is imperative."

At first, the captain sat frustrated in his chair. He let the people argue and protest. It gave him a minute to overcome the shock of looking death in the eye. A bead of sweat cut a white streak down his face. He had been a breath away from his demise. Bob would never forget staring down that hollow barrel.

"All right, that's enough!" Benson blared, turning to his first officer. "Now, what do you have to say about yourself and your deceased partner, Lieutenant Willas? I do believe you've lost not only your sole witness but the complainant, too. The only man still on trial here is you, sir, and I would venture to say your claims of innocence haven't a leg to stand on."

Willas jumped to his feet and shouted, "You can't treat me like this! Neither I nor the town's business owners will settle for it. This is my fort! I made it what it is."

"And so you keep saying," Captain Benson replied. "What would you have me do with Perry Weston's partner, Mr. Levi Johnson?" His eyes went to the mountain men's table. "I can't help but believe they had everything to do with Mrs. Johnson's subjection to human rights violations. It was a terrible thing, all that happened to your wife, sir. It's now clear who is the greater evil."

The owner of the trading post stood unwarranted, but the captain ignored formalities at this point. Once he had a dead man in his courtroom during a hearing, the nature of everything changed. He stared at his first lieutenant as Sergeant Walton swaggered back into the mess hall, but this time, he pulled up a chair, dropped it beside Willas, and sat.

"Now, be forewarned; you're in my reach, Lieutenant, sir," Jack whispered, smiling. "If you make a move, it'll be my pleasure to thump ya in the face and break your nose."

"Lieutenant Willas has been holding our businesses hostage," the trading post owner, Chance Wesson, said. "I brought the issue before the last fort commander, but he didn't seem to care. It was as if he was in another world. Not long after, he shot himself. Then again, maybe he *didn't* kill himself. What we've learned today makes us all wonder. If you look through the captain's log, you'll no doubt find my complaint. I'd be interested to see what the ex-captain said in his notes. They may further incriminate Lieutenant Willas."

"Let's have the fort prosecutor give us an idea of what he believes is going on," Captain Benson said. "Despite the situation, I would like to proceed in as orderly a fashion as possible. I know we have only had a day to dig deeper into the claimed suspicions, but we still uncovered enough illegal activities to merit a speedy conclusion."

A stone crashed through an unbroken window, spraying the floor with more broken glass. The shadow of somebody flashed by, but it was no more than a silhouette in the shade of the roof.

"Sergeant, see who the hell it is now," Captain

Benson ordered. "We're never going to get through this trial if we continue as we are."

The unexpected explosion filled the mess hall and came as a total surprise. Nobody knew where it came from. Everybody's ears rang from the blast in a contained room—for a second time, people checked to see if they were shot. Dozens of eyes glanced across the hall, but the gray-green gun smoke solved the mystery. On the floor, behind his little square table, Lieutenant Phil Willas lay in a puddle of blood. Red spread across his white shirt, growing to his blue pants and leather belt. His saber glinted in sunlight from the side windows.

Spurts of thick claret pumped from his busted heart. Willas looked at Levi Johnson, then at his wife, and tried to smile before he died. The hot gun froze in his fist. The edges of the bullet hole glowed orange as the fabric singed his jacket and smoked, and the small fire went out. The room reeked of gun smoke, blood, and sweat.

Rusty Steel swept clawed fingers through his hair and smiled. "So, what do we do now, Captain Benson? It seems like your problems are all solvin' themselves. Can Dahteste go with us? I've had just about enough of civilization to last me until next year. I agree with ya; she broke the law, all right. But don't you think that after what Corporal Bennet and Private Nebraska did to her, she's had punishment enough? You do know we won't leave here without her, don't cha? That ain't a threat; it's just a fact."

"Take it easy, boys," Will said soothingly. "You've got to understand, Captain Benson. Where we live, there's no law at all except for Rusty Steel here, and we follow his lead. My friends get nervous when we come to a place with over a dozen buildings. It's strange what livin' in the wilderness does to you. Don't get me wrong; it's a good thing and not a bad one. We aren't threatening anyone, but what's fair is fair. What do you say, Captain, sir?"

Forrester's eyes pleaded for it to end then and there. There had been enough bloodshed, and no matter what they did, what was done couldn't be taken back. He also knew there would be much more blood spilled if the captain said he wouldn't allow Dahteste to leave. The clan of mountain men and women didn't take it kindly when somebody abused the women. The fact that Benson was an army captain didn't appear to bother them.

"Mrs. Johnson?" Captain Benson said inquiringly.

"Yes, sir?" Dahteste replied. Her face filled with uncertainty.

"You are hereby released into the custody of your husband, Levi, and Captain Will Forrester," Benson ordered. "I will hold you both responsible for keeping this young lady out of trouble. Do you men understand?"

"Yes, sir," Levi said begrudgingly as Rusty nodded and smiled.

Johnson wouldn't be satisfied until he saw Dickie Bennet die. It was a fact the mountain man didn't try to hide. It was there in his eyes for anyone to see.

Heading Home

The fort's towering adobe walls and watchtowers were rain-washed and sloughing into slow decay. The Hudson's Bay Company flag hung limp at the top. Cumulonimbus reflected off water puddles scattered across the courtyard. Horses' hooves sank in the muddy square as the seven riders headed across the courtyard and toward the gates.

Captain Bob Benson stood on the barracks porch as rain slanted across the plaza, denting hats. Will pulled up his horse, wheeling it around. The young army officers saluted. Each respected the other for their honorable ways. They nodded knowingly; they would be seeing each other the following spring. Maybe then they could sit and enjoy a friendly visit. This trip had been all nerves and violence. Then again, they were in the wilderness, where danger awaited around every corner.

With the end of the Rendezvous, the location of the mountain men's supply sources changed. Now that the beaver pelts were worth a tenth of their original price and still dropping, they chose a new direction to earn a living. They would head for the great herds of buffalo. Maybe they could work out an arrangement with the Indians for a portion of the hunt so they wouldn't be considered trespassers.

The Snake River led a corridor of trees downriver. The party of frontiersmen watched the current lazily run westward as they headed east. Tiny bombs exploded on the water's surface, but the first break in the clouds allowed patches of light to shine across the countryside. Soon, the glowing disk pushed away the clouds, and bright sunlight took its place.

The rain stopped as suddenly as it started. Wet hat brims lay limp, drooping near shoulders. Fur caps smelled of wet hair. Everyone had gotten soaked to the skin, but it was summer, and as soon as the sun began to shine, they stopped to dry their shirts, jackets, and hats on leafy bushes.

Their campfire leaned downwind as they slept in the quiet forest. Joseph and Rusty sat and talked late into the night. The rest of the mountain men and women snored gently as flames caressed logs like long fingers in the campfire. Cinders swirled upward with the smoke, disappearing a few yards into the night.

As the days passed, they rode farther east as the forest appeared and became denser with every day. At night, they now lie on cones and needles from the ponderosa pines. Hot chains of sparks ran along the shrubs, then quickly disappeared and got swallowed by the night.

Well before dawn, flies landed on Rusty's face as they walked across his mouth and peered into his nose. He waved his hand, sending them flying. He sat up like he was jolted, and then he remembered where he was, making him smile. His dream had said he was still back in Fort Boise. Steel had seen enough of civilized people for a time. He got along with Mother Nature better.

The air smelled of horses and burned wood mixed with pine needles. They all noticed the absence of the smell of humans, like back in the fort. They went from the small, overpopulated space of Fort Boise to their chosen wilderness full of shades of green. The racket of locusts came and went as suddenly as the previous rainfall.

Dahteste rode on red-eyed and sullen the first days, but as they closed the distance to home, she slowly began to face what had happened and tried to get on with her life. Levi felt the difference in her, but now he knew all he could give her was patience, and she would need a wagonload.

By midday, they began to climb toward the summit in the gap between the mountains. An eagle's shadow crossed the earth at unimaginable speeds just above the string of riders. The humans looked up across the faultless blue void. They crossed the gap and entered a high pine forest that led across a long valley and through the mountains.

The horses cocked their ears and stepped quickly as they rode on, despite the strange noise. Marshal Walker swung his head, squinting one eye with loose lips.

The blistering sun advanced calamitously. They nooned at a mineral spring, taking time for stale biscuits, hot coffee, and a smoke. Finally, Angus poured the last of the kettle on the campfire, making it spit and sputter, going out. The fire steamed and darkened as a gray cloud rose. Black smoke raced heavenward before disappearing.

In minutes, they were back on the trail home again. There was still a week's ride. Horses' hooves clopped, echoing across the canyons. Dust filled every wrinkle of their faces and clothing. Even their mounts had a heavy coat of dirt on them at the day's end.

Levi Johson pulled his animal to a stop, halting the seven riders. He inhaled deeply, wrinkled his nose, and whispered, "Buffalo."

"Where there's buffalo, there'll be Indians," Rusty whispered with narrowed eyes. "You two best to have a look."

Will and Levi turned their horses, quirting them into a fast trot, as the rest of the party followed at a walk. They could hear millions of flies from over the ridge.

"I'm gonna ride over there and check that smoke out," Marshal Walker said. It spiraled into the sky.

"Is that your final say, Joseph? Ya really wanna stick your nose into somebody else's business after all that fuss back at Fort Boise?" Rusty asked. "No sense in goin' looking for trouble when all we need seems to find us all on its own."

"As final as the word of God," the marshal replied. "I'd rather run into a problem on my terms than have somebody sneak up on us later and catch us with our guard down."

"Virgil, you best go with 'im," Rusty said. "Make sure he don't start that trouble he's talkin' about." Steel chuckled. "The rest of us will climb that hill and see if them ain't buffs we smell."

Bottle flies buzzed over the heads of tens of thousands of buffalo as they silently grazed. The group made a camp on a mountain ledge near a talus slope. Below them, bulls bellowed as cows pulled at grass and slid their jaws. It was a difficult spot for Indians to approach, and it allowed them to observe such a wonder of nature. A half-million bison grazed across the green valley below.

The buffalo ate the grass to the nub at the valley's far end. The buffalo mowed down the vegetation as they migrated and ate, leaving nothing green in their paths. Their weight and numbers trampled everything else into dust. Barren land lay in their wake.

Betty Forrester lay on her belly while holding the heavy fifty-caliber Tennessee rifle carefully with both hands. She stared down the gun sight and pulled the trigger, letting off shots slowly and carefully. At four rounds per minute, she dropped one buffalo after another.

Dahteste was so amazed by Betty's accurate and precise way of hunting, for a moment, she forgot what had recently transpired. It was like she was dissecting the herd of hundreds of thousands, one piece at a time. The rest of the bison hardly stirred. The men also watched in amazement at the calm way she shot, reloaded, and went on to the next target. Her actions were almost mechanical.

A gunshot rang out and Rusty gave Levi a knowing look. The marshal was taking care of business.

When Joseph found them after following their track and the signs Rusty left that only Joseph would recognize, he pulled up, nodded to the mountain man mentor, and jutted his jaw. The marshal swung his white-sox quarter horse around again and walked off. Rusty grabbed Flossie, his Andalusian gray, and rode bareback behind Walker. Steel knew what to expect from the vultures that were already circling their next meal—another thing that was visible for miles.

The dead Shoshone lay on the creek bed wash. Joseph dropped off his horse and carefully pushed over the dead man with his boot. He could see where his lead ball passed between two ribs and struck the man's heart. The warrior's hair was long and black. When the painted face came up, pebbles stuck to his cheeks.

Lice scuttled the dead body like a sinking ship. He wasn't a young man and bore the scar of an ancient knife wound from his cheek to the corner of his eye. This warrior obviously wasn't new to the game of life and death. He wore a raven's wing eye shield above vacant eyes.

"This must have been a spy sent out to keep an eye on us," Rusty said. "This fella's a Shoshone warrior."

They heard a twig break and looked at the grazing pony that was oblivious to the intruders and its dead owner. Like a fur blanket, the grass was thick and plush and swirled in the breeze.

"Well, it don't surprise me none that the Shoshone and every other Indian out there knows we're here," the marshal grumbled.

"If we didn't have the horses and mules, we could have traveled unperceived," Rusty said. "Then again, we hadn't planned on going to Fort Boise. I wonder if anybody showed up at the Rendezvous in the end."

"That racket y'all make shootin' buffs already let everybody within miles know we're here," Joseph spat. "Especially with the heavy, fifty-caliber rifles."

"And what about the vultures overhead? You, my friend, are responsible for that one. If we're huntin' buffs, the local Indians will know we're here anyway," Rusty said. "We best let 'em know sooner than later when we're more occupied skinnin' them buffalo Will's wife just shot."

"What do we do with 'im?" Marshal Walker asked. He used his pistol to open the dead Indian's shoulder bag and peeked inside—the smell of herbs seeped from the dark goatskin. Bones and trinkets rustled around.

"It's one thing killin' a warrior all fair and square, but it's another matter messin' with his body after he is dead," Rusty huffed. "We better be respectful of the deceased, old pard. If we bury 'im like White folks do, they'll probably get angry. As it is, he was killed in the line of duty just like he could have killed you, Joseph. There's no right or wrong here among White or Red warriors. It's just the survival of the fittest among nature and all of us wild animals."

Indian Treaties

It really didn't come as a big surprise when a small party of Shoshone warriors and war chiefs showed up at the edge of the ledge. They tied a white bandana to the end of a long lance the man riding point carried. A dozen men with painted faces sat astride squat, stocky ponies. They all brandished tomahawks, bows, arrows, and lances. The leader had a single pistol shoved into a wide leather belt.

"Don't anybody go for your guns, now, family," Rusty whispered, smiling with open arms. "These folks have come to parlay. Y'all be as nice as ya can, and that means you too, Joseph."

A middle-aged red man nudged his horse nearer the old mountain man, who was obviously the White men's tribal elder. He nodded, kicked his foot over the pony's neck, and dropped to the ground. Little clouds of dust rose around his moccasins.

He covered his chest in different lengths of white and blue beads. A breechcloth fell from his waist. Metal bands covered his biceps, and his long black hair hung below his waist and fluttered in the breeze.

He wore a war bonnet of golden eagle tail feathers and a browband embroidered with porcupine quills on his head. His face was no more than a neutral mask, but his eyes were full of confidence and dared anyone to challenge him.

"I am Cheveyo," the Shoshone warrior barked. "Who are you, White man?" He pointed his lance at Rusty Steel. "I am the Spirit Warrior. Maybe you have heard of me in the songs of the elders."

"I reckon I have, Chief Cheveyo. You've made quite a reputation for yourself. My name is Rusty Steel. It's mighty fine to meet cha."

"I, too, have heard of you—the White warrior," Cheveyo replied. "It is said that you, too, live as do we. Was it you that killed my spy?"

"No, sir, it wasn't, but if I'd have seen 'im first, I'd have done the same. I reckon just like you would have, Chief. There wasn't anything dishonorable in that warrior's death. He passed to the other side a brave man."

Cheveyo stood before Rusty and proffered his hand. Rusty grabbed the man's lower bicep and the Shoshone his, and they greeted each other as Indians.

"Are you still friends with Crow Chief Hachta?" Cheveyo asked. "Or has the old fool retired or died?"

"You know as well as I do, he ain't dead, and I don't see the chief retiring anytime soon, either. Why, he, like me, is in the prime of his life," Rusty replied. "Why, it'd be all over the Indian gossip if he was. I reckon you know he's more than just my friend, too. We're blood brothers."

"I have always found that odd." Cheveyo chuckled. "A White man and an Indian chief being blood brothers. But then again, stranger things have happened."

"Ain't that the truth." Rusty grinned. "Actually, we were hopin' you would stop by for a friendly parlay. I want to offer you and your people part of our kill. We have high-powered weapons and can easily shoot the buffs from a safe distance when compared to runnin' 'em down on horseback or stampedin' a few hundred off a cliff. Personally, I find the latter a waste of such a noble animal. Too much food and hides go to waste, and for what? We only shoot what we're gonna skin and for food."

Cheveyo chuckled. "You are a clever man, Rusty Steel. I have heard as much. How many of *our* buffalo do you propose to *gift* us?" He laughed as did his men.

"One of every ten, and we'll even skin 'em and cut out the sweetbread and tongues for ya." Rusty smiled. "Ain't that right, Betty?"

"What did he say?" Betty whispered into Will's ear. She was as nervous as a dog with ticks and no hind legs.

"I don't know, but I think they're speakin' Crow," Will said. He glanced at Levi, and he knowingly nodded.

"This woman shoots like a White man?" the Shoshone war chief asked. His face showed his surprise. "I don't have a single warrior who is such a shot with a rifle. Then again, red men don't have lead and black powder to waste practicing."

"She shoots better than *most* men, exceptin' yours truly. Why, you've heard of Davy Crockett, ain't ya?" Rusty asked. "She's his niece, and he, her uncle, so they are blood, and you know that makes for big medicine."

The name of the famous frontiersman who fought at the Alamo was repeated among the warriors as they whispered behind their chief's back. The ponies snorted and sidestepped nervously. There were few people in North America who hadn't heard of Davy. He was one of the original frontiersmen and was respected from the Great Plains to Washington, DC.

"It looks like they're more impressed by Betty than they are by you, pard." Joseph chuckled as Mrs. Forrester looked even more confused.

The Shoshone war chief shot the marshal a questioning and somewhat unfriendly glance. He wondered who this man was and why he spoke when he wasn't spoken to.

"Don't mind him." Rusty laughed, taking advantage of the fact that the marshal didn't speak Crow. "He's a fool and ain't right in the head. We usually don't pay attention to what he says, but you know as well as I do that it's bad luck to mess with crazy people. That's why I took the poor soul in and fed 'im. Sometimes, he says something intelligent through all the jabberin'."

The war chief nodded and replied, "I have men like that, too. They come with every war party and every camp, but we, too, must suffer such fools."

Rusty had to bite his lip to keep from laughing. Dahteste suddenly appeared in the middle of the mounted warriors with her bloody hands full of warm sweetbreads. She handed out cuts to the hungry Shoshone men. A hint of a smile showed on her lips as she listened to her husband's mentor charm the enemy with his wit.

"Whose wife is the Crow woman?" Cheveyo asked as

he raised an eyebrow. "She looks like a warrior, too. Are all White people the same?"

"She's Levi Johnson's wife," Rusty replied, pointing to his massive apprentice. "And I'd hardly say that there be many White men like us at all, Chief."

"I've heard of Johnson, too," Cheveyo said, nodding. "Your reputations are of honest men. We will take one in ten buffalo and *half* the sweetbreads and tongues. Is that a deal, Rusty Steel?"

"That's fair enough, Chief," Rusty replied. "How is it you speak such good Crow?"

"My mother was a Crow woman," Cheveyo replied. "My Shoshone father stole her from her people when she was seventeen summers old. She taught me her language in secret. My father forbade it, but she was clever and knew it would come in handy in the future. As usual, she was right."

Rusty smiled so wide you could see down his throat. The others, except Dahteste and Levi, had puzzled expressions on their faces. They hadn't understood anything except for their friends' names.

"And it *was* you that killed Wood Duck, then," Cheveyo said. "Maybe this holds more water than anything else. That Comanche renegade was all the peoples' enemy. Now his reign of terror is past.

"Shundahai," the war chief said. "Peace to you, my new neighbor. My warriors will leave you in peace as long as you honor your word. But don't kill any more of my spies, fair fight or not, or the treaty will end. We have a right to keep an eye on our land every day and every night."

"Fair enough, Cheveyo." Rusty smiled. He spat in his

hand, proffering it to the Indian. "This is how White men agree, Chief."

The war chief hesitated momentarily before spitting into his hand, but then they grasped their palms together and shook. The Shoshone leader nodded in approval.

Without another word, Cheveyo swung onto his pony's back and turned, stepping off the ledge. His warriors gigged their horses and stormed off. A cloud of dust followed in the horses' wakes as hooves hammered the ground. Shoshone war cries slowly vanished in the distance.

"What was all that about?" Will asked.

"I didn't understand a word," Joseph said, "but it appeared to have gone well, didn't it, Rusty? And what were you sayin' about me? I saw ya pointin'."

"Let Dahteste or Levi tell ya." Rusty laughed. "Beaver speaks Crow about as good as I do nowadays if not better. There's nothin' like an Indian wife to learn the language quickly."

"Rusty made a treaty with the Shoshone so we can hunt here without losing our scalps." Levi smiled.

"And what did he say about me?" Marshal Walker asked.

"Rusty was just sayin' what a fine fella you were, Joseph," Levi lied as mischief danced in his and Dahteste's eyes.

Buffalo Herd

They spent that night on the ledge over the sleeping herd of a few hundred thousand animals. Rusty snored nearly as loudly as the buffalo bulls. Bison roared during the night, and coyotes sang in their never-ending choir. Late at night, a pack moved over a ridge, the shadows visible in the moonlight.

Dahteste and Levi sat with their legs dangling over the edge of the ledge. Her head leaned on his shoulder as she wrapped her arms around her husband's bicep. They stared at the wonder of Mother Nature in a comfortable silence. A lush green valley stretched for miles from animal to animal to the very end.

"Are you feelin' better, darlin'?" Levi asked after a time. "I know it's only been a couple of weeks, but I want ya to know I worry about cha, girl. For me, you'll always be the same."

His Crow wife shrugged and replied, "Life has always been hard. Nobody ever told me it would be easy. I have no expectations, so I have no disappointments.

Do you understand, Levi Johnson? Still, I feel dirty just the same, even though I know it's not my fault."

"Don't say that. Don't you ever say such a thing again." Levi huffed. "Not to me, you don't. When I married ya, I did so for life, and nothin' short will do. So, push all that out of your mind and shush. We'll suffer this together, all right?"

His Crow wife nodded, and her shoulders relaxed for the first time in weeks. It wasn't but fifteen days earlier that she was ready to walk up the steps to the gallows and hang by the neck until dead. Even worse than that, at least for her, was the brutal attack in the jail cell. Still, she was a war chief and knew she had to push aside her emotions and deal with life like she always had.

"It's somethin', ain't it?" Levi said. "I remember the first time I saw a herd as far as I could see, but even then, I had no idea how big the herds got. They're like oceans of brown fur."

"I can't remember the first time I saw a buffalo." Dahteste smiled, relaxing more. "It must have been when I was a baby. My mother would go to the killing fields with me, her papoose on her back while she gutted and skinned the animals. Everybody in the tribe pitched in when the buffalo hunting season came. For us, they are as constant and important as the sun, moon, rain, and wind. She would feed me sweetbreads as a treat."

Dahteste stopped for a moment as she looked back on her youth. For a young woman, she *had* lived a hard life, especially as a war chief. It was difficult for some men to accept women as their leaders, but she had repeatedly proven herself until all the men in the Crow stronghold respected her.

"Our entire world revolves around the bison," Dahteste continued. "From our houses to our clothing and, of course, food. My mother made fishhooks from the small bones and needles, too. Ribs make good bone handles. Our Crow creator, Isáahkawuatte or Old Man Coyote, gave us the best gift of all—everything we needed rolled into the buffalo. That is why he created such herds of millions, so they would never deny us food and homes. The elders say when man is gone, the buffalo will remain. When or where have you seen so many Indians as there are buffalo?"

"It's funny, ain't it? Here I come from back east and yearn to have what you've had all your life. I reckon I'll never understand nature like you do, and I grew up in the forest with no neighbors. But living in the western wildernesses is a whole new challenge, and I learn every day."

They continued to sit silently, watching the herd sleep. The occasional mother's calf would cry for milk. Not much later, Levi heard Dahteste's breathing deepen, and finally, a whisper of a snore came from her lips, making her husband smile. He gently picked up his petite wife and lay her on her bedroll. She was so at ease she didn't stir.

Maybe we'll make it through these tough times, after all, Levi thought.

Johnson lay down gently beside his wife with his head propped up in his hand, resting on his elbow. The love showed in his eyes when he looked at her sleeping. She seemed so peaceful and innocent; you would think she could never hurt a thing, but Levi Johnson knew the truth. He wasn't even sure he could beat her in a fight.

When someone angered Dahteste, she was as ornery as a honey badger. You could have asked Perry Weston about that, but now it was too late. None of the mountain men felt regret for Will shooting him dead. The animals belched and passed wind through the night.

The following morning, just before sunrise, the western sky appeared to be alight. Heat wavered on the edges of the disk of fire as it climbed into the sky, chasing away the dark while creating long, thin shadows across the land before them. Angus squatted on his heels as he spooned coffee grounds into the burned-black gallon kettle. Ten minutes later, the smell of java filled the air. It even covered the odor of two hundred thousand hairy animals.

Everything had been quiet that night. The men had taken two-hour shifts doing guard duty, but there wasn't a sign of anybody watching them. Still, they knew they were there. A wolf howled, and three more answered. A male owl hooted, and its female partner replied, who? They sat at dawn as the light deepened.

By the time the sun departed the horizon, rising into the sky, everybody was awake and hungry. McFarlin was a good cook, but he didn't like them rushing him, because then the results weren't the same. Of course, nobody in the group was impatient except for Virgil who had the patience of a saint, and Joseph that of a sinner who was no patience at all.

Every morning, he was the one who grouched and grumbled until he touched his coffee to his lips. Then his humor changed for the better, like a switch.

Rusty fished out a flask from inside his buckskin shirt. He pulled the cork with his teeth and poured a splash into his dented tin cup. Steam poured from his coffee as he tested it, burning his mouth. He smacked his lips at the taste of whiskey. A quid of tobacco perpetually occupied his cheek.

The bluish light suffused the mountains and tallest peaks. As the fiery disk rose, the rest of the valley still lay in darkness. A bull bellowed below as obscure figures moved nervously. From the corner of their eyes, they spied the silhouette of the first rider. He wore a quiver of arrows across his back. Four more Shoshone hunters took chase. Ponies' hooves hammered the earth, grinding dust into the air.

The lead horse panted, and its lips blew, nearly out of breath. The entire herd began to run as one. Five brave young men, fleet on their mounts, split off a dozen buffalo. The first rider pulled even with the last bison as he drew back his arrow, bending the bow double. It burrowed into the running beast just below its heart. In seconds, five arrows followed in rapid succession, and the buffalo's knees gave way, and it tumbled head over heels. Seconds later, it lay groaning, taking its last breaths.

Two more braves targeted a large bull as they nudged their horses nearer to send the deadly arrows home. One brave let his projectile fly, missing his target as his pony stumbled. When the other neared, the buffalo swung its head, burying his long horn into the hunter's stomach. Before throwing him into the air, it gutted him from his crotch to his throat in one muscular movement.

His friend veered off and let the rest of the herd race

by, trampling everything in their path. The rumble sounded like constant thunder, and the dust became so thick it was hard to breathe. The Indian hunters disappeared from the valley floor until the morning breeze brushed the cloud away.

When the stampede of animals passed, the four rode over and dropped off their horses. Their friend was as flat as a tortilla—not much more than a stain. The buffalo had pounded his face into the dirt, and his horse lay dying beside him, broken bones jutting from its hind legs. Hunting bison from the back of a racing horse was a dangerous business both for man and animal.

One hunter scraped his dead friend's hair into a skin sack and added any personal items that survived. There wasn't much left after being trampled by tens of thousands of hooves. Several white teeth shone from the dirt, reflecting the early morning sun.

Moments later, the remaining Shoshone hunters began to gut and skin their kill. They cut away all the valuable meat and tongue. Blood dripped from the bundle on the pony's back, running down its sides and legs. They removed the buffalo's hide in a single piece to use to patch up worn teepees or make warm blankets back at the big camp.

Grizzly Bears

When the clan climbed the final steep stretch of trail to home and reached the buck-and-rail fence, they saw the three cabins standing in the center of the compound. They all breathed a sigh of relief when they realized there were no signs of fire, so the Blackfeet Indians hadn't been at it again.

Rusty wondered what had kept them busy because, lately, they didn't stop pestering the White men on the mountain. Still, small miracles were always welcome. Maybe they went to the Rendezvous to sell their pelts and found nobody there, just like Rusty's clan. Then, they would have had to do what everybody else did: find a new place to sell their furs and skins.

Despite the dangers of leaving the cabins alone, they sometimes had little option, especially now, as they had changed jobs not by choice but out of necessity. As soon as Rusty saw the door of his cabin open, he began to grumble. Broken bottles, torn sacks of flour, dented tin cans, and busted barrels were scattered across the yard.

The door was torn from its hinges when they got to

the porch. Deep claw marks raked across the heavy timber, and metal lay broken on the floor. Balls of curly brown fur hung where the intruder had scratched its back on a hanging rake.

"Only a large male grizzly bear could be strong enough to tear that door off like that," Rusty said, visibly angry.

"We're lucky he didn't tear up more than he did," Angus said. "It looks like he couldn't get into the new dry cellar. That's where the bulk of our stock is stored."

"Look at the size of those claw marks." Rusty smiled. "Maybe I ought to go out and hunt that bugger down. I could use a new grizzly fur coat for next winter. Whatcha say, Joseph? How about goin' with me on a grizzly hunt?"

"I ain't confronted a bear in years, let alone a grizzly," Marshal Walker replied doubtfully. "It doesn't exactly sound like fun to me."

"Ah, stop peckin' and scratchin' in the dirt like an old hen." Rusty cackled. "That'll give the rest of our people time to clean up all this mess. You and me can go out and make sure it don't happen again. For sport, I can't think of a better wild animal to hunt unless it's a mountain lion. They're not as big, but they're much sneakier."

"I thought Levi was your huntin' partner," Joseph grumbled. "We've been ridin' for weeks, and now you wanna run off again and chase down a furry monster? And for what, you say, for the sport? You must have lost your mind."

"Levi and Will have wives to tend to, and Angus, Dennis, and Virgil gotta clean up the cabin." Rusty grinned. "You know old McFarlin won't rest until everything is back where it belongs, and he'll be needin' your help, Lovejoy—you too, Dennis. So, that just leaves us to track this rascal down. We've gotta make sure he don't come back with us home and do somethin' worse than tear off our door. If we're not careful, he might sneak up on us and tear off one of our heads. You boys might wanna look at a new set of hinges first. We don't want the cabin standin' open come nightfall."

"All right, but let me fill my flask with a spot of whiskey before we leave," Marshal Walker said. "My backsides hurt from sittin' in my saddle for days. A little sip will help numb the pain."

"And you wanted to cross the Oregon Trail?" Rusty laughed. "That sounds like six months of rubbin' leather. You must be gettin' soft in your old age, Joseph. And now you want to shy away from nabbin' a bear. You must have Mr. Paranoia sittin' on your shoulder again, just like you did when I first met ya, when we were young."

"Aw, stop hackin' on me, Rusty. I'm comin', so don't fret. You would think a man your age would have something better to do."

"Levi, you and Will be good boys and tend to our mules and horses," Rusty said. "We shouldn't be gone too long because I doubt this critter's afraid of anything so he won't be runnin' for cover, and he sure as shootin' won't be runnin' from us. From the looks of the cabin, I'd say he'll be as brazen as the marshal here and not at all shy. Come on, old pard. I always wanted to take ya huntin' grizzly with me. Ya can't have much more fun than that."

"I always thought you were crazy, but now I know you're nuts," Joseph complained. "Only a madman would think huntin' monster bears was fun. For me, it's sittin' on a saloon porch, drinkin' whiskey as I watch the ladies go by. Your idea of a good time is runnin' hell bent for leather with a wild grizzly bear on your tail. I'll never figure you out."

"If you don't stop waggin' your jaw, we're never gonna find this rascal." Rusty laughed. "Come this way, pard. We wanna stay upwind of this critter, or he'll be the one doin' the huntin'."

The forest instantly swallowed up the grumpy pair of friends. Even their movement and footsteps were immediately muffled by the dense vegetation. Only the slightest smell of bear fat lingered. Rusty wore it to keep him warm on chilly nights sleeping out of doors, but it came in handy when you were on the trail of large wild game.

The men held their rifles in white-knuckled fists as Joseph's breath came short and fast. The vein on his temple pulsated like a bullfrog, and his mouth suddenly went dry—it felt like it was full of sand.

Rusty led the way as he carefully crept forward. He got the feeling the bear was closer to the compound than he expected. This one appeared to be more confident than your average grizzly. It almost looked like he was waiting for them to come and play.

Rusty drew back the hammer on his rifle. Cold chills shot up Joseph's back when it clicked, and beads of sweat sprouted on his forehead, rerouting through wrinkled lines. A second cocking hammer followed. In the quiet, it sounded even louder than the first. The marshal had to remind himself to breathe. His palms felt sweaty against the gun's grip. He smelled polished wood as he raised the rifle to his shoulder.

Suddenly, the odor of bear overwhelmed Rusty, making him freeze. Joseph was looking everywhere but in front of him, so he walked into Steel's back, nearly dropping his gun.

The mountain mentor swore, and the marshal turned. He caught sight of the massive, furry paw closing in on his head before he could flinch. Then came the playful impact from a clawless mitt.

The soft pad hammered Joseph on the side of his head, dropping him to the ground and sending his mind spinning as his eyes blinded with stars. When the marshal rolled onto his back and looked up, a nine-foot-tall, eight-hundred-fifty-pound male grizzly stood roaring over him, his arms slashing the air. When he drew back and roared, spittle sprayed from his mouth, covering Joseph's face.

The marshal watched as claws popped out like switchblade knives. He locked eyes with the thing he dreaded most, and he was too close to bring his rifle to bear and knew his pistols would make him angry.

The blast came unexpectedly to Joseph. The next thing he knew, Rusty was holding his rifle as smoke wafted from the barrel, and the colossal beast dropped to the ground face down. A neat hole appeared in the grizzly's back. The shot hit its heart dead center, stopping the blood to his brain, and mortally wounding the bear.

A breathy wheeze escaped the snout full of yellow fangs. Its breath smelled like rotten meat. It twitched as its nervous system began to shut down, and the grizzly was rendered harmless. Its feet and paws jerked a few times more, then it shuddered and died.

Marshal Walker scrambled backward like a crab on

its back, digging in his heels as he tried to scoot away from the deadly animal. Joseph wasn't all that sure it was harmless even when dead and didn't plan on taking any more chances.

"Are ya gonna sit there in the dirt all day, or are ya gonna help me skin this grizzly?" Rusty laughed at his cowering friend. "Don't worry, Marshal. There ain't nothin' embarrassin' about being afraid of such a big bear." Rusty's cackle echoed among the trees.

Despite what Rusty said, Joseph knew he wasn't joking. The marshal was aware he wasn't one of them—a real frontiersman—unlike the others. At first, he came for a visit, but then his dream of taking the first wagon train across the Oregon Trail went up in smoke. Then the fur business blew a gasket, and pelts were worth pennies. Now, they had turned their attention to hunting buffalo, and he knew he wasn't skilled enough to pull off something like that on his own.

"Why is it you always give me a hard time, Rusty?" Joseph asked seriously. "You're always so kind with the rest of your bunch, but you still treat me like I'm an outsider. Why don't you ask me to leave if you don't like me? It won't be the first time and probably not the last, either."

Rusty continued to laugh and answered, "Why, I like havin' ya around, Marshal. Without you, who am I gonna hack on? Virgil is too meek, and Angus is too old, and Dennis—well, he don't pay no attention. And the young boys might just kick our butts. I reckon we're stuck with each other, pard. Like it or not."

That afternoon, the couples retired early to their cabins and left the older men at the porch table. Gray cigar smoke hovered two feet from the ceiling, and there wasn't a breath of air. Rusty was looping the last claw onto his pigging string necklace. Virgil read his book by the candle flickering on the windowsill. He mumbled as he sounded out the words in his mind. Angus walked out with a pie pan full of steaming biscuits and a bottle of homemade raspberry jam.

Happy Times

Levi and Will unsaddled the horses and removed their bridles then brushed them down, ensuring they didn't chafe under areas covered with tack. They cleaned their hair to help avoid skin problems like thrush and scratches. They carefully did their chores, using stiff brushes to remove dead skin and soft ones to clean the dust away.

Grooming the mules and horses was a daily chore, and they couldn't put off until tomorrow. If their mounts weren't tended to when Rusty returned, there would be hell to pay. The aging mountain man always took special care of Flossie, his Andalusian gray, and the young man knew what he expected—nothing less than perfection.

"How is Dahteste handling the situation?" Will asked, knowing it was a delicate subject, but he felt he had to say something as his best friend. "If you need me, all you must do is ask. I know I don't know very much about women, but whatever you need, I'll give it a try."

"I think it was too hard for her to talk about it—

even to me," Levi replied. "I learned more from Tatanka than I have from her. I think admittin' it happened out loud is more than she wants to deal with. I'm surprised by how much it affected me, too. At first, I wondered if I would get over what he told me and what my mind invented. I wish I hadn't forced him to give me all the details because now I have it burned into my memory."

Levi stopped and sipped on his whiskey to wash the bad taste from his mouth. He rubbed his nose with his fist and blinked away the water. Johnson finally cleared his throat and spat a yard of brown juice off the side of the porch.

"I can't even imagine what Dahteste went through, and she's a tough girl," Levi whispered. "Most women would have cracked under such stress with the court hearing and jail, not to mention the thought of hangin'. Then those two topped it off with their depraved acts."

"The important thing is you get through this intact and don't let it break up your relationship," Will said. "Despite your differences, you two were made for each other. I knew it from the day you met."

When they finished with their mounts, they started on the mules. Unlike the high-spirited fighting horses the mountain men rode, the mules were usually easier to tend to. The mountain men knew they had to be on par with the Indians, and their ponies were second to none. Afterward, they bedded them all down with some fresh hay and headed for the porch. They could smell the coffee and baked blueberry pie. Steam rose from two pans sitting on the windowsill, cooling off. The men's stomachs grumbled, and they suddenly felt like they were starving.

"I could eat a whole pie," Levi said as he closed his eyes and sniffed the air while rubbing his belly.

"I've seen you eat, and you could gobble up three pies if offered to you." Will chuckled as they walked across the yard from the stables. "Honestly, I've never seen a person eat so much, especially after recovering from that gunshot wound. You're worse than ever. I hope you don't start to grow again. I doubt I would fancy having a friend much bigger."

Virgil hammered sixteen-penny nails into the new hinges as Dennis used a brick and plank to hold the heavy timber door in place.

"Hold on now, fellas." Levi laughed, rushing to the rescue.

Johnson and Will grabbed the door and lifted it off the ground, kicking away the brick as a black hand swung the hammer and drove the last two nails home. When they swung it shut to test, the new hinges squeaked like they were rusty, but it closed, sealing perfectly to keep out the wind and rain.

"That'll do it, but leave it open to air out my kitchen." Angus grinned. "That grizzly left a mess, but he didn't get that much food nor the rest of our furs. I figure we probably just about run into 'im. I believe if we had arrived an hour earlier, we'd have found ourselves face-to-face with that bear." He fingered the deep claw marks in the two-inch-thick door and frowned.

"Just imagine what those claws can do to a man." Levi huffed. "I bet they look like yellow steel nails."

Everyone there except Levi's Crow wife, Dahteste, and Betty Crockett Forrester had been mauled by a bear. They all remembered the fear they felt when it happened. Despite making fun of Joseph, everyone knew how terrifying an encounter with a grizzly was and were glad they weren't home when this one visited.

When Rusty and the marshal returned with the massive grizzly bear hide thrown across Joseph's shoulder, he stared crossly at his friends giggling and snickering on the porch. All the fun-making of the marshal was rubbing off onto the others. Rusty was scraping a bear claw with his pocketknife to add to his necklace. He looked up at his friends, and the smile reached his eyes. Mischief danced there, too.

"The first thing I want is a stiff shot of whiskey and some tobacco to smoke or chew, and I don't care which," Marshal Walker growled. "That bear nearly tore my head off, and that was before he got angry."

Joseph rubbed his neck with his fingers, obviously rattled by the encounter, but Rusty roared so hard he got a stitch. His body convulsed with laughter, his eyes swelled with tears, and a thin spool of saliva hung from his mouth and dangled in the breeze. He held his side as the stitch intensified with his thundering cackles.

When Angus brought out the cooling blueberry pie and a gallon kettle of coffee, everybody stopped joking and grumbling, and they all sat at the large table with their eyes as large as saucers. It had become a custom for them to break bread together daily, if possible. Sometimes, they ate all three meals on Rusty's porch. Little by little, they had become like one big happy family.

As usual, while the boys hacked on each other, Virgil followed the sentences in his book with his finger, never losing his place. He occasionally raised his head and smiled as he read, but he often barely heard what they said.

When he read his Bible, he was one hundred percent invested in the story and didn't find anything more interesting. He was the holiest person living in the compound.

"You *do* know that sometimes books lie, don't cha?" Joseph baited Virgil. He gave him a knowing smile. He was dying to hack on somebody.

Lovejoy was the easiest-going person of the bunch, so he was naturally the marshal's softest target. Lately, Rusty had been playing Joseph like a puppet on a string, and Joseph felt the need to complain about something to somebody.

"God don't lie," Virgil snapped sternly and shot Joseph a dirty look. "And the Good Book is made of His words. Are you sayin' God tells fibs?"

Again, the marshal's attempt at hacking on one of the family blew up in his face, and everybody on the porch turned their punishing eyes to the Kansan.

"Dagnabit, I didn't mean the Bible!" Joseph huffed. "Oh, I don't really know what I meant."

The puzzled look on his face brought another round of laughter, but the marshal joined in this time. He had gotten so flustered from the close call with the bear, he didn't know what he wanted to say.

"I've got to admit, that grizzly bear nearly gave me a heart attack." Joseph chuckled. "I don't think I've ever been that scared in my entire life. Not even Comanche are that terrifying, and I've seen 'em up close and personal. Still, they ain't got nothin' on a male like the one we tracked down. The fact is it ended up following us. That's how it got a swing at my head. Lucky for me, it seemed to be playin' at first and didn't use its claws."

Joseph looked at Rusty, who was fingering the new additions to his necklace. The marshal chuckled nervously, but soon enough, they were all laughing again and slapping each other on their backs.

They had won against all odds, and every one of them returned home safe and sound, even Dahteste, who almost hanged at the executioner's hands.

The day passed, the sun dove off the end of the world, and darkness once again dominated the land. Yellow lamplight spilled from the cabins' windows, lighting up the yard.

A sizable lamp hung from the porch ceiling, casting a yellow circle out to the edges of the floor. The cabin's front door stood open, as did the window. Green vines wrapped their way up the sides of their home, blending in with the environment and making it more challenging to see at first glance.

Little Dahteste sat on her massive husband's lap as they ate from the same plate. Levi used a fork, but she ate with her fingers, licking them clean when done.

Although Levi and Dahteste tried to maintain a constant in the group conversation, they often forgot the rest of them were there and seemed to live in their little world. Rusty couldn't remember Beaver Johnson so happy, nor could Will.

Will and Betty weren't much different, although the captain always stood erect, and if you didn't know him, you would think he had a chip on his shoulder, but that was the military officer drummed into him for years. Still, the frontierswoman from Tennessee with the famous uncle was what he had been looking for all this time.

The following day, just after sunrise, a pot went flying through the window of Levi's cabin. Breaking glass covered the doorstep, flashing in the sunlight. A string of indecipherable words came from a tiny voice inside, almost in a scream. It appeared Dahteste had gotten a second wind and was on the warpath again. A rooster crowed, and hens scrambled across the yard and to safety.

Rusty and Angus dropped four bits on the table. "I put my money on the Crow woman," Joseph said. "I've seen her fight, and she's somethin' fierce when riled."

"From the looks of things, she's riled all right." Virgil snickered. "As long as it's in good fun."

"Put your money where your mouth is, pard." Rusty smiled. "If ya want, we can make it an even dollar."

"That's too highfalutin for me—too rich for my blood," Angus grumbled. "You know I ain't a big gambler. You would have to go and ruin it."

"All right," Rusty replied. "Four bits is the limit. If you weren't so frugal, you'd enjoy life more."

"Look at the pot callin' the kettle black," Angus retorted. "You're so tight, your wallet squeaks when it opens."

When Mrs. Forrester came tumbling out the door, the men jumped to their feet and began to cheer on their favorite. In the past, Dahteste and Betty had nearly killed each other in a grudge about respect. Since then, they occasionally had spats, and none knew which one was more ornery, the Crow Indian or the Crockett from Tennessee.

"I wonder what they're fightin' about this time—

anybody got a wild guess?" Angus asked. "I've never seen two women who profess to be best friends fight so much. You'd think they'd tire of thrashin' on each other."

"Ah, it's just the Indian ways for Dahteste," Rusty said. "Crow war chiefs are expected to throw a tassel with a disgruntled brave on the odd occasion, and just because she's a woman don't cut her no slack with the tribe. She got the position of war chief by fighting other braves for honor. I doubt Betty had to fight her brothers."

"Anybody that's got Crockett blood runnin' through their veins has to be the best in a scrap, just like Davy," Joseph said.

The four men dropped to the floor and sat on the edge of the porch's wood planks. Rusty's feet dangled in the air. A buckskin-clad wild animal with black hair came tearing out the door on the path of a White woman with blond hair.

Rusty sniffed the air, turned, and smiled. "I was wonderin' where you two were hidin'," Rusty said as his eyes twinkled.

Levi and Will stayed out of sight in the dark shadow of the roof. They spied on their wives from around the corner.

"What are you two chickens whisperin' about?" Rusty asked, snickering. "Don't y'all go hidin' behind us. Go out there and dive into the fray." The mountain mentor grinned like a monkey.

"Well, are ya gonna stop 'em or not?" Angus asked. "You two big fellas can't be afraid of a couple of women."

"That would be the right thing to do," Virgil said.

"You should teach them how to turn the other cheek, like in the Bible."

"You be my guest," Levi said. "As a matter of fact, I dare ya to try."

Tables and chairs clattered as the two women tumbled like two stray cats. Claws flashed, and they even bared their teeth like rabid dogs. One moment, the blond was on top, and the next, the woman with coal-black hair. They grabbed each other in a bear hug and rolled in the dirt, but still, neither one advanced on the other.

"Come on, Will." Levi huffed. "I reckon this falls on us, since we're the husbands."

"I thought if one of them won, it would be over, but it looks like they're tied even," Will said. "I suppose we'll have to do like last time and drag them off each other."

"From the looks of it, I think I might have to tie Dahteste's hands and feet," Levi said. "I guess I knew what I was gettin' into when I married an Indian woman, but I have no idea why Betty is such a scrapper. Do you know, Will?"

Will shook his head and replied, "And she looks so lovely when she's asleep."

Then, the best friends broke out laughing, followed by the older men on the porch. Only Virgil continued to frown on the lack of will to act when they were all watching something that shouldn't be. At least, that was how Lovejoy saw it and interpreted it from what he read in his Bible. He thought women should behave themselves just like the men had to.

Levi shook his head and stepped off the porch, and boot heels followed. He turned his head and saw they were all following him. He frowned and shot his friends a dirty look.

"Come on, Will," Levi said. "Don't you dare shy away and leave this all to me."

Beaver Johnson walked up behind his wife, picked her up, and held her suspended in midair. She thrashed her arms and kicked her feet like a trapped cat, but Levi just looked bored with it all. After a few moments, her temper settled and her husband let her down, but he held onto her arm to ensure she didn't lunge at Betty again.

Will had to wrestle Betty to the ground to the great enjoyment of all the men. She was almost as big as him and fought like a cat trying to escape a dog. Their blond hair and blue eyes tangled in the struggle, eventually becoming a tickling contest.

By then, the women were too tired to continue to fight, and the men had their laugh. It was good for them to return to normal again, as strange as their ways were.

A Look at Book Ten:
Buffalo Hunters: A Western Double

When one way of life dies, another rises in its place.

Buffalo Hunters

The fur trade is gone, and with it the life the mountain men once knew. Levi Johnson, Rusty Steel, and their companions turn to the only opportunity left—buffalo. Millions roam the distant plains, promising fortune to anyone willing to risk the hunt.

But those herds are more than profit to the tribes who have depended on them for generations. As the mountain men ride far from their Rocky Mountain compound in search of unclaimed herds, they must learn a dangerous new trade while treading on ground already claimed by others.

The Searchers

When outlaws rob the Fort Boise payroll, a posse and an army patrol give chase across wild country. The thieves flee south into Yellowstone Valley, hoping the wilderness will swallow their trail—and anyone foolish enough to follow.

Back at the compound, tragedy strikes when another member of their tight-knit community dies. Loss weighs heavy on the mountain men and their families, but the frontier allows little time for mourning. Trouble is already moving through the high country, and Levi and his friends may soon find themselves in its path.

AVAILABLE JUNE 2026

Thank You

Thank you for taking the time to read *Wood Duck: A Western Double here*. If you enjoyed it, please consider telling your friends or posting a short review. Word of mouth is an author's best friend and much appreciated.

Thank you.
Ash Lingam

About the Author

Ash Lingam was born and raised in Southern Ohio, not far from the mighty Ohio River. He had somewhat of an isolated upbringing on a family farm with his sisters. His best friends were his horse, Sugar, and his grandfather.

Born in 1886, the family patriarch grew crops, raised cattle, and doted on the young boy. At his grandfather's side, Ash learned about livestock and firearms at an early age. His grandad carried an old Colt with him at all times. It helped spawn a young boy's dreams of yesteryear.

Ash was only eight years old when his grandad taught him how to trap muskrats to prevent them from draining the farm's ponds. He gave him a double-barreled shotgun at twelve and taught him how to hunt to put food on the table.

It wasn't long before Ash was breaking horses. His spirited Tennessee Walker never allowed any other rider on her back. Together, they searched through the plowed fields in the spring, looking for Miami Indian arrowheads to add to his grandfather's ample collection.

Ash's family was among the early settlers in pre-

Revolutionary America. He has traced his lineage back to around 1746 when his ancestors immigrated from Europe to the aspiring American Colonies.

A retired marketing executive, Ash devotes his spare time to training police dogs and writing novels. He has found his niche in the Western, historical fiction, and adventure genres. With his vast vault of experience, he never runs out of sources for new stories. He has lived in eleven different countries and worked in a total of forty-six to date, Ash has written approximately 130 novels, short stories, and poems. More than one hundred of his eclectic titles help the American frontier come alive for his readers.

https://www.ashlingam.com/

Join the Lawless Waters Western Readers & Writers Facebook Group